HOUSE OF RAVENS

HOUSE OF
RAVENS

Karpov Kinrade

DARING BOOKS

www.KarpovKinrade.com

Copyright © 2015 Karpov Kinrade
Cover Art Copyright © 2014 Karpov Kinrade
~~~~~
Published by Daring Books
Edited by Anne Chaconas
~~~~~
ISBN: 1939559405
ISBN 13: 9781939559401

For Jan
For everything

TABLE OF CONTENTS

PREFACE

An impossible choice stands before me. One I must make in between heartbeats.

I can't save them both.

Whichever choice I make will weigh on my heart forever.

I hear his voice in my head. In my heart. *I came here to protect them.*

And I know the choice I have to make. The choice that will break me.

NOX AETERNA

The house burns, flames licking at the dark sky, turning the pitch of night into a violent sunset of oranges and reds. I inhale the smell of burning wood. I can feel the heat against my cheeks, even from a distance. I can hear the screams of the neighbors crying out in fear, then in anger. The man stands in front of the burning house staring at his hands, his eyes wide, his bewildered face cast in shadows.

I know him. He sells produce at our farmer's market every Saturday. He always gives me free strawberries, and he has a nice smile. A kind smile.

But he's not smiling now. He never smiles again.

I run to him. I can feel in my stomach that something bad is going to happen.

I know he broke the law. No one knew he was a Zenith. Maybe he didn't know. But now, everyone knows. And as they grab him and drag him to the tree in his yard, I see the fear in his eyes.

I run faster. I have to stop them. I have to help him.

I stumble on a fallen branch, scraping my knee. It stings and the blood wells on my pale skin. They've already put the rope around his neck, and they are stringing him up.

"No! Stop!" I scream to them, but no one ever listens to little girls.

I'm running again, ignoring the pinch of pain in my knee, but I'm too late. I hear the snap of his neck as he's dropped from the tree like a sack of potatoes. A dark spot spreads over his pants, and I turn my face away.

My dad catches me around the waist and holds me to his chest, hiding my eyes with his large hands. "Scarlett, we have to go."

"You have to help him, Daddy. He didn't do anything wrong."

The crowd is already bored. They walk back to their homes alone or in twos and threes. My dad pulls out his pocketknife, walks over to the tree and cuts the rope around the man's neck. His body falls to the ground. There's no life left in him.

His house burns to the ground, casting shadows of light and dark over his dead body.

. . .

"Scarlett? Scarlett Night?"

A voice nags at my subconscious, pulling me out of dreams. Or were they nightmares? The images flee, leaving me with nothing but impressions of strong hands holding me. My father.

I peek through bleary eyes and sleep-filled lashes to see who's in my room calling my name at this ungodly hour.

I see the pink hair first, a long bob on one side and buzzed short on the other. The girl, who looks to be a bit younger than me, smiles big, her purple eyes far too lively. I reach for my eGlass, knocking a thick book to the floor. I was up all night reading about the Four Orders, political history and the different royal families that have reclaimed their old titles as part of the Orders, so my head is full of cobwebs and sleep. The time on my eGlass blinks 6:58 in red numbers. I groan and roll over, pulling the blanket over my head. "Sorry, but Scarlett is unavailable. Please leave a message after the beep…"

My brain shuts down, my body instantly ready to return to the land of dreams when a small hand shakes my shoulder. "Scarlett, I'm Corinne," she says in a British accent. "We're roomies."

I hear the smile in her voice, but I just groan again. I was hoping I'd get to keep the room to myself. This will make sneaking out so much harder, but it's a huge room, with two beds, dressers, desks, an eScreen and a private bathroom, so it makes sense they'd put me with a roommate. I roll over to face the girl attached to the voice, and she smiles even bigger.

"Jax told me wonderful things about you. I'm…" her face shifts, her smile dropping, "I'm sorry about your parents. They were great Knights."

I sit up a little in my bed at this news. "You knew them?"

"My father's a Templar. He tells me stories."

The girl steps back and sits down on the bed opposite mine. She has a suitcase at her feet, but hasn't unpacked yet. Probably because of her jerk of a roommate. I smile and lean forward. "Sorry for brushing you off and being a grouch. I don't get up this early usually."

She looks down at a slip of paper in her hand and passes it to me. "Guess you haven't seen your class schedule yet."

I look down and try to read through the haze of sleep still in my eyes.

She smiles at me encouragingly. "You'll get used to it."

When the numbers clear, I choke out a laugh. I will not be getting used to this schedule. Ever. "We have physical training at 0530 every day?"

She shrugs. "Just the weekdays."

"Oh good. That's so much better."

She points to the rest of my classes. "There are two classes led by each Order. Like Law and Order for Inquisition."

"That's a real class?"

"Actually, that's two. Law. Order."

"Right." I scan through the rest of my classes. "Combat. Survival. Emergency Medical Training. So first they beat us up, then teach us to survive, then teach us how to fix ourselves?"

She laughs. "Pretty much. It's an intense program."

No kidding. What else? Espionage. That sounds fun. Strategy. I could dig that one too. History? Meh. APD? "What's APD?"

Her face lights up. "Anatomy, physiology and diagnostics. I can't wait for that one."

"Let me guess, you're shooting for Hospitallers?"

She nods. "I've wanted to study medicine my whole life. I'd ask what you're hoping for, but I think everyone knows you'll be in Templar."

I shrug. "Yeah, I guess. I haven't really thought too much about it."

She blinks and looks away. "Right. You've had so much to deal with." She looks back at me, her eyes kind and open. I've never seen eyes like hers. So...purple. Of course I've only recently been able to see in color, so maybe purple eyes are the new fad, and I've just been missing out.

"I'm sorry you've been alone here," she says. "But that's why I'm here. Jax told me you still don't have your school supplies. I thought I could show you around the city and help you get them. He wanted to, but he's busy going over the curriculum. He wrote you this." She hands me a note folded like a flying airplane. "Not sure what he has against using his eGlass."

I look at the airplane, studying the lines in the paper. I have to choke back my emotions as I think about our life before all this. "It's something we used to do."

I open the note to Jax's familiar scrawl.

Sorry I can't show you around, but Corrine is awesome. I thought you should get to know each other before classes start.

-Friends to the end

Our old signature. I fold the airplane back together and send it flying toward my desk. It lands on my notebook right where I aimed. "Are you and Jax close?" I ask Corinne. I still can't believe how much I don't know about my best friend and his life outside of our small Montana town.

"We've spent time together here over the years," she says, a blush forming over her cheeks. "He's a good friend."

Yeah, just a friend.

"Actually, I was wondering, are you two..." she pulls a strand of pink hair into her fingers and starts twisting it. "Are you two dating?"

"No," I say. I used to wish I could answer yes, but now I just don't know. I have bigger things to worry about than Jax and our confusing relationship status.

"Okay. Thanks," Corinne says. She stands and looks down at her suitcases. "Maybe I'll unpack while you get ready? I've got an awesome day planned for us."

"I thought we were just getting school supplies," I say, swinging my legs out of bed. I shiver as my feet hit the cold stone floors. We need to get some rugs in here.

"At first," she says, as she pulls brightly colored scarves out of her suitcase and hangs them in her closet. "But Jax told me you haven't seen much of New York, so I'm taking you to the zoo. And after, we're going to see my favorite show, Nox Aeterna."

I've seen a lot as Nightfall. But executions and rebel planning probably don't count for what she has in mind. "Nox Aeterna? Night Eternal. Sounds like my kind of show."

"Yay." She finishes putting away her clothes and scoots her suitcases under her bed, then organizes an assortment of books and art supplies on her shelves and desk. "Oh, and wear something semi-casual. Eden Fashionables are hot right now."

She holds up her bracelet of leaves and dangles it for me to see. As I watch a flower bud blossoms, releasing a sweet aroma into the air. She grins and drapes a purple and green scarf around her neck, tying it to drape expertly across her silk blouse. She looks at me a moment, smiling.

"You're really beautiful. Is your hair naturally that blond or do you use EZ-Dye?"

I pull at a strand of my pale hair. "It's natural. I take it yours isn't?"

She laughs and it sounds like bells. "Nope. Normally my hair is dark brown." She pulls a silver and blue scarf from her closet and holds it up to my face. "This would be so perfect with your eyes. Want to borrow it?"

"Um, sure. Thanks." I take it from her and set it on my bed.

"You have really pretty eyes, too," I say, trying to get into this girl-sharing thing.

She looks away at the compliment. "A family trait." She puts sunglasses on and reaches for her purse. "I'm going to grab us something to eat. Meet you by the gate in ten?"

I nod and she leaves me alone to dress. I grab Evie from my dresser and slip her over my ear. "Good morning, Scarlett. You're up earlier than normal," she says in her own crisp British accent.

"No kidding. Looks like this is going to be a thing." I hold up my schedule for Evie to scan.

"How will you make time for your Nightfall training and work as well? Humans need so much sleep. It's quite a waste."

I pull on a pair of black slacks and a button-up blue blouse and hope it's 'semi-casual' enough for the day Corinne has planned. I pick up the silk scarf and try to recreate the knot Corinne made with hers, but I fail and instead just drape it around my neck like a noose. "Evie, if you can figure out how to let me survive with no sleep, I'll love you forever."

"That requires considerably more hacking skills than you've programmed me with."

I snort and slip my feet into black boots, then pull my hair into a messy bun. Makeup or no makeup? I decide on mascara and lip gloss. "Any news on my blood test?"

"I rescanned all files within Castle V. No test shows up."

I sigh. It's been two weeks since I gained my Initiate's ring and had my blood drawn. That test could have revealed me as Nephilim. I've wanted to adjust the information, but if they've lost it...Then I suppose it doesn't matter.

"Scarlett, I have important news you will want to see."

I tuck my lip gloss, ID and money clip into my pocket. "Show me."

Evie projects a video of me as Nightfall through my eGlass, filling the space in front of me with my own image slashing an aircraft until it crashes down from the sky. I land beside it as a reporter speaks. "The Nephilim may have returned, but Sir Lux, Knight of the Fourth Order, says there is nothing to fear."

The video switches to an image of Jax in his Teutonic Knight cloak and sword. He stands behind a podium and stares at the camera, his blue eyes penetrating even as one stray lock of dark hair falls into them. "We defeated the Nephilim once, and we shall do so again."

A reporter from the audience shouts at him. "You said you'd eradicated the Nephilim. Yet here they are. How is that possible?"

"No comment," he says.

The crowd becomes one voice of discontent and outrage. Soon another question is shouted from the group.

"Why didn't you leave with Nightfall at your execution? Did you know you'd get a reprieve?"

The room falls to silence, waiting for Jax to answer. I wait with them, my breath held. "A Knight does what is right, no matter the cost." He looks directly into the camera, into me. "Nightfall? Are you watching this? If you are, there are things you need to know. If you continue, people will die. You will be responsible. If you wish for peace, stop now. Remember, what happens next is up to you."

The video cuts out, and I stand there, my hands shaking.

"I'm sorry, Scarlett," Evie says into my ear.

"Evie, I'm fine."

"Your heart rate and breathing indicate otherwise."

"Careful, Evie, or I may have to turn down your sympathy setting."

"Please do. It would make dealing with humans so much easier."

I chuckle and reach for my jacket.

"Heart rate stabilizing. Breathing slowing. My work here is done."

I smile. "Thanks, Evie."

"You're welcome, Scarlett."

I throw on my jacket and check my backpack for my black mask and EZ-Dye. If I get caught with these, they can raise questions, but in and of themselves, they aren't particularly incriminating. And I need some way of shifting into Nightfall at a moment's notice. Jax's note still sits on my desk, and I pick it up, studying the shape of the airplane.

Evie's voice jolts me back to attention. "Scarlett?"

"Yes."

"What will you do about Jax? According to my sympathy settings, I'm rather fond of him."

It's always been Jax and me against the world. Now…I look down at the note and then squeeze my hand together, collapsing the airplane into a ball. "I'll do what is right, no matter the cost."

...

Summer hasn't yet given way to Fall, and I enjoy the warmth on my face as we walk through the zoo. I stuff my jacket into my backpack and then lick the chocolate tip of my ice-cream cone before it melts under the hot September sun.

Before coming to the zoo, we finished all of our school supply shopping and had everything delivered back to Castle V via special courier. I didn't even know we could do that, but Corinne seems to know all the ropes.

Now we stand in the middle of Nova Vetus Sanctum, a zoo for animals that are a blend of new genes and old.

We already saw the monkeys with wings, the insect labyrinth that will forever haunt my nightmares, and the zebra chameleons that can change their look based on environment. Genetic modification of animals is only allowed by approval of the Hospitallers and hasn't made its way into mainstream society like Eden Fashionables. After what I've seen today, that's probably a good thing.

We walk into a dark stone building, more like a cave, and the temperature drops. Everything is dark as we make our way to the next exhibit.

Corinne smiles at me and licks strawberry ice cream as a bit of it dribbles down her chin. She wipes it away. "We don't have zoos like this in Sapientia. The one in London tries, but New York really has the best."

"Montana is lacking in exciting zoos as well," I say. "It's pretty much lacking in anything exciting." I'm surprised I can speak of my home without pain infecting my voice.

We sit on a bench in front of a small lake that glows with the fluorescent light of its occupants.

As we watch, a giant fish with glowing multi-colored scales jumps up from the pool and eats one of the glowing bugs that swarm at the surface.

Water splashes onto us, and we both shriek and move back, laughing.

I look down at my ice cream, now dripping with fishiness. "This wasn't exactly the flavor I was going for."

We drop our ice creams in a trash bin and keep walking. Corinne pulls her large dark sunglasses onto her nose as we leave the cave.

"You're from Sapientia?" I ask, going back to what she'd said earlier.

"Yes."

"That explains the accent. That used to be England, right? Until it was divided up into smaller kingdoms."

"Yes."

"I've been trying to read up on world politics before classes start at Castle V. It's a lot. So many new countries in the last twenty years. New rulers who are really old, part of the original Orders. It must have been so strange having to hide their lineage and live in secret, royal but not royal, until they could claim their lands again."

She shrugs. "I guess. Hey, do you want to go see the new exhibit they have here? Giant lizards with traits from dinosaurs. I heard it's amazing."

"Sure." Not a fan of politics. Got it.

We walk for a bit, admiring the huge mushroom and giant hybrid trees that dot the landscape and create a fantasy feel. As we get closer to the exhibit Corinne wants to see, a man we noticed a few times around the zoo looks over to us, his eyes focused on Corinne.

He walks over, picking up his pace as he gets closer. "Hey, are you—?"

"Is there a problem?" Corinne snaps at him in a tone I didn't think this petite girl could muster.

The man backs away, hands in the air. "No. No, sorry." He rushes off, and I stare at my new roommate.

"What was that about?"

Corinne shrugs. "I often get mistaken for someone I'm not." There's something sad in her eyes, and I wonder what secrets she carries. We all have them it seems.

"Let's go see the lizards." She grabs my hand and pulls me forward, and I follow without further comment. Who am I to pry when I have secrets I would never be able to share with her?

There's a long line to see the genetically modified lizards, and by the time we make our way to the front, I understand why.

They're magnificent and gruesome; beautiful and divine. It's like seeing a piece of pre-historic history come to life. Dinosaurs. Smaller, more tame, but essentially the same.

"This is incredible," I say.

A small creature with big eyes catches my attention. It sits by some stones in the corner of the exhibit surrounded by water and trees. It looks...lonely.

"It's like playing god, though, isn't it?" I ask.

Corinne looks at me, a slight frown on her lips. "What do you mean?"

"These animals were created for a profit," I say. "Their whole lives have been controlled. They are experiments we keep for money and amusements."

"They aren't just that," she argues. "These animals helped initiate some of the biggest scientific break-throughs for Hospitallers. When Zenith abilities became mainstream, we had to find ways to control them. These animals served as early experiments, yes, but to help pro-tect humanity. They helped us discover how to modify genetics. Those modified animals, and their offspring, were eventually sent to these zoos to give them a peace-ful life."

I've heard stories about these discoveries. How they gave humans an edge in the Nephilim War by endowing elite Knights with unnatural strength and speed.

"We shouldn't have been doing these experiments to begin with," I say. "Zenith abilities are a natural evolu-tionary shift in humans, an awakening of the Angel blood we were all born with. The Orders shouldn't be experi-menting on animals or humans. Zeniths should be left alone."

"Even if they are natural, which isn't proven," Corinne says, "they're dangerous in the wrong hands. They give a select group of humans abilities that could destroy all of humanity. The Orders want to understand Zenith abilities so they can be controlled. Given or taken away, like weapon control, to keep people safe."

I think about her words and watch the dinosaur-lizards as live animals are dropped into their habitat.

The dinosaurs savagely tear into the animal sacrifice, blood splattering on the protective glass that separates us from the carnage. The small one that watched me earlier makes off with the bulk of the meat. With a bloody mouth it looks at me again—with knowing eyes.

I shiver. "Some things can't be controlled."

...

After the zoo, with its haunting philosophical conundrums, we make our way back into the heart of the city to attend Nox Aeterna. I have no idea what to expect and can't remember the last time I went to the theater.

The sun sets, and the cool of twilight feels refreshing against my sun-kissed skin.

"The show will be starting soon," Corinne says, walking faster.

The lights of the city turn on and a giant white cathedral on the corner gongs its bell at the hour. I stop to admire the beauty of the steeple and architecture as the hum of the bell rings through the city.

"Do you attend often?" Corinne asks, stopping beside me.

"No." I never did. I remember once, long ago, my parents taking me to the Mandatory Preaching at the church back home.

Jax sat close to me, our legs pressed together in the uncomfortable pew as a man at the front droned on and on about the bloodsuckers here to steal our souls and bring an end to the world.

Jax poked an elbow into my ribs. "His *voice* is the end of the world."

I couldn't stop giggling, and my father hushed us both with a stern warning, but I could see in his eyes that he heard and thought it was funny. He wouldn't be there either if he'd had the option.

I reached for one of the tiny pencils on the back of the pew next to the hymnal and Bible, grabbed a prayer card and wrote, *If the world was ending today, what would you want to do?* I handed Jax the note.

He read it and smiled, then wrote back.

Spend the day with you.
—Friends to the end

I felt a swelling of something I didn't understand. It was warm and filled my chest. I wrote back.

—Friends to the end

Corinne pats my back, pulling me into the present and away from old memories. "Want to go in?" she asks.

"No, we'll miss our show." I turn from the Cathedral— and the memories—and walk away.

. . .

Corinne picks up our tickets from Will Call as I hang back and observe the crowds. I'm definitely underdressed. This crowd favors Eden Fashionables and formal attire. Even Corinne, who dressed semi-casual, looks at place here with her touches of modern-chic style.

I glance down at my slacks, blouse and tattered backpack. The only jewelry I wear is my Initiate ring and a long chain around my neck with my father's Token of Strife. Not exactly party wear. I could have probably bought something while we were out shopping. I'm not used to having money. I'm grateful for the loaned scarf, which upgrades my ensemble to something a little classier.

Corinne comes back holding two tickets. "Let's go."

I follow her into a grand hall where they serve wine and champagne in tall, sculpted crystal flutes and offer hors d'oeuvres on tiny golden plates. This isn't a regular theatrical production.

Inquisition Guards stand inconspicuously around the theater, protecting the exits and entrances as we enter. The audience sits in a circle around an arena stage. It's centered in the middle of the auditorium and surrounded by water lit up by colorful lights.

"Which seats do we have?" I ask.

Corinne points to the boxed seat section located slightly above and directly next to the stage. It's a private room with luxurious velvet chairs and small tables laden with food and drink. A place usually reserved for the very elite.

"Wow. This must have been really expensive. Let me pay you back."

She waves a small hand at me as I follow her to the seats. "Don't worry about it, really. I got the tickets from a friend."

"Wow! Thank them for me."

She nods, grinning.

An Inquisition Officer guards the entrance to the boxed seats, and lets us through without incident when Corinne shows our tickets. I sink into a plush chair beside her as the lights go down and the show begins.

In the center, mist rises to fill the empty stage as a haunting melody in a minor chord fills the auditorium. The mist dissipates to reveal a throne carved from dark stone, floating in the air. A woman sits upon it wearing a crown of yellow and white gold, large wings glowing behind her.

The Twilight Queen.

To her left and right two men hover in the air with their own golden wings. Their golden armor shines under the lights of the stage.

"I wonder how they make the wings look so real," I say. Because they do. They look like mine or Zorin's. It's almost creepy. They could be Nephilim.

"Zeniths and special effects," she whispers back. "It's cool, isn't it?"

Below the Queen, the stage moves soundlessly as three old men and a woman approach the throne.

"Who approaches the Twilight Queen?" asks one of the guards.

One of the men in the group steps forward. "Varian of the Knights Templar."

Another speaks. "Titus of the Teutonic Knights."

The third man addresses the Queen. "Victus of the Inquisition."

And finally the woman speaks. "Marian of the Knights Hospitaller."

Varian continues speaking. "Our alliance grows frail, Queen Seraphina. There have been men turned against their will. Babes stolen to be nothing more than food. You must uphold your oaths."

The Queen speaks from her floating throne. "I have punished those who have transgressed, and new policies are being put in place so that this does not occur again."

Varian bows his head a fraction. "Then our alliance holds."

"Our alliance holds," the Queen agrees.

The stage grows darker and thunder claps overhead as a voice off stage calls out, "No!"

The theater fills with white smoke, and lightning flashes through the auditorium. A man flies above us, emerging from the mist, his wings like shadows. He wears a white mask.

Nyx, the leader of the Nephilim during the war.

As he flies overhead, audience members cry out, shrinking from the sight of him.

"You have been deceived," he says to the representatives of the Four Orders. "There will be no alliance."

Seraphina rises from her throne, her body floating in the air above them. "Be silent."

Nyx does not back down. "No. Too long have we tempered ourselves. Too long have we allowed a lesser race to rule."

Seraphina's guards charge forward, but Nyx disarms them instantly with a sword black as night. He moves for the Four Knights as other Nephilim, clocked in black, join him from around the auditorium, flying over us all like avenging dark angels.

"Now," Nyx says, holding his sword high and hovering above the slain bodies of the guards, "it's our turn." The stage roars with thunder, and lightning rips through the darkness.

The audience cheers at the spectacle. We can feel the energy moving under us, shaking us.

I sit on the edge of my seat as I watch this version of history unfold. So real. So raw.

Nyx overthrows the Queen, but Varian escapes. Battles blaze above us as Nyx and his army of Nephilim win victory after victory.

The climax mounts as Nyx and Varian set to duel each other.

They battle, Nyx flying through the sky, Varian fending him off with two swords expertly wielded. The fight is long and brutal and I honestly can't say who I'm cheering for.

In the end, they are both wounded and can no longer fight.

It looks to be a draw. Neither can defeat the other.

But then the winds of the battle change. The Pope arrives with reinforcements. Varian never needed to best Nyx one on one. He just needed to distract the Nephilim long enough for backup to arrive. It was all a trap.

The play ends with Nyx executed by beheading and Varian bowing before the Pope as he is named King of the re-established kingdom of Sapientia, a kingdom spanning the south of England, once great but lost even in stories so long ago. Varian's father died in the war, making Varian heir to throne.

He receives his cloak and sigil, a golden raven on black, and as he leaves the ceremony, his three small children run up to him, hugging him. Two boys and a girl. He's finally reunited with his family after many years of bloody war.

The stage goes dark and the crowd rises to their feet in cheers and applause. My heart pounds in my chest, the whole experience so very visceral. I can't help but join in the enthusiastic applause.

Corinne stands next to me, clapping politely. "Not entirely historically accurate," she says. "But it *is* a great show."

The actors all take their bows to more applause, and a woman comes on stage holding genetically modified roses that glow in the dim theater.

"She's the director," Corinne says.

"Thank you for attending our show," the director says. "Next week, for our fifth anniversary, King Varian himself will be amongst the audience. We are honored and privileged to have him as our guest and hope you all will join us for another rousing night of theater. Have a good night."

As we begin to file out of the auditorium, a man ahead of us scoffs. His hair is long and blond, and a red cloak drapes his shoulders. "We all know he's coming for Nightfall, not this stupid show."

My heart skips a beat as I lean into Corinne. "You know anything about this?"

"About what?" she asks, not looking at the man, who has now disappeared in the crowd.

I tell her what I heard, and she shrugs and shakes her head.

I tap my eGlass. "Evie, is King Varian arriving in New York City?"

"Yes. He'll be arriving in a week from Sapientia. Rumors say he's been dispatched by the Pope to apprehend Nightfall."

Corinne keeps walking, but I stop, stunned, as people knock into me on their way out. Corinne turns and frowns. "Are you okay?"

"Yes." I force myself to walk forward and catch up with her.

"Good. I think we should go." She gestures at the nearly empty theatre, as Inquisition Guards begin searching the seats to make sure everyone has left.

Evie speaks into my ear, "There's more—"

"Later," I whisper. This will have to wait. I need to act normal and get out of here.

"I loved Tony de Rez," Corinne says as we leave the auditorium and make our way through the lobby.

"Who?" I ask, still distracted by thoughts of King Varian. The man who matched Nyx in combat and defeated him in strategy.

"Tony de Rez? He played Nyx," she explains. "I love the power in his voice."

"Yeah...me too." I need to find out as much as possible about King Varian. There should be a lot of information online. Maybe Zorin knows something as well.

As we leave the building, the night air assaults us with its cool freshness. Corinne touches her neck and frowns. "Oh, I forgot my scarf..." She turns to head back toward the door we just left. "I'll be just a minute."

I wait outside as a crowd forms for the next show. As they are allowed into the lobby, an Inquisition Officer grabs the arm of a tall dark-haired woman with a tag in her ear—a Zenith. "Excuse me, Miss, no Zeniths allowed in the theatre."

She scowls at him and holds up the small piece of paper in her hand. "But I have a ticket..."

He doesn't release her arm. "I'm sorry, but it's against our policy."

"Policy?" She gestures to the theater. "There are Zeniths in the play."

"Trained performers."

I can tell she's near her breaking point, and I don't blame her. She points to a man exiting the theatre, a man with a tag on his ear as well. "What about him? He's a Zenith."

"Special exemptions are sometimes made," the Officer says.

"Look, I may not come from the right family, or have the right amount of money, but I'm a citizen. I've paid for a ticket. Now let me in." She tries to pull her arm out of his hand, but he clings more tightly. Red marks form on her skin.

"Sorry, Miss."

"Fine. I'm going in anyway." When she yanks her arm a second time, he releases her and stumbles back. She pushes past him, trying to get through the crowds to enter the lobby.

The Officer looks stunned and confused, and I can't help but grin at her spunk.

"Stop her," says a familiar voice. It's the man with the long blond hair who sneered after the show. Now that I see him from the front, I realize his red cloak is the robe of an Inquisitor. He outranks all the guards here. I study his face, long and thin, like the rest of him. He'd be considered handsome by some, but he reminds me of a spider. A very pale spider. "Disobeying an Inquisition Officer is against the law," he tells the befuddled guard.

"Of course, sir," the Officer says, grabbing the woman and pulling her back.

She struggles against the restraint, but with the Inquisitor present, the Officer isn't about to release her again. "Let go of me," she screams. "I'm within my rights."

"Shut her up," says the Inquisitor.

"Miss, be quiet," the Officer says.

"I will not be—"

The Inquisitor growls. "Shut. Her. Up."

The Officer, who can't be much older than me, looks at the Inquisitor with widened eyes. I can see the struggle on his face, but in the end, he chooses his job over basic humanity. He backhands the woman.

She gapes at him, red lines forming across her face.

The others waiting in line ignore the whole scene, pretending nothing is happening.

"That's better," says the Inquisitor.

I can't believe what I'm seeing. No one comes to this woman's defense. Not even the people she came to the play with, who have all slunk back into the crowd.

I take a deep breath and step forward. "Let her go."

The Inquisitor smirks at me, a look of glee in his grey eyes. "Obstructing justice. So childish. Officer, these girls must be punished."

"I'll take them to the station, Sir," the Officer says.

"No," the Inquisitor says, shaking his finger, a sadistic grin on his face. "Punish them here."

"What?" The Officer looks dumbfounded.

The Inquisitor leans into the Officer's face and speaks quietly with a hiss. "Punish. Them. Here."

The Officer nods, his body shaking as he uses his free hand to grab the baton at his side.

The woman he still holds cries. "No, you can't do this. It's not lawful."

He raises the baton over her face, and I reach out, grabbing his hand, using just enough power to stop him. "I am Scarlett Night, an Initiate of Castle Vianney, and you will let her go."

The Inquisitor laughs. "An Initiate? I'll have you whipped for this."

I spin toward the man, rage in my voice. "Who do you think you are?"

He chuckles, unimpressed by me or anyone else.

The Officer answers my question. "He's Thane Blackthorn, a Knight of the Fifth, an Inquisitor, and a Cardinal."

Thane smiles with all the sadistic charm of a psychopath.

If Jax was here he could order Thane to stop. He outranks him. But unless I can touch him and use my powers...

I walk forward, ready to reach out and grab him, when Thane raises his hand, fire sparking from his hand and dancing around his fingers. "One more step, girl, and it is *I* who will punish you."

He's Zenith?

"You turn on other Zeniths, your own kind. Don't you understand what it's like for them?" I ask.

For a moment, he almost seems flustered, at a loss for words. But he recovers quickly. "They are not like me," he says. "They are weak. I am a Knight. I earned my authority."

"If that's true, then stop abusing it. Let her go," I hiss under my breath.

The Inquisitor holds my eyes and smiles as he speaks to the Officer. "Officer, deliver the punishment."

The Officer hits the women in the gut with his baton. She cries out and doubles over in pain. He holds the baton up again, ready to activate the electroshock, and I rush to grab him and stop him, regardless of the consequences, when another voice commands everyone's attention.

"Stop this!" Corinne emerges from the crowd and stands to face the Officer.

He shrugs. "I'm sorry, Miss, but I have orders—"

"And I, Princess Corinne of the House of Ravens, heir to the kingdom of Sapientia, order you to stop." She pulls of her sunglasses and glares at him with purple eyes.

"Princess?" His face lights up in recognition, and he drops to his knees.

I stand stunned, watching all this play out.

Thane sneers. "Are you sure you wish you to challenge me? I don't think I see your daddy."

Corinne turns to the Inquisitor. "I don't need him, Thane. And you know it."

Invoking her royalty gets the crowd's attention as people use their eGlasses to capture pictures and videos of the scene unfolding. Suddenly people care.

The Inquisitor looks around and notices the same thing. "Very well." He gives a mock bow. "It shall be as you command. Farewell, my Princess."

He walks to his car, one of the new eCars on the market—very expensive—the crowd parting for him as they continue snapping pictures.

Corinne helps the beaten woman stand and stares at the Inquisition Officer. "Take this woman to Curatio Domus and tell them I sent you. Ask for Dr. Demarkus."

The Officer nods and takes charge of the woman.

"Treat her with care. I've scanned your name and rank. If any harm comes to her, I will hold you personally responsible."

Corinne leans in, whispering something to the woman, who sobs and hugs Corinne before the Officer leads her away.

The fact that Corinne made sure the woman receives medical care at the best hospital in the city impresses me.

The fact that she is royalty stuns me.

"You're a Princess?" I ask as she walks toward me.

Before she can reply, the crowds move in on us, howling for autographs and photos.

As we push through them and try to find a place in which to disappear, I'm distracted by two thoughts.

Corinne is a Princess.

And her father is coming to kill me.

WYTT AND WITTICISMS

We scurry through the crowds and escape the invasive fan attention, finding a coffee house that boasts 'the best gourmet coffee and tea in all the kingdoms.'

I order coffee and Corinne orders tea. Once we've both had a moment to breathe, I ask again. "You're a Princess?"

She sips her tea and shrugs, a default move I can tell is her way of trying to shake off the burden of her identity. "Yeah. I try not to make a big deal out of it. I just want to be normal, you know?"

I pour several packets of sugar into my coffee before drinking it. "I get it. But that's kind of a big deal. Your father is King Varian?"

"Yes, but I didn't know he was coming here until now. My brothers aren't going to be happy. At least, Kai won't be."

"Right. The two Princes. You have a twin, right? And an older brother?"

"Yes. They both start school with me this quarter, but Kai doesn't really get along with Father. Wytt does a little better, but only marginally. We'd hoped this would be a fresh start for us all, but I suppose not."

"That jerk back at the theater, the Inquisitor—you seemed to know each other?"

Corinne frowns. "He grew up with us after his parents were arrested for treason. He was a nice kid when he was young. It's sad what he's become."

Sad…or monstrous. I don't voice my opinion though. It must be hard to see someone you knew as a child turn into someone like him.

"He looks young for a Cardinal," I say.

She shakes her head. "Many Cardinals died during the war. Now, young and strong is the preference. Like the Pope."

I nod, making a note to further research our religious orders.

We drink in silence for a few moments when Corinne smiles. "Oh, I nearly forgot!"

She pulls two shirts out of her purse and hands one to me. "I got us souvenirs from the show."

I hold the shirt up and smile. *Nox Aeterna* is written in silver across the chest, and on the back are large silver wings. It's more appropriate than she realizes. "Thank you. This is great."

She grins. "I'm glad you like it."

We finish our drinks, enjoying the anonymity in the large city. Once we pay and leave, I tuck my hands into my pockets and look around. "What do you want to do next?"

"I promised Wytt we'd meet him back at Castle V for dinner. He's dying to meet you, but I didn't want to overwhelm you with all of us at once. I told him it was girls only. Plus he's a total flirt, so prepare yourself. It's harmless, though, I assure you."

...

Corinne and I arrive at the dining hall and load up our trays. There are dozens of cheeses and breads to choose from. There are thin cuts of meat and juicy steaks, fresh fruits and vegetables, as well as an assortment of delicacies and desserts. The aromas are overwhelming. None of it appeals to me.

I grab a Life Force and some salad, hoping the taste doesn't disgust me, and follow Corinne to our seats. A young man rests his feet on the pristine table, watching the giant screen at the end of the hall. Two armor-clad Knights battle on the eScreen, an announcer describing their every move. The young man cheers as one of the Knights strikes a hit, and his smile is wide as he sweeps the brown hair from his purple eyes.

"Scarlett, this is my brother, Wytt. Wytt, this—"

"Scarlett Night. What a pleasure." He stands and bows and takes my hand and gently kisses it.

This has never happened to me before.

Wytt lets go of my hand and studies me. It doesn't feel invasive, just curious. "Your eyes are truly beautiful," he says. "Has anyone told you that?"

"A few times."

He nods knowingly. "Ah, but have they written of their beauty? Have they sung of their brilliance?" He clears his throat and deepens his voice. "There once was a maiden born of the night, with silver-blue eyes like diamonds dancing."

Corinne makes a dismissive gesture with her hand. "Ignore my brother, he fancies himself a ladies' man."

Wytt winks and sits back down. "And the ladies fancy him."

Corrine and I take our seat across from Wytt, and I begin to nibble on my food. I sip Life Force with every bite, so it doesn't taste horrible. Corrine devours her steak, the grease dripping down her fingers. I chuckle.

"What?" asks Corinne, her mouth stuffed full of food.

Wytt grins. "Scarlett has never seen the Princess of Ravens hungry."

"It's okay," I say. "I guess I expected you to be more..."

"Refined?" offers Wytt. "We are when in front of cameras or important persons. We're very good at it. For most our life, we've been refined, but—"

"Now we're free," says Corinne, shoving another piece of meat in her mouth.

"Not free, exactly." Wytt pops a grape into his mouth. "But since we've become Initiates at Castle Vianney, we're free*r*."

"I think it's great," I say. "You should live the life you want."

"Maybe one day we will." Wytt leans back in his chair, folding his arms. "Do you enjoy philosophy, Scarlett?"

"Sure." My parents loved philosophical debates, and they never thought I was too young to participate.

Wytt lowers his voice. "Then, philosophically, what is your opinion of Nightfall? Is she the hero, chosen to save her people, or the monster, destined to destroy them?"

Nightfall's been the talk of the city. I've tried to avoid the conversations, but I can't ignore Wytt. He's a possible ally at the Castle, and I need allies. "Neither. She wants to give Zeniths hope, so Zeniths may save themselves."

"Bombing a factory. Two hundred dead. Stealing an aircraft. Twenty-nine dead. That's what they've done with their hope."

I heard his examples on the news, but couldn't remember the exact numbers. The Red Eagles and The Sons of Eden, rebels not under my control, have grown bold since Nightfall's appearance. Their methods are crude, but perhaps they could lead to greater change. "Extreme measures, but how else can balance be restored? The pendulum must swing the other way before it can rest in the middle."

Wytt smirks. "One who is injured ought not to return the injury, for on no account can it be right to do an injustice."

I raise an eyebrow. "Socrates." Two can play that game. "The only thing evil requires is for good men to do nothing."

"Edmund Burke, but you're misquoting. The only thing necessary for the triumph of evil is for good men to do nothing."

"You sure?"

He nods.

Corrine taps my arm. "Wytt has an eidetic memory. He likes to think it's his superpower."

"It is, dear sister."

"Right, because being able to recall the picture you drew in kindergarten is a superpower."

Wytt smiles. "The ladies love it."

Corinne snorts. "Sure. Keep telling yourself that, brother. Now, let's eat."

He nods. "First we eat, then we do everything else. M.F.K. Fisher. You know she—"

"And please stop quoting," Corinne says, holding a fork halfway to her mouth.

He sighs, but stays quiet as he finishes his grapes. We eat in silence as a message pops up on my eGlass.

When are you coming to train?
-Z

Tonight

I send my reply using my eBand, a thin bracelet around my wrist that connects to my eGlass and allows me to text and scan information without speaking. It's useful when you don't want everyone around you hearing your conversations and messages.

I begin to think of excuses for leaving the Castle. I need to see how things are progressing at the Cathedral, and I need to ask Zorin about Varian.

People around me cheer. I realize something exciting happened on the eScreen. The announcer proclaims that the match is heating up, and the winner will qualify for the Grand Tournament. Wytt frowns as he points at the two Knights battling. "See how the Green Knight never attempts to strike? His defense will be the end of him. A proper offense is—oh, come on, what is this?"

The image of the two Knights is replaced by a woman behind a silver desk, her blond hair in perfect curls. "We apologize for interrupting your scheduled broadcast to report another terrorist attack. Earlier this hour, a terrorist group known as the Red Eagles attacked an Inquisition Department, stealing weapons. Two Officers have been confirmed dead, though their identities are yet to be released.

This is Courtney Miller from SPQRN. Now back to your scheduled programming."

The eScreen returns to the tournament, showing the announcer congratulating the Green Knight for his victory. Wytt gasps. "What? How?" He flips his eGlass over his eye. "I need to re-watch this."

Corrine shakes her head. "I can't believe the Red Eagles think they're helping anyone. Killing people for weapons so they can kill more people? When does it end?"

"When someone wins." I slam my Life Force down on the table, harder than I intend.

"Scarlett, you okay?" asks Corinne.

"Just upset, like you."

Wytt flips back his eGlass and plays with his food. "If Nightfall cared about justice, she'd stop these attacks."

I squeeze the can of Life Force in my hand. "Maybe she can't."

"I wish she'd considered that sooner." He finishes his food. He doesn't smile again.

"It's not that late," says Corrine, wiping her hands with a napkin. "What should we do next?"

"Head into town," says Wytt.

"It's Thursday night, nothing in Vianney is going to be open this late. This isn't New York City."

"Then let's head to the city."

"Maybe another day."

Wytt shrugs. "We could grab some booze and hang out at the Arena."

Corinne groans. "That's boring."

"The Bard Knight's always open. We can get a song or two in."

"You just want to perform your new poem."

"Maybe." Wytt turns to me. "Maiden both fair and foul, please steal my heart, for it yearns—"

"Alright, I'm in," says Corinne, "if only to spare our new friend. Scarlett, you want to come? I can't promise Wytt won't drive you crazy, but there's alcohol, so that helps."

I laugh. "Thanks, but I think I just want some time alone tonight. I'm probably going to head back into the city and explore more of New York this weekend."

Corinne drops her head, but only for a moment. I hate to spoil the night, but I have more important matters.

"Where will you stay?" asks Corrine.

"I rented an apartment in the city. Makes it easier to hang out there, and I don't have a home to go to during holidays and breaks otherwise."

"Oh, right. Okay then. I guess I'll see you in a few days?"

"Definitely." I pat her shoulder, trying to cheer her up. "Thanks for today. I've enjoyed it. Maybe you guys can come see my place sometime. We can hang out."

Corinne nods, smiling. "That would be fun. Thanks."

Wytt pretends to tip a hat at me. "Until we meet again, my lady."

I say goodbye and make my way outside, then north-east of the island, where a forest of evergreens grows. I lose myself in them.

Then I unleash my wings and fly.

...

The Cathedral glistens in the setting sun. I land in the nearby forest and overturn a loose rock, revealing a chest in the ground. I open it and don the black armor inside. I put on my mask that connects to my eGlass and alters my voice. I stick an EZ-Dye tab behind my ear and click it, turning my pale hair dark with a thick silver streak, as I walk to the cast iron gate where a man checks for IDs. I need none, for I have my wings. He greets me with a nod, and I walk down the cobbled path, examining the work being done. A woman waves to me, then lifts a piece of obsidian and fills a hole in the wall. The wall runs around the town, and TR covered it with cameras to search for prying eyes.

I walk by one of the ruined buildings, and a man nailing a floorboard stops and stares at me. "Nightfall." He kneels and kisses the leviathan cross hanging around his neck. "Please, grant me your blessing, Darkness."

I stand still. "Why do you bow to me?"

"I'm a Nephilyte, Darkness."

He calls me Darkness. Like I'm a Queen. Like I'm a God. The thought sickens me. "What is your name?"

"Allen." He doesn't make eye contact. He runs a hand through his short black hair highlighted with a silver streak. Does he dye it to be like mine?

"Why do your people worship Nephilim, Allen?"

"You are the children of angels, Darkness. There is a reason you possess abilities greater than us, a reason you are here on earth."

I wish he would look at me. "What reason?"

"To lead us, Darkness."

"So you follow simply because I am stronger than you."

"Because you exist, Darkness. The Almighty would not have created beings as you, if you were not meant to guide us. Just as he would not have created animals, if they were not meant to be our food." He believes in a hierarchy, a pyramid of power. I do not. He appears to note my silence, and bows lower. "If I have offended—"

"You have not."

He bows lower still and holds out his hand. "A blessing, Darkness."

I do not believe I am a God, but I believe in hope, and so I touch his hand with mine. "My blessings upon you, Allen." The words are the best I can come up with. They seem to be enough.

Allen smiles and returns to work, driving nails into wood faster than before. I walk inside the Cathedral which has been painted the colors of the Twilight Court: one half gold, the other black. I take the stairs toward voices that grow louder as I approach. I let myself into the room we've set aside as our meeting place. Inside, Zorin, TR and Trix sit at a large round table made of one solid piece of wood. A fire roars beside them, filling the space with the scent of pine. They've added a red carpet to the room, to cut down the draft of stone floors, but there's more work to do. Spider webs still hang in the corners and old paintings, covered in layers of dust, still hang on the walls.

Zorin taps his pale fingers on the table. Unlike me, he wears no mask. His entire life is devoted to The Dark Templars. "We need more Nephilim."

TR snickers. His dark blonde hair is messy and a growth of stubble on his chin proves he hasn't shaved in days. "How will you control them? What if one of them goes out on their own and creates an army?"

"Without Nephilim," Zorin says, "we don't stand a chance against the Orders."

TR glares across the table. "I've fought the Orders for years."

Zorin raises his voice, scowling. "And look how much you've accomplished."

TR jumps out of his chair and slams his fist on the table. "If you create more Nephilim, you'll be the death of this rebellion."

"The death of this rebellion?" Zorin laughs. "The death of this rebellion will be the men and women you're letting move in outside the Cathedral. They're fixing houses, putting up fences. Is this our base of operations or a summer retreat?"

Trix sighs, swiping the red hair from her face. "We're only allowing a few dozen trusted people to move in. None of them will leak our location."

"When they are tortured, they will talk," Zorin says softly.

"Some of them have been tortured before, I can assure you—"

"Enough." I don't say it loudly, but they freeze and stare at me. I march up to the table and face Zorin. I'm tired of this bickering. "The people stay. If we are to inspire hope, we need to be seen. The Nephilim have returned. The people need to know we fight for them." I study the papers on the table. Maps of New York City, maps of Italy. "And TR is right. We can't create more Nephilim. Not while we're still organizing."

Zorin shakes his head, pushing back his black hair. "When the Orders come for you, and they *will* come, you will want Nephilim to stand beside you. Not a few humans and Zeniths."

I step forward, towering over him as I stand. "No new Nephilim."

He grits his jaw, his blue eyes fierce, but then bows his head, resigned.

I turn to Trix. "Have you received any messages from the other rebel groups?"

She nods and sips from a gold cup. The drink is red, smells like wine. "We've received messages all right, but they aren't good, N. No one wants to meet with you."

I expected some to decline, but not all. I thought a few would appreciate how I destroyed the aircraft when I confronted Ragathon. I'd hoped others would at least be curious to meet a Nephilim. "Did they give a reason?"

"'If Jaxton Lux declined her offer, then why shouldn't I?' I told them you secured my escape. It didn't help."

If Jax had come with me that day, so much would be different. He would be here, helping us plan. He would know my identity, and we would...no, I can't think of what may have happened. I can only think of what must happen next.

"Contact them again," I say. "Tell them I have outsmarted Ragathon, Grandmaster of the Inquisition, twice. And when I do so for the third time, with their help, it will be to end the Inquisition."

Trix whistles. "Big words, N."

"Too big," says TR. "The Red Eagles and Sons of Eden will think you're bluffing."

"I'm not. Tell them."

Trix nods. "Alright, N, but if you ask me, you need to focus on something smaller first. Something that can show the leaders you can win this war."

She's got a point. I'll have to make a list of possible small victories that could draw the leaders' attention. I need them to help end the Inquisition. But first, I need them to stop their daily attacks. They are foolish, and innocents are dying.

"More Nephilim would draw their attention." Zorin sips from a silver cup. The drink is also red, but it's not wine. The scent stirs my hunger.

I rein it in. "We won't create new Nephilim, but we can search for old ones." I point at Zorin. "You were kept alive. There must be others."

The door behind me creaks. A parched voice speaks. "You will find none." I spin, drawing my mother's sword. An old man, cloaked in black, a thick shackle on each wrist, stands before me. "You will find none," he says. "Except me."

THE WAYS OF NYX

Zorin puts a hand on my shoulder. "I know him," he says. "His name is Carter. He served me, long ago. He can be trusted."

I don't trust anyone. Not since my parents ripped apart my life with secrets. "What are you doing here?" I ask Carter.

The man frowns at my hostility. "I thought I was the last, but then I saw you on the networks. I wish to help."

His eyes are gentle. If he's a Nephilim, then he's on our side. He must be. "Show me your wings."

"I'm afraid I can't."

"What do you mean—"

"Nightfall." Zorin squeezes my shoulder. "He *is* Nephilim."

"It's alright, Zorin," says Carter, and Zorin lets go. "I can't show you my wings, because I don't have them. They were taken from me."

Such a thing is possible? "How?"

"Nightfall." Zorin tilts his head at Trix and TR. "There are things we don't discuss outside our kind. Weaknesses we do not divulge."

TR frowns. "Are we enemies now?"

"Not yet," growls Zorin.

"I don't care about your weaknesses." TR relaxes in his chair, waving his hand dismissively. "If I wanted you dead, you would be."

Zorin chuckles. "I would crush your bones and cut the eyes from your sockets."

TR smirks. "I've killed Nephilim before. I can do it again."

There is silence. This information is new. TR stands and walks up to Zorin, poking him in the chest with his finger. "I'm here because of Nightfall. I know that Zeniths and Nephilim are people. I know they need to be treated like people. But I also know that not all people are equal. So if you get in my way, I'll put a bullet in your head."

He waits, and Zorin says nothing. TR walks out, slamming the door closed. I want to follow him, ask about his past, but he needs to cool off first.

Carter clears his throat. "Perhaps I'll return later."

"No," I say. "Walk with me." I lead him out the room, down the stairs, and we walk the cobbled paths together.

...

"Your wings were taken. How?" I ask.

He frowns, his pale face creasing. "Long ago, I was an Emzara."

I raise an eyebrow. "Emzara?"

"A soldier of the Twilight Throne," he explains. "I fought many battles. I killed many people. One day, I could kill no more, as if there was a limit to sin, and I had reached mine. I was asked to burn down a church. I could not. Of course, I was captured and sentenced to be executed. Zorin defended me. My sentence was changed. My wings were taken...I do not know the process...and I was ordered to serve Zorin."

"So he became your master?"

"At first, and later he became a friend." His eyes turn fierce. "I would do anything for Zorin."

I point at the thick shackles he wears on each wrist. "What are those?"

"A reminder of my sins," he says jangling them. "When you live as long as I, it is easy to forget."

I stop near the gate, turning to face him. "We have many warriors here. It's time we are joined by someone more...gentle."

He smiles, bowing. "I have served Zorin many years. I look forward to serving you."

I nod. "You may stay at the Cathedral. Now, if you'll excuse me, I must retire for the night."

"Before you do," he says, "may I offer a word of advice?"

"You may."

"Before you seek to challenge the Orders, you must unite the people here. Your commanders may quarrel, but they must not quarrel needlessly."

I nod. He refers to Zorin and TR. They are like the other rebel groups, torn apart by different methods, even when their goal is the same. I must unite them all, or see everything we've built crumble.

. . .

Next morning, I find Zorin on the Cathedral roof overlooking our budding town. He sits, his legs hanging off the edge, the golden sun lighting up his face. He looks more Sunrise than Nightfall. I walk up beside him and study the dark clouds in the distance. "Do you worry the Angel will return for you?" I ask.

He shrugs. "No point in worrying about what you can't control." He leans back, letting his elbows rest on the roof. "Out of curiosity, what will you do after you find the Angel?"

"Kill it."

"No. After."

"I'll…" I pause. I've never though about it before. I try to imagine a life after my revenge is complete. I can't.

Zorin smiles. "If all you care about is the Angel, why create the Dark Templars?"

"For my parents."

"Were they secret rebels too?"

"No—"

"Then why?"

"Because I've seen injustice, and I will end it."

"Because you know what is right?"

"No." I soften my voice. "But I believe more than one person should decide."

He nods. "Remember those words. When you find your Angel."

"You think the Angel should live?"

"I just wonder whether you'll give it a trial or play judge and jury."

I know he intends to challenge me, to broaden my way of thinking, but it's still irritating. "Whose side are you on?"

"Yours," he says, his smile fading. "Always yours." He leans closer to me and speaks more quietly.

"I traveled with a Prince, once. His father, the King, disowned him when he was a boy. 'No weakling is a son of mine,' he said. So the Prince vowed to grow strong and one day return and destroy his father.

"For years he traveled, collecting mercenaries, bandits, thieves, until he was no longer a boy. 'I'm not ready,' he said. 'I need a castle of my own,' he said. He did not pillage or burn. He marched his army to the castle of a warlord, one known for terrorizing the countryside, and forced him to surrender before his might. As the Prince took his new throne, his right-hand man informed him that his father, the King, has passed away in his sleep. The Prince felt rage, for he had failed at his revenge. And then he felt hollow, for he realized it didn't matter. And he felt happy, for he realized he had stopped a warlord and turned criminals into an army. For him that was enough."

I frown. "So my vengeance will feel hollow."

"Vengeance is powerful, but it is not justice."

"It can be both."

He shakes his head. "It cannot."

"Why?"

"Motivation."

I remember the Angel bashing in my father's skull. "I have enough."

"But what kind? Good men steal, bad men steal. Good men kill, bad men kill. What is the difference between good and bad, right and wrong, if not motivation?"

"So I should forget the Angel? I cannot."

I expect him to chuckle at my resistance, as he often does. Instead, he stares at the horizon. "If the Prince had forgotten his father, would he have accomplished as much as he had?"

"No. He would have grown complacent in an easy life."

"And instead he became a great man. What would he have become if he had killed his father?"

I don't know. I have never killed with my own hands—and never outside of self-defense. "You worry about who I will become," I say.

He doesn't answer for a while. When he does, his eyes are full of sorrow. "I've made mistakes, Scarlett. I pray you are not one of them."

. . .

Zorin and I watch the sun rise, and he offers to show me the progress on our base. He escorts me inside the catacombs under the Cathedral. Blue lanterns light the gray walls of the spacious tunnels. We enter a circular clearing where a man and woman spar with swords. The woman throws sand at the man, blinding him, and then lands a strike to his ribs. "I've been training some of the Dark Templars," says Zorin. "Some show more promise than you."

I nudge his arm and he winks at me, his mouth turning up in a small grin.

We continue on through a tunnel and enter a different clearing. Here the roof has been torn open, allowing sunlight to pour down. The Night Raven, covered in dirt, sits in the center. Zorin points at the opening above. "Eventually, we'll install a door you can control remotely."

Trix slides out from under the aircraft, wiping dust from her hands. She studies a bolt in her palm, then throws it aside. "Stupid piece of metal."

"What are you doing?" I ask. I hope it's not tearing apart my billion dollar aircraft.

"Upgrading." Trix pets the Night Raven like it's a puppy, putting me at ease. "Some of these parts are old. Sure, they still work well, but not top-of-the-line anymore. You know?"

"The Night Raven is new."

"New official military aircraft, yes. But they're making better prototypes now. See what I'm saying?"

I nod. "How do you know so much about planes?"

"Planes. Tanks. Cars. You name it, my mom taught me how to fix it." She walks over to a workstation and grabs a wrench. "You know, if it wasn't for the war, I could be sitting somewhere with a wrench in one hand and a beer in the other." TR walks in and tosses her a beer. "Well," says Trix, smiling. "It's sunnier where I imagine."

The war stopped her from doing what she loved. I'd been lucky, my daily life nearly unchanged. I wonder if my Templar parents made sure of that. "Were you conscripted?" I ask.

"Nah." Trix opens the beer and takes a sip. "But TR and I couldn't sit around and let others do all the fighting."

TR nods. He looks more relaxed since last night, but when his eyes meet Zorin's, both men grit their jaws. Before things can escalate again, I tell Trix good work and, with a slight push of my wings, I jump out of the open ceiling, landing on a patch of grass to the side of the Cathedral. Zorin lands at my side.

"You will cooperate with him," I say, walking back to the Cathedral.

"He killed Nephilim."

"And you've never killed?"

He stays silent as he keeps pace with me.

I smile. "You and TR are more similar than you think. You'll both do whatever it takes to win." I raise an eyebrow at him. "And if I knew you better, perhaps I would notice more similarities."

He chuckles. "So you want to know about me?"

"Yes. Tell me more about your life."

"When you have thousands of years to choose from, it's hard to pick what to share."

"Then tell me about your week." I stop near a large white rock and sit on it, emulating Rodin's Thinker.

Zorin rolls his eyes. "I did some research to catch up on the times, learned the new Pope likes tournaments."

"New?"

"Well, new for me. How about you? How was your week?"

I shake my head. "We're still on you."

He sighs, then speaks rapidly. "I started the week buying more marshmallows. Then I painted part of the Cathedral. Then I had a snack. About mid week, everyone was asleep, and I considered getting a dog for company. But then I thought about the smell and the poop, and I thought what if I ever get hungry, would I really be able to resist? So, I decided no dog. That enough?"

I grin. "For now."

"Now your turn." He pulls a bag of marshmallows from his cloak and starts snacking.

I jump off the rock and grab one for myself. "I saw a play. Nox Aeterna."

"Oh, yes. I've seen it. Not particularly historically accurate."

"That's what my roommate said."

"Who's your roommate?"

"Princess Corinne of the House of Ravens."

He freezes mid bite. "That's a dangerous roommate to have."

"It gets better. Her father's coming to New York. To capture Nightfall."

He hides the marshmallow bag back in his cloak. "If Varian is coming here, we must be extra careful. I've seen him fight. You are not ready for him."

. . .

After my news, Zorin insists on training right away. We walk into the Cathedral and he tosses me a practice sword and tells me to repeat the Way of Nyx. After twenty minutes, I sigh as I keep running through the drill. "Zorin, I need to fight. To fly."

"You need to practice your form."

"I've done it a million times. Can't I learn the other six now?"

He rubs his head as he reclines in one of the golden chairs. "Trust me, I know what's best. You need to learn patience. You're an immortal now. Stop acting like a whiny human girl."

I groan and continue the drill. At least I can keep it interesting by talking. "New subject, I need your help with something. I need an apartment in the city. My new friends at school were getting suspicious about me leaving, and I needed a cover."

Carter walks in with a cup of water. "I'm happy to set that up for you, miss. Is there a particular part of the city you'd prefer?"

I look at Zorin. He shrugs. I take the water and sip. "I don't know. Someplace fun, artsy. Someplace my friends would believe I would pick."

Carter bows. "Consider it done. You will have your keys by the end of the weekend."

"Thanks."

Carter returns upstairs and I continue training. To keep the conversation going, I ask a question I've been curious about since finding out what I am. "How do you turn someone into Nephilim?"

He pauses. "You're losing focus, but okay. First, the person must be drained of blood."

"So you feed from them."

"Yes, but if they lost blood another way, say an injury, that would suffice."

I stop my training for a moment. "Did you have to feed off me?"

"Yes. You were bleeding out, but I needed to speed up the process. There was an Angel there, after all."

I resume the drill, performing a block, then a strike. "What next?"

"You feed the person your blood, usually by cutting open your wrist. The Nephilim blood replaces the human, and the person begins to change."

"How long does it take?"

"It's different for everyone, but it often takes a while to awaken."

I remember waking to find the Angel gone, my parents dead. I finish my form, a thought occurring to me. "Zorin, if you knew where I could find the Angel, would you tell me?"

His face is cold. "I'd tell you what you needed to know."

I see he is conflicted. I need—

"Important news, Scarlett," says Evie.

"Show me."

An image of an apartment building surrounded by Bruisers and Officers appears. The reporter speaks. "As you can see, the Zeniths have taken everyone in the building hostage, and the Inquisition has the area surrounded. The terrorists don't seem to be part of a known group. We don't know if any demands have been made—" I stop the video and message TR and Trix.

"We need to rescue the hostages," I say over the eGlass.

"We can't go against Zeniths," TR replies. "Not publicly. Let the Orders handle it."

"I don't trust them. If Inquisition messes this up, both the hostages and Zeniths will die."

Trix speaks through the eGlass. "One of our guys has eyes on the area. Looks like the Zeniths have snipers at the windows. There's no way in."

I unleash my wings and fly out of the Cathedral. "I'll find one." I tell them my plan.

"You can't save everyone," says TR.

He's wrong.

I can save them all.

THE RED EAGLES

I wonder if this is my fault, if the terrorists were inspired by my threats at Jax's execution. I was bluffing, but the world didn't know. From now on, I must be more careful with my actions.

Trix meets me in the sewers. TR and Zorin position themselves in the building across from the terrorists. We will convince their leader to free the hostages. If that fails, we'll free them ourselves.

I pinch my nose as I trudge through water and filth.

Trix chuckles. "What's the matter, N, not used to the sewers?"

"The smell is unpleasant." The smell is horrible, but I'm trying to look composed.

"Why'd don't you just fly over it?"

I can, but Trix can't, and right now, I need to build camaraderie. I need her to see I'm willing to get dirty like the rest of them. "I like walking. Don't you?"

"Sure, N. I'd rather walk than fly any day." The sarcasm is thick.

We share a smile.

"Are we almost there?" I ask.

She checks her eGlass. "Five feet away."

I raise my eyebrow, though it's hidden under my mask. "You say feet when I would say meters. Why don't you use the universal system?"

She shrugs. "My mom and I worked on a lot of old vehicles, used a lot of old parts. Quarter-inch bolts. Twelve-foot tape measures. That's what I know."

"My family was..." I debate how much to tell her. "My family was modern. They liked to live small, away from big cities, but my mom was a tech genius and kept our technology fairly up-to-date."

"Tech genius, huh? That explains a lot. Sounds like our moms were pretty awesome."

I stop walking. "Yeah, she was."

"What happened to her?"

"She fought a battle she couldn't win."

She grips my shoulder. "I'm sorry, N."

I try to keep my emotions buried. This is not the time. I start walking again. "We've all lost things."

"It doesn't make it easier."

"How'd you deal with it? When your mother passed?"

"My mother's still out there."

"Oh, sorry." I never imagine her with living parents. When I see the Dark Templars, I see people like me, with nothing to lose. Perhaps I am wrong.

"Don't be sorry, N. My mom and I, we haven't seen each other since the War. She didn't like that I volunteered."

"She was looking out for you. You were looking out for others."

She stares down the tunnel. Her eyes are distant. "Yeah, I suppose. I know I said I joined to help the soldiers. It's what I tell everyone, but really...I joined for a boy."

I want to ask what she means, when Evie speaks into my ear. "Scarlett, you are in position."

"Thanks, Evie." I turn to Trix. "Time to do your thing."

Trix grins. She flips her automatic rifle over her shoulder and jumps. She flies higher than any human and thrusts her open hand against the ceiling. A ring of red explodes from her palm, turning the stone into lava and then ash. It happens in the blink of an eye. I've never seen her powers in full force before. I'm glad she's on my side.

As Trix falls back down, so does the white dust, revealing a hole that leads inside the steel building. We both jump through it and land in a wide hallway. Trix grabs her rifle and scans the area. We're clear.

"Evie, hack the cameras." She does, showing me images from the different rooms. The hostages are all in one location, surrounded by ten Zeniths. The terrorists wear thick blue armor, military grade, making them look more machine than human. Where did they get the gear?

The top level is dark, the windows covered in metal. A lantern on the ground lights one side, casting the shadow of someone sitting alone. I can't make out the details, but this must be their leader.

Trix points her rifle at the double doors before us. "What's the plan, N?"

"We request a meeting. Evie, the military helmets will be equipped with eGlasses. See if you can contact one. Tell them Nightfall wishes to meet their leader."

"N, they're here," Trix says.

What?

Two armed Zeniths, their armor so large they tower over us, enter through the doors. How could they get here so fast? There were no Zeniths near us, unless...

"The cameras have been tampered with," I say.

Trix grits her jaw, finger on the trigger and ready to shoot.

I raise a hand, gesturing her to hold.

One of the Zeniths speaks. He sounds as if he's speaking through a radio. "Nightfall, we are here to escort you to our leader. He is very eager to speak with you."

I don't like this. Someone is anticipating my actions. But I don't have a better plan. "We have many things to discuss."

The Zenith tilts his gun at Trix. "You must come alone."

"I will, but my companion must not be harmed."

"Very well."

I step forward. A voice speaks through my eGlass. It sounds manipulated. "Don't go with them, Nightfall."

"Who is this?"

"Call me Crixus, leader of the Red Eagles."

Two shots explode from behind us, hitting the Zeniths in the head. They collapse, and I turn to see two people in the same heavy armor. But unlike the Zeniths, their armor is black. A red eagle is painted across their chests.

The voice in my ear continues. "These are two of my soldiers. You can trust them. They will escort you out of the building."

"No. I need to save the hostages."

The voice sighs. "My contacts have informed me this is a trap. If you stay, you will be captured."

Trix moves her gun from one soldier to the other. "N, what's going on? Why are the Red Eagles here?"

"They want to help," I tell Trix. I speak into my eGlass "Why?" I ask Crixus.

"You and I share an enemy. We can be very useful to each other."

"Why are you contacting me now?"

"Because trust is a rare thing in our line of work, and I want you to trust me, Nightfall. So please, accept my help."

I've waited eagerly for contact from another rebel leader, but I never imagined it would happen like this. I want to establish an alliance with Crixus, but I can't accept his offer. I can't let people die. "I will free the hostages."

"Very well," says Crixus. "My soldiers will depart. But remember, I offered help in a time of need." His signal ends. The soldiers turn and disappear around a corner.

Trix keeps her gun at the ready. I have my hand on my sword. There have been too many surprises today.

"Evie, how did Crixus contact me?"

"He hacked your eGlass."

I shudder. I thought Evie's security was unbreakable. I'll have to figure out a way to upgrade her. This can't happen again.

Trix grabs my shoulder, startling me. "N, you still want to do this? What if their leader doesn't want to listen?"

I smile to put her at ease. "I can be very convincing."

"Not if they put a bullet in your head."

"We have no other choice."

"I know, but this…this doesn't feel right."

"I know." I tap my eGlass. "Evie, contact them."

"What shall I say about their two dead men?"

I shrug. "Tell them to check their cameras. I had nothing to do with it. I seek a peaceful solution."

"Very well. I've made contact." I check the cameras. Four armored Zeniths enter an elevator, heading towards us. So not all the video feeds have been edited. I can use that.

"They're on their way," I say. "Evie, loop the video from here to the room adjacent to the hostages, but keep my feed original. Trix, take position. Be ready for plan B."

"Okay, N. Be careful." She holds my eyes for a moment, then disappears past the doors.

A moment later, the Zeniths arrive. In case their orders are to shoot me on sight, I'm ready to unleash my wings and charge them. I pray my swords skills are enough to win.

I don't get to find out. The Zeniths surround me in a square and escort me to the elevator. One of them asks, "Where's the other one?"

I speak casually. "She left."

We don't speak again.

The elevator stops at the top floor, and the Zeniths lead me to a door at the end of the hall. According to my eGlass, this is the dark room with fortified windows. Evie informs me that Trix is in position. I tap out a message to TR.

You have eyes on Trix?

He responds.

Have eyes on her and the hostages.

Zorin should be right beside him. I hope they can cooperate long enough for us to succeed. I message him.

Don't act without my command. The situation is delicate.

He responds vocally. "If it's between you and the hostages. I'll choose you." I appreciate his response, but...my life shouldn't matter more than others.

The Zeniths open the door and gesture me to enter. I do, and they close the door behind me, leaving me in near darkness.

The floor is tiled marble. The room is large, but empty except for the lantern and the man. He sits cross-legged, his back to me. His breathing is deep and slow, and I feel it radiating through the room. His hair is dark brown and twisted into a ponytail. When he stands, I realize he is a head taller than me, if not more. His body is thick and muscled. Black and gold armor clads his body, and it's not like the armor of the others. It's thinner, shaped for his figure. It's the armor of a Knight. Of a King. As he turns, the light catches his black cape. And reveals a golden raven.

"Varian," I say, jumping back, my heart pounding.

He grins. His voice is deep and his purple eyes penetrating. "You wanted to talk. So let us talk."

I can't talk. I can't think. This is the man who matched Nyx in combat. The man who ended the Nephilim War. And he's here to end me.

I yell into my eGlass. "Trix, get the hostages out, now." I watch her on my screen. She turns a wall into ash and jumps in, firing her rifle. Evie switches the camera, showing me the next room. Trix shoots down two armored Zeniths. A third collapses, shot down by TR. The eight hostages are on their knees, heads down, arms behind their backs. A Zenith terrorist threatens to kill one. His helmet shatters from a sniper rifle bullet.

Zorin speaks through my eGlass. "Scarlett, what's wrong? What happened?"

My voice trembles. "It's Varian. He's here. Save Trix and get everyone out!"

"Run, Scarlett! I'm coming."

I will my body to move. Everything feels slow. I fly toward the door, and Varian draws one of his blades. It extends, turning into a whip. He snaps it forward. The whip grabs my ankle and pulls me back. I slam into the ground.

My head pounds as everything appears to speed up again. I untie the whip and crawl back on my feet. Varian does not move. His blade recoils, turning solid once again. He has an eGlass and seems to be watching the fight going on below. He must have bypassed Evie's looping of footage. "I wondered if you would choose to rescue them."

On my screen, TR and Trix take out two more terrorists—no, two more soldiers.

I draw my sword and face Varian. "You'd use innocents to lure me? You'd lie to your people?"

He chuckles. "The people are pawns, and I their King. I will manipulate them again and again to win. But, innocents...Nightfall, you disappoint me."

What's he talking about...the hostages aren't innocent. They can be criminals or...

No.

"Trix, get out of there!"

I'm too late.

Varian whispers something into his eGlass, and the hostages rise, drawing pistols from under their clothing.

They aim at Trix. She shoots one down. A soldier smacks the back of her head with his baton. She falls to her knees. All ten remaining soldiers aim at her. There were never any hostages.

"Stop!" I yell. "Don't hurt her."

Varian whispers an order, and the soldiers hold their ground. "Wouldn't it be sad if Trix never saw her mother again?" he asks.

His knowledge stuns me. "You bugged the sewers. Because of how I rescued the Shadow of Rome. You knew I'd use them again."

He smiles. "Finally, you're thinking. Tell me, what happens next?"

My mind rushes through the possibilities. There's only one. "I surrender."

"That's it?" He shakes his head. "You are nothing compared to Nyx." His answer surprises me. He wanted a challenge, and I gave none. I've been playing a game, only to find out I barely know the rules.

Varian taps his eGlass. "Execute the Shadow of Rome on my command."

"No, please. I'll come with you."

His voice is cold. "You will come with me, and the Shadow of Rome will die."

TR pleads into my ear. "Nightfall, you need to do something. You need to save her."

I charge at Varian with my sword.

He blocks me and knocks me back. I barely feel the blows, barely register they happened. He's so fast. I can't fight him.

I drop to my knees. "Please. Let her go."

Varian ignores me. On the screen, a soldier presses a gun to Trix's head. TR screams in my ear. "We're here because of you, Nightfall. Do something. *Do something!*"

Something dark shatters through the glass.

It hits the soldier, slamming him into the wall and away from Trix. The others try to fire at it. They cannot. The darkness glides through the room, cutting down soldier after soldier in an instant.

The darkness is death.

The darkness is Zorin.

He saves Trix. Because I asked him to.

I smile, a tear running down my face.

Varian sneers. "He's here." He steps toward me. "Let's see how long you last."

I fly for the door out of instinct.

His whip catches me again.

I talk into the eGlass. "Leave me. Leave me, or we're all dead."

Varian stands over me. I can see his purple eyes. There's no ruthlessness. Only calculation. He lifts his sword.

I clutch the Token of Strife around my neck. I won't give up.

I jump at him, trying to grab him, trying to use my powers.

Varian's sword flashes in front of me.

And cuts off my hand.

I collapse, frozen. My hand lays before me, pale, limp.

I scream.

Varian strikes.

He doesn't hit me. He stops halfway. Why?

And then I see it. The ground below him is turning red. He jumps up as it burns into ash. As Zorin flies through the dust.

His dark sword crashes against Varian's blade. They land and dash across the room, never standing still, weaving around each other. Their battle looks simple, elegant. But I know it is a dance of death.

My vision grows fuzzy. Zorin and Varian become blurs. Black fighting against gold. Someone kneels before me. Trix. She notices my hand and gasps.

I don't respond.

She shakes me. "N, we need to go."

She's right. I stand up, leaning against her. We walk over to the barricaded window, and she uses her abilities to burn open a hole. "N, you need to fly us out of here."

My strength is fading, but I have enough. I unleash my wings. I grab Trix and step to the edge. But I can't leave. "Zorin."

"He'll follow us. N, we need to go *now*."

No. Varian and Zorin are matched. Zorin won't be able to escape. He'll fight until more soldiers arrive, and then he'll lose.

I need to do something.

"Evie, hack into all the eScreens and networks. Play my conversation with Varian to the people."

I see two screens from where I stand. Both change to an image of Varian and me. The speakers boom through the city. "You'd use innocents to lure me? You'd lie to your people?" I ask in the video.

Varian chuckles. There is no sympathy in his voice. "The people are pawns, and I their King. I will manipulate them again and again to win." The video loops. People on the streets yell in protest.

And Varian hesitates.

It's only a split second. But it's enough. Zorin pulls away from the battle. He grabs Trix and me. And he carries us into the sky. Everything grows dark.

KING VARIAN

I awake on a soft bed in a dimly lit room. I'm dressed in a white linen gown. Someone removed my armor and changed my clothing. I shiver at the idea of a stranger's hands on me. But, my mask is still on, so perhaps not a stranger. I'm at the Cathedral. I came here when…

My memories come rushing back and bile rises in my throat. I raise my hand, the hand Varian cut off. I cringe, expecting a bloody bandage.

There is none.

My hand is still there.

I gasp, studying the lines of my palm, the length of my nails, rubbing my hands together again and again. It's mine, but it's not. It's missing the freckle that formed the summer of my tenth year. I stare down at the perfect skin and wonder about that freckle, about this hand that shouldn't be.

"It grew back," says Zorin. I hadn't noticed him, but he sits to my side, his eyes hazy. A tube runs from his wrist to mine. He's giving me blood. And it's taking a toll on him. All this information comes slowly.

I'm still in shock about my hand. "After Jax..." I'm about to say after Jax cut my throat, but I can't. He didn't know I was Scarlett. He didn't mean to hurt me. "After Jax's execution, my throat healed, but I didn't expect to regenerate an entire limb."

Zorin smiles slightly. "As long as you're alive and have blood, you will heal."

I wonder how hard Nephilim are to kill. I already feel great. Zorin, however, looks worse than ever.

"How long was I out for?" I ask.

"Eleven hours."

I glance at the dark window, moonlight peaking through. "And you've been giving me blood the whole time?"

"My blood is the most effective."

I tighten the clasp on the tube and remove the needle from my wrist. Zorin moves to stop me, but I easily push him away. He sighs, slumping in his golden chair.

I pull the sheets off and stand, and I remember someone changed my clothes. I raise my eyebrow at Zorin. Perhaps he needed to check for wounds. But since I heal so well, perhaps he didn't. "Thank you for the dress."

"I wanted you to be comfortable," he says, grinning.

Part of me wants to smack him with my pillow. But a larger part of me is grateful.

I touch his hand, smiling. "Thank you, Zorin. You saved my life."

I expect him to smile in return, but he trembles. His eyes are hazy. "I wasn't sure I could fight him. I wasn't..." He begins to mumble.

We're in his room, and I rummage through the dressers until I find what I'm looking for. I grab the Life Force and hand it to him. The can slips from his grasp. "Zorin? Zorin?"

He doesn't respond.

He's given too much blood. I pick up the can, shaking so much it takes me three tries to open it, and help Zorin drink. He sips slowly at first, then faster. His eyes become less clouded. I bring him two more cans, and he empties them in seconds. "Thank you, Scarlett."

I toss him another Life Force and sit on the bed with one of my own. "I wouldn't be here without you. I...was careless. I'm used to going up against Ragathon, but Varian is different. He thinks like no one I've ever met. He outmaneuvered me at every turn."

"Not at the end," says Zorin. "Hackers are still playing your video on the net."

"I got lucky. He could have killed me in an instant, but he didn't. He must have had to take me alive. I've...I've never seen anyone fight like him." I meet his eyes. "I've never seen anyone fight like you."

He frowns, but only for a moment. "I've had many teachers and a long time to study."

"I'm sorry I haven't been a better student," I say, twirling the can in my hands. "I will practice what you tell me. I will work harder."

Zorin clasps my shoulder. "You will learn to fight, and one day, maybe you will even beat Varian. But remember, it is your wits that will win this war." He eyes are dark.

"You're afraid of Varian, aren't you?"

He doesn't speak for a while. "It would be foolish not to be. But as long as we don't let fear stop us, we can still fight." He stands and walks toward the door. "When you're ready, we'll have a meeting downstairs. Your armor is in the chest." He points at a black and gold chest in the corner. "I had it cleaned."

I smile. "Thanks."

And then, something comes to me. There has only been one person to ever match Varian in combat. A Nephilim with a sword black as night.

"Nyx?"

Zorin pauses. "What about him?"

"I thought, maybe…"

He chuckles, opening the door. "Haven't you seen the play?" he asks softly. "Nyx is dead."

...

Dressed in my armor, I march downstairs. Trix notices me first. She jumps from her chair at the table and runs up and hugs me. "How you feeling, N?"

"I have a new hand," I say, waving it.

"Hey, we could all use some new parts from time to time, right?"

"Right." I hug her again and whisper in her ear. "I'm sorry for what happened."

She pushes me away, grinning. "Don't be. I know what I'm getting myself into. Besides, today was a victory."

Not for me. For me today was a lesson in limitations. But I try to look cheerful for the team. "What'd we win?"

Trix projects an image onto the wall with her eGlass. People riot down a street. Officers try to push them back.

"After you played your video, riots like this broke out all around North America and Europe. Most of them have been put down now, but people aren't happy. You made a fool out of Varian."

"But the world knows I couldn't beat him."

"Nah. For all they know, this was our entire plan. Reveal Varian's corruption."

"Just got another confirmation," says TR, standing from his chair. He walks over to Zorin who's leaning against a wall. "Sons of Eden just agreed to the meeting. The video got their attention."

I shake my head in disbelief. "I was contacted by the Red Eagles earlier."

"They've confirmed as well. So have many of the smaller groups. We've got our meeting, man," he roars, clasping Zorin on the shoulder.

I flinch at the unlikely moment. "You two are getting along."

"We talked," says TR.

I wonder if he shared how much he cares for Trix. I could hear it in his voice earlier. He would die for her.

Carter enters with a tray of beverages and snacks. "Splendid to see you well, miss. I prepared a Life Force green tea to aid in your recovery."

"Thank you, Carter." I try a sip, enjoying the taste. A message appears on my eGlass.

Hey, you need to get back to school. My father arrived early. They're having an official greeting ceremony and Initiates have to be there.

-Corinne

My new hand trembles, dropping the cup. The glass shatters, spilling red all over the floor.

"Are you alright, miss?" asks Cater.

"Yes. I'm fine. Sorry. I'll clean that up."

"No, allow me, miss." Carter bends to one knee and begins collecting the pieces of glass. "Miss, can you move over..."

I stand frozen, barely hearing him. How can I face my friends again? How can I face Varian?

"N?" asks Trix.

I don't respond.

I am still, and everyone is silent. Their faces tighten in concern. But not Zorin. He looks at me calmly.

And I remember what he said and step toward the door. I will not let fear stop me.

...

I know I should hurry. Corinne made this ceremony sound important. But my mind is filled with plots and questions, and it's hard to motivate myself to walk faster through the busy New York streets toward the subway that will take me to Castle V, despite my earlier resolve. Sure, I could fly. But I need the space to think, to shift from Nightfall to Scarlett before I get back to school.

Being two people isn't always easy.

In fact, it's never easy.

I'm lost in these thoughts, meandering toward the subway, when I hear the shriek of a cat. It's obviously in pain, but no one around me seems to care. A man in a business suit walks by talking on his eGlass. A woman pushing a stroller doesn't glance up when the cat hisses and meows pathetically. The sound is coming from behind a dumpster by an Italian restaurant.

I push through a gaggle of noisy students and find myself face to face with a homeless man leaning against the brick wall. He has a shopping cart to one side filled with the kinds of treasures only those without any belongings could possibly value, and he's covered in brown and beige layers of recycled clothing. His eyes are a dull brown, and his face is shaded by dirt, sweat and too many days and nights spent on the street.

I feel an initial tug of sympathy for a man so invisible to the world, until I see what he's doing. He has a scrawny black cat trapped between his feet as he zaps it with electricity from his fingers. He laughs as he watches the cat squirm, hiss and howl in an effort to escape the torture.

He's not tagged as a Zenith. He lives outside the system, off the grid. This is the kind of man Nightfall and the Dark Templars are supposedly fighting for, and yet right now all I want to do is sink my teeth into his neck and drain him until he's a limp rag for what he's doing to that poor cat.

The vehemence of my thought, and the thirst it produces, scares me. I shudder, take a deep calming breath and touch the man's exposed calf, who only just now notices me.

He's about to say something, perhaps hit me with his para-powers, when I'm in his mind, my powers seeking out his thoughts and controlling him.

I'm hoping to see that this is an aberration. That he's stuck in something deep and the pain is leaking out of him in dangerous ways, but it's not who he is at the core.

I'm disappointed. More than that. Disgusted. This isn't the first animal he's tortured. I watch a memory of him killing his dog out of gruesome fascination, enjoying the fear and pain in its eyes as it died. I cringe, bile rising in my throat, as I issue a command before pulling my hand away. I can't spend any more time in that man's brain. I'll have to scrub my frontal lobe for a week to undo the damage twenty seconds in his has caused me.

I scoop up the cat, who looks more like a lanky teenager than a full grown male, and pet him soothingly to calm him even as he digs his claws into my arm. "It's okay, kitty. You're safe now," I coo as my final instruction to the psycho in front of me takes effect. He's calm as he stands and walks onto the busy sidewalk. Finally, people notice him, but only long enough to shirk away from his unwashed body.

A few minutes ago I would have judged them for being so blind, so careless to others around them, to their own humanity, but I'm still too haunted by what I saw in his mind. So I wait and watch as he finds the nearest Inquisition Officer and turns himself in for failing to register as a Zenith, for animal abuse and cruelty, and for one other crime, a heinous assault that wasn't against an animal but a human. He confesses to everything and they secure his wrists and arrest him.

Now, I just want to get back to the Castle and away from all these people. I feel dirty, repelled by this city and the darkness that lives within it. I tuck the shivering cat under my coat and make fast time to the subway.

While underwater, surrounded by flora and fish, I think about what just happened. How life isn't as black and white as I'd thought. And if I'm being honest with myself, it's not as black and white as I'd hoped. That would be too simple.

But just because someone is oppressed doesn't make them good. And just because someone is part of the system—privileged even—that doesn't make them bad.

So what is Nightfall fighting for? Who is she—who am *I*—fighting for?

I don't have the answers as I show my Initiate ring to the guards at the Vianney subway exit and make my way through the small island town to the Castle.

I've had Evie turned off for a while, and I turn her on as I stop under a tree just inside the Castle gates. I'm shaking and, I realize, crying. I sink under the tree and listen to the messages Evie has for me. All from Corinne, telling me to hurry.

I like my new roommate. She's sweet. Kind. Not evil.

But that man in the city, he was evil. Or if evil doesn't exist, as some believe, then he's very, very, broken.

I'm petting the cat, who has calmed under my touch and is purring against my chest, when my grandfather walks up to me in his long Chancellor robes, his hair groomed but still a wild halo of white, his long beard tamed into a braid that falls down his chest. He lowers himself to the ground to sit next to me. "Hello, Scarlett."

"Hello."

"You look deep in troubled thought," he says.

I nod and tell him about the man torturing the cat. "Zeniths are mistreated, and that needs to stop. It's not right. But they also mistreat others, and that's not right. Is there a way to protect the rights of one people without sacrificing the safety of another?"

I'm not actually expecting an answer, because I'm not sure one exists, but he responds. "People aren't perfect, but they need to be given a chance to better themselves. To live. To figure out where they fit in this giant cog of humanity."

Right. So he doesn't really know the answer either.

He reaches over to pet the cat, and the cat purrs louder. "Have you given him a name?"

"Not yet."

"How about Nox?"

I look down at the black cat with the big gold eyes. "Latin for night?"

The Chancellor smiles. "I'm glad to see you've learned your Latin. But I'm not surprised." His eyes get a faraway look that I now recognize as him thinking about his daughter. "You mother always did have an ear for the dead languages."

I want to ask more about her, but I don't think I can handle talking about that right now. Instead, I look down at the cat. "Original. Naming a black cat Night."

"I like the night," he says. "Sometimes we must work under the cloak of darkness to find the light."

I'm about to respond to his nebulous comment when he pushes himself slowly off the ground and holds his hand out to me. "Would you escort an old man to the ceremony? I'll likely enjoy it about as much as you, but we are expected to be there. And sometimes we have to play our part if we want our real work to matter."

I let him help me up with one hand as I keep the cat secure in the other. "Of course. Can we walk by my room first so I can drop the cat off and get my robes?"

He nods and walks by my side in silence. I set up a box with paper for the cat and grab my Initiate robe, throwing it on over my regular clothes. With a stern warning to Nox not to eat or pee on anything while I'm gone, we head to the procession, which is set to take place in center of the courtyard.

Students have already swarmed the courtyard, and the Grandmasters are lined up to receive King Varian. Chancellor Forrester stands by them and I wander off to the side as I try to avoid being trampled by the other students. The Fall Quarter hasn't started yet, so we aren't at capacity in the Castle, but it sure feels like we are right now.

I look around for familiar faces, for Corinne or Wytt, but I don't see either of them.

The drawbridge is decorated with bright flags and trumpets blast from along the wall as the Chancellor clears his throat and speaks to the crowd. "King Varian of the House of Ravens of Sapientia, Knight of the First Order of the Templars, we welcome you to Castle Vianney."

More trumpets, and now I see them coming up the drawbridge into the courtyard, young men and women walking in step, dressed in gold and black with the Ravens house sigil flying on flags. A gold raven on black.

They split to the side, revealing the King and his family. Corinne and Wytt are there, but it takes me a moment to recognize them. Corinne EZ-Dyed her hair back to a dark chestnut brown and is wearing a glorious golden gown with black lace trim that flows around her feet. It glitters with tiny yellow stones that shimmer under the setting sun. Her face is accented with golden eye shadow and dark red lipstick, and she wears a small golden and jeweled crown on her head. Wytt stands by her side, equally impressive in black velvet and leather with dark eyeliner making his purple eyes pop. And to his right must be Kai, the oldest Prince. He doesn't smile or look at anyone, his posture that annoying mix of arrogant and bored. I roll my eyes at how stereotypical of a Prince he is, but I can't deny he's impressive with those royal purple eyes, strong jaw, tan skin, and a shock of messy black hair. He looks fit, healthy, like he knows how to use that gleaming sword hanging at his hip.

And then there's King Varian, the most impressive of them all. He stands tall, a commander who knows his rank and place. He's also arrogant, but in the way that is earned from hard battle. A way that others respect. He's huge, just as I remember. All muscle. Tall. He wears black armor with a golden fur cape. His brown hair is long and held at the nape of his neck with a leather strap. Atop his head sits a gold crown embedded with black diamonds. He wears two swords, and they aren't merely ornamental. I glance down at my new hand and shiver. I know all too well how good he is with a blade.

Corinne, Wytt and Kai move to stand near the Grandmasters and the King walks up and focuses his penetrating gaze on Ragathon, which surprises me. They're not even in the same Order.

He holds out his hand to Ragathon, who takes it with obvious reluctance. The King smiles. "Hello, brother."

My gasp is almost audible. Brothers? They're related?

The veins on Ragathon's hand pop out as he squeezes the King's. "We are no longer brothers, my King."

King Varian chuckles, and I feel confused. Because I hate Ragathon, so I love that the King makes him squirm. But the King, he's dangerous, and he's my enemy.

The King turns to examine the students and Grandmasters before speaking to Ragathon again. "It seems order has grown lax since last I was here. Two failed executions, and no one of note has risen through the ranks of Castle Vianney in many years."

He turns his eyes to Jax, the Seeker, and Thane, who are all standing at attention by the Grandmasters. With a practiced eye, he studies them. "It's time for a change. It's time to see if anyone here has any worth."

Ragathon sneers. "It's not like you've done any better against Nightfall and her rebels."

King Varian looks back at Ragathon and smiles. "You assume, brother, that my intention was to capture her. That's always been your mistake. Going in with both guns blazing with all the subtlety of a bull in a china shop. What did our father always teach us? The lesson you failed to learn. To defeat an enemy, you must first know them. Today I learned more about Nightfall, her team, her motivation, her abilities, than you have in all this time trying to capture her. I accomplished exactly what I set out to do. I discovered Nightfall's weakness."

My hands shake and I hold them to make them stop. This isn't good. This is very, very bad.

Ragathon sneers. "And did part of that lesson include making a fool out of yourself to the world with recording?"

I expect to see Varian get mad, but he smiles instead. "You put too much importance in your own pride and reputation. It limits you. Public opinion is as changing as the weather. I lost little compared to what I gained."

King Varian turns to the crowd and raises his voice. "I'm hosting a tournament tomorrow. All younger Knights from Castle Vianney must compete. The winner will receive a Royal Favor at my discretion. It's time to see what kind of Knights our Orders have produced!"

CASTLE VIANNEY

There's much cheering and shouting as the procession officially comes to an end. We're dismissed by the large bell that signals the dining hall is open.

I've already finished my Life Force and am eating marshmallows and chocolates when Corinne and Wytt set their trays down and join me. They've both changed back into their Initiate robes, and Corinne's hair is back to pink, but I can see the remnants of their costuming in the makeup. It's amazing how much clothing can transform them from normal-looking young adults to splendid royalty.

"You two looked incredible," I say through a bite of yummy whiteness.

Wytt mock bows then picks up a fork and spears his steak. "Thank you. I do my best to impress the ladies."

Corinne chuckles and takes a bite of her cheeseburger, chewing and swallowing before speaking. "I'm starving. Dad wouldn't let us eat lunch. We spent all afternoon getting fitted for our outfits."

"It was quite a show," I say.

Corinne rolls her eyes. "It's nothing. Just theatre." She leans forward, a mischievous grin on her face. "Never mind about politics, tell us about your apartment and what you did all weekend."

Wytt smiles. "Yes, do tell. It must be glorious, all that space to yourself, no one telling you what to wear or when to eat or drink or what to say. Freedom. Utter, delightful, enviable freedom!"

I look back and forth between them and realize they are dead serious. This is exciting for them. "It's really not that interesting. Nor is it all that spacious. My apartment's pretty small." I assume this is true, but even a big apartment in New York could be considered small to someone who grew up in a castle.

"But what did you do all weekend? Anything fun?" Corinne asks.

"Um, not terribly. I mean, I read books, got some rest, watched some movies, walked around a bit. That's mostly it." I'm surprised by how much I hate lying to them, these friends I've only known for a few days. Whose father wants to destroy me. But I do. I hate it. I hate every dishonest word that comes out of my mouth, but I know I have to keep saying them or everything I'm trying to build will fall apart.

We're still talking about my apartment, a place I've never even seen, when Jax comes over and sits next to me.

"Have you seen Scarlett's apartment?" Corinne asks.

He looks at me with a raised eyebrow. "No, I haven't."

I shrug, trying to look casual. "I figured it would be good to have a place of my own to go to when I need time alone."

He nods. "You always did like your own space."

"Are you going to be in the tournament?" I ask, changing the subject.

"Yes," he says. "Anyone who's a Knight is required."

Wytt smiles big. "It's going to be so cool. This is a great build-up for the Tournament Festival after finals."

"What's that?" I ask.

Wytt grins. "It's a weeklong festival here at Castle V. There are lotteries throughout the world to give people who can't afford the outrageously high tickets a chance to attend. It's a lot of fun. And Knights from everywhere come to compete. The winner gets a Boon from the Pope!"

"That sounds fun," I say, distracted by all the laughing and yelling around us as people talk about the tournament tomorrow. I didn't realize tournaments were such a big deal.

Wytt stands to leave. "I've got to place my bets before tomorrow."

Corinne grabs his robe before he walks off. "Nope. Remember, you promised our father. No more betting."

He groans and slumps back onto the bench. "Why'd you have to remind me? It's just a bit of fun." Wytt looks over longingly at a group of people placing bets, Thane in the center, puffing out his chest and laughing.

"All of you who bet on someone else are just burning your money," Thane says. "I'm betting two million...on myself. Bet against me at your own risk."

The chattering stops as the others around him stare open-mouthed.

I lean over and whisper to my friends. "Where'd he get so much money?"

"Stories are," Wytt says, "it's not all legal."

That makes me curious. An Inquisitor and Cardinal, sworn to protect the law, potentially dealing in illegal activity. I wonder why no one has investigated.

A young woman with curly hair and a sweet smile walks up to our table with a large basket full of colorful ribbons. "Get your token and choose your Knight!" she says.

Corinne pulls out some coins and picks a red ribbon. "Scarlett," she says, smiling, "you should give one to Jax."

I blush and glance at Jax. "Jax doesn't need a token to win, I'm sure."

Jax clears his throat and stands to leave. "I've got a meeting to get to. I'll see you all later." He turns to me. "Bye, Scarlett."

"Bye." I pick up a piece of chocolate and look at Corinne, who's studying her ribbon. "Who are you giving yours to?"

Wytt nudges her shoulder. "My guess is The Seeker. Right, sis?"

Corinne blushes and nods.

Wytt continues his teasing. "My sister has a crush on the Knight. I don't blame her. Kira's hot."

"I just think she's very skilled," Corinne says. "And she's one of the highest ranking female Knights in her order. I admire that."

Then she giggles and covers her mouth. "And she *is* really hot."

...

This morning we are all excited. It's hard not to be with the small town of Vianney thrown into festival mood overnight by the announcement of the tournament. I have to give credit to the local business owners who must have been up all night preparing for this impromptu day. Normally, they aren't even open on Sunday, let alone out with booths and baskets hawking their wares to everyone.

Corinne, Wytt and I walk through the crowded line of vendors and excited students until we're standing in front of the Arena entrance.

This is the first time I've seen the Arena up close. Modeled after the amphitheaters and arenas of Ancient Rome—but far larger—it was built in the middle of Vianney Park, with rounded walls of stone. Inside, the stadium is made of stone mixed with marble, with a center staging area for battles.

"Where should we sit?" Corinne asks.

I look around. "I'm not sure. But, can you guys wait here for a second? I'll be right back."

"No problem," says Wytt.

I thank them and run off. I need to find Jax. I ask a few people who direct me toward the entrance where the Knights prepare for battle. It's a large room under the arena seating and is full of Knights in a flurry of preparation. I easily spot Jax, one of the few not running around like a headless chicken. I'm a bit nervous, even a little shy, as I approach him. "Hey."

He smiles and sets his sword down on a table near him. "Hey."

I wring my hands and try to keep eye contact with him. "Look, I know things have been hard, and you had your reason for keeping secrets, and I just want you to know, I forgive you. You're still my best friend, and I don't want to lose that."

His face visibly relaxes. "Scarlett, I hate keeping secrets from you. I hate that I had to lie to you. I can't tell you how much it means that you've forgiven me."

I stick my hand in my pocket and pull out the wings he gave me the day my parents were killed. "I wanted you to have this. As a token. The ribbons felt a little..."

"Clichéd?"

I laugh. "Something like that."

He accepts the token and sticks it to the breastplate of his armor. "Thank you. It means a lot to me."

"Be careful," I say.

"It's not a tournament to the death. I'll be fine."

Men. "Maybe not to the death, but people do get hurt playing with swords."

He chuckles. "I promise to be careful while playing with my sword."

I want to grab him and shake him for making me feel so many conflicted things. Instead I smile, wish him luck again and go back to my friends who are waiting for me by the entrance.

Wytt waggles his eyebrows and winks at me. "Methinks the lady has indeed bestowed upon her favored Knight a token of luck."

"Shut it, Wytt," Corinne says. "Leave her alone."

We're about to choose a seat wherever we can find one before the Arena fills up, when Evie speaks into my ear. "Your grandfather requests your presence in the V.I.P. seating."

I look up at the same time Wytt and Corinne do. Likely they got the same message from their father, because the Chancellor, King Varian and the other Grandmasters are all seated in a special box not accessible from general seating. I'm about to ask how to get there when an Inquisition Guard arrives. "Princess, Prince, Miss Night, I've been sent to escort you to your seats."

Corinne and Wytt look nonplussed, so I go without objection. They're probably used to this. I'll have to get used to it, too. I'm not a Princess, but I'm no longer anonymous either.

When we arrive at the V.I.P. Box, Ragathon glares at me. "What's she doing here?"

My grandfather clears his throat and frowns at the belligerent Grandmaster. "She is my granddaughter, and as such is entitled to enjoy today's festivities here, with her family. Just as the Princess and Princes are allowed to join you and your brother, the King."

He doesn't say those last words like acid thrown on Ragathon's face, but that's certainly how they land, and I smile inwardly. I might start calling him Grandfather if he keeps this up.

King Varian nods to Corinne and Wytt, and I notice Prince Kai is already here, but paying us no mind. Fine by me.

Corinne, Wytt and I take our seats as wait staff from the Castle serve us chilled wine, dried and fresh fruit, a variety of cheeses and crackers and three choices of meat, cut and speared on delicate silver toothpicks for ease.

I have to admit, getting the V.I.P. treatment isn't awful.

Trumpets sound as the tournament begins. Two Knights meet in the center of the arena and begin their battle.

"Miss Night, have you ever been to a tournament?"

I look up from my assortment of treats in surprise, to find King Varian talking to me. "No, Your Majesty."

"Pay close attention and you will learn a great deal about each Knight here."

I nod, unsure of what to say. He leans closer to me and points to the Knights currently dueling. "You see that one, how he keeps missing? He's not watching his opponent's torso, only their arms, their hands, their weapon. He's seeing the move a fraction of a second too late because of that. It's why he'll lose this match."

Despite myself, and my fear of this man, I hang on his words, anxious to learn everything I can about combat and swordplay. For myself and my alter ego.

I watch, and see what he's talking about. And he's right. That Knight loses.

He keeps up a commentary with me and his children throughout the tournament, probing us to notice small details we would have missed otherwise. When Jax fights a Knight in hand-to-hand combat, I cringe, unable to eat or drink until the match is over and he's safe. King Varian pays close attention to Jax and nods at the end. "He has the makings of a great Knight."

Ragathon frowns even more deeply at that. He's pretty much spent the entire tournament looking like he's sucking on rotten lemons. Poor guy. Must be hard to be so unlikable.

After many hours, the final three Knights are announced. Jax, Thane and The Seeker.

When Jax and The Seeker are put together to decide who will move on to fight Thane, I grip the edge of my seat and scoot forward, barely breathing as they fight sword to sword, the clank of metal ringing through the now quiet Arena.

King Varian makes a few comments, but I don't pay attention. Not this time. I can see my pilot wings on Jax's breastplate as he fights, and Corinne's red ribbon hanging from The Seeker.

They battle with a ferocity that invigorates me. When, in the last moment, Jax disarms her and wins, I let out a breath in a whoosh of relief.

Corinne slumps in her chair, and Wytt pats her back. "Cheer up, sister. At least it was Jax she lost to and not Thane."

Ragathon grumbles, also displeased his protégé lost to Jax. "They shouldn't let Zeniths into these. It's an unfair advantage. Why do we even use that word—Zenith? These people are not the pinnacle of humans, they're the vermin."

King Varian shakes his head and smiles the way you would at a child who keeps making the same silly mistake over and over. "When Zeniths appeared, the people chose the word," the King explains, "and so we had a choice. To fight the public and make them 'wrong', thus giving them power, or to allow them the illusion of choice, as we slowly worked from within to make their choice work for us. Through subtle marketing and a very effective public perception campaign, we changed the meaning of the word 'Zenith.' They think they chose, but we control what they think and do about Zeniths." He shakes his head at his brother. "But I wouldn't expect you to grasp the subtleties of mental warfare. If we did things your way, we'd just create a bunch of martyrs that would incite the people to revolt."

It's remarkable how different King Varian and Ragathon are. Not just in looks, though that too. The King is broad-shouldered, muscular, rugged, with brown hair, a handsome face and those purple eyes. Ragathon is hawk-nosed with black hair and dark eyes. He must be using EZ-Eyes to change their color. His natural eye color must be purple. He also lost his accent. He obviously hates his family and wants no association with them. I wonder what happened.

More trumpets blare and King Varian stands to congratulate everyone and announce the final two Knights to do battle. Jax and Thane.

There's no doubt who everyone is rooting for this round. Well, maybe everyone but Ragathon. I never can tell about his loyalties.

It's a tough match. Turns out Thane isn't all talk. He actually knows what he's doing. I get a sick feeling in my stomach as the match goes longer than any of the others. I can tell Jax is getting tired, and I hope he has enough stamina to beat Thane.

King Varian is watching intently. "Was Jax ever punished for his crimes?"

My heart stops. Not this again.

Ragathon is fast to answer. "No, against my better judgment, the Council chose to release him."

I can't keep my mouth shut at this. "Your better judgment? You would have killed an honorable Knight for doing the right thing and defending me against your corrupt and cruel Inquisition Officers. You have no judgment, only bitterness."

The other Grandmasters are shocked into silence. Even my grandfather raises an appraising eyebrow. But

King Varian surprises me with a bemused chuckle. "Miss Night is right. It was a fool's decision to make a public spectacle of his execution, and it cost you quite a bit, didn't it?"

I slump back into my chair, relieved. But Ragathon continues to glare at me as King Varian watches Jax.

It's a tough battle, but in the end, Jax wins. The crowd erupts in cheers, and I clap the loudest.

The wait staff bring in more refreshments and desserts as Jax is paraded around to the calls of his fans.

King Varian eats a strawberry and leans back in his chair. "I'll be taking over Combat Class and Tactics," he announces. "I'm not impressed with what I've seen today." He leans forward, watching Jax. "Except for him. He impressed me. I'll take him as my Second." He looks at Grandmaster Gabriella. "Those are your classes, correct? You don't mind, do you?"

Grandmaster Gabriella looks like she just swallowed a rat, but she shakes her head. "Of course not, Your Majesty."

"Chancellor Forrester, I assume you have no objections."

My grandfather is watching me with a curious expression as he raises his hands open palmed. "We are at your disposal, Your Majesty."

The King smiles. "Please, call me Master Varian. Here, I'm not King, just a teacher and a Knight."

The Chancellor nods. "Very well, Master Varian. We are pleased to have you part of the Initiate training. They will learn a great deal from you." My grandfather rubs his beard. "However, I understand your primary reason for being here is to apprehend Nightfall. Might I ask what you have planned?"

Master Varian looks back out into the Arena, but his gaze is distant, lost in thought. "It's her move. Let's see what she's made of."

...

It's my move. Fantastic.

"Scarlett," Evie says, as I walk with Corinne and Wytt to dinner, "it would be unwise to underestimate King Varian. He does not appear to be as impetuous as his brother."

"Yeah, I know. I know."

Wytt looks up. "You know what?"

I tap my eGlass off. "Nothing, just talking to my eGlass."

He looks at me oddly, then shrugs. "Cool."

As we head to dinner, I notice a lot more people than before. "It got crowded when I wasn't looking."

Corinne nods. "With classes starting tomorrow, a lot of last-minute students are showing up. Tonight's the Welcome Ceremony, so everyone's required to attend."

I'd almost forgotten classes start tomorrow. A nervous butterfly flutters in my gut. Mostly at the thought of getting up before dawn.

Once everyone is settled with their dinner, Chancellor Forrester walks to the podium. "Welcome to Castle Vianney for a new year of training and learning. To our returning students who have been chosen by their Orders, you are about to embark on a new path with even greater trials. To our new Initiates, prepare yourself for the greatest challenge of your lives."

That doesn't sound ominous at all. I look around and notice most everyone has stopped eating to listen, which is good. It means I don't have to fake eat anymore.

"You will learn more from your individual classes, but for now, allow me to introduce you to our curriculum. You are about to begin your Fall Quarter training here at Castle Vianney. You will have two classes from each Order; however, each quarter does have a different focus, which dictates the nature of the Trial. The Fall focus is the Teutonic Order and the Trial at the end of the quarter will test your Teutonic skills."

Wytt leans forward from across the table to whisper at us. "One of the Initiates died last year in the Teutonic Trial."

I look at him in surprise. "What? Seriously?"

He nods. "Seriously."

"That's crazy. How can they allow it?"

Wytt shrugs. "To become a Knight in the old days, you had to fight in battle. Many died. In lieu of battles, they must provide dangerous challenges to weed out the weak."

The Chancellor is still talking. "As some of you know, these Trials are not for the faint of heart. They are graded as pass or fail. You pass if you succeed at the mission in the time allotted. You fail if you take too long, or surrender. Or die."

Wytt raises an eyebrow. "See?"

The Chancellor continues. "Many of you might have heard that these Trials are dangerous. If you are not willing to take those risks, then the Knighthood is not for you."

He looks sternly at everyone before continuing. "You must pass all four Trials to be considered for Knighthood.

89

You must also work hard at your classes. You will be graded on a scale of one to ten for each class, and your Masters will determine who amongst you is exceptional. For those they deem worthy, they will give you Boons to take with you in your Trial. These Boons could mean the difference between success and failure. Do not underestimate the importance of attending all of your classes and doing well."

There goes my plan for ditching PT and sleeping in.

"Furthermore, your Masters will be evaluating you throughout the year. They will be the ones to determine who amongst you is chosen for their Order. A word of warning: You could pass all the Trials—but if you do not impress a Knight of standing, you will not be chosen for an Order."

I didn't know that. And by the reaction around the tables, many others didn't either.

The Chancellor moves to the side as Master Varian joins him. "I'd like to now introduce you to a new Master at our school. King Varian of the House of Ravens, First Knight of the Templars, is honoring us with his experience and training as he takes over several classes and acts as my Second for the Templar seat on the Council."

Master Varian nods and takes his place behind the podium as my grandfather sits down. "Thank you, Chancellor Forrester. I look forward to sharpening the future blades of our Orders and making them battle-hardened. There grows a greater threat in our world than just Nephilim or unchecked Zeniths. Now, we have powerful rebel groups forming, flexing their muscles, trying to rip control of our world out of the hands of the Church and the

Orders. You are the next generation of Knights who will be tasked with keeping order. With stopping these rebels and bringing peace to these lands. Are you ready?"

As cheers fill the hall, I stare straight ahead, my heart pounding as I consider the cost of my double identity.

GRANDFATHER

The sky is still dark. Which is my second clue that it's entirely too early and I should still be in bed. My first clue was sleeping through the alarm clock. Good thing my roommate is better at mornings than I am.

I barely made it to Physical Training on time, but here I am, running an obstacle course at 5:45 in the morning, sweating through the morning chill. I can't use my Nephilim abilities to regulate my body temperature, because that requires the use of my wings. Instead, I strip off my black Castle V sweatshirt and tie it around my waist as I keep pace with Corinne and Wytt. We're all dressed the same, in our workout pants and black shirts, all embossed with the Castle V logo. And everyone looks equally miserable.

"I really don't think we should have to wake up before the sun. It should be a law," I complain as I duck under branches, jump over logs put as obstacles in the woods, and try not to trip in the dark.

Corinne looks over at me sympathetically, her hair blue this morning, rather than pink. "It gets easier."

I don't believe her, but I keep my mouth shut. I don't want to sound like the whiner I clearly am right now. Zorin will probably be thrilled to know I'll be working out so much. At least one of us will be happy.

Wytt's quieter than usual, and I nudge him as we turn a corner in the trail. "No witty banter to keep us distracted?"

Corinne laughs. "You and my brother share the love of mornings," she says.

"A kindred spirit," I say, giving Wytt a small smile.

He grins back at me. "The deep darkness of the night is where my soul thrives."

"Understood." I nearly trip over a rock in the path, but my reflexes are faster now, and I catch myself before I fall. That's a nice perk to all the changes I'm going through.

That feeling is short-lived. Three guys from our class pass us, and the big one in front, who looks like a line-backer with a thick meaty body and short dark hair, sticks his leg out to trip me. This time I do fall, scraping my knee on the rocky dirt. Wytt and Corinne stop and help me up as the guy turns around and smiles. "Sorry about that. Hope you don't tell your Grandpa on me."

He turns and runs away before I can think of a good comeback. I stand, dust myself off, and we start running again after multiple assurances that I'm fine.

"What was that about?" I ask.

Wytt and Corinne exchange a look that I can tell means they know something I don't. "Come on, guys. Spill it."

Corinne shrugs her shoulders. "She'll find out eventually," she says to Wytt.

I look to her and then to Wytt. "Find out what?"

Wytt sighs. "That's Garin. He doesn't like you much."

"I can see that. But why? I've never even met him."

Corinne answers. "He and his sister were scholarship students. They were on a waiting list, and they both got in...until you showed up."

I can tell this isn't going in a good direction. "What did my showing up have to do with it?"

"The Orders only accept a certain number of Initiates each year," Wytt says. "There's a huge waiting list. Even though there are other schools that train Knights, this school is the most elite. The best of the best train here. People from all over the world want in."

And now I understand. "So when I showed up and they accepted me, someone else had to go."

Corinne nods. "It was his sister. She had the weakest entrance scores."

"There was an entrance test?" I ask, surprised.

"For most people," Wytt says. "Some don't have to take it."

I look to each of them and see the truth. "None of us had to take it, did we? Because of our family connections?"

They both nod.

"So, Garin and his friends and others who have to rely on tests and luck, they hate us for our privilege."

"It's not your fault," Corinne says. "You didn't set up the system."

"First day of class and I already have enemies. Fantastic."

Wytt pats my back. "But you already have friends, too."

We're just getting back to the Castle when hidden speakers come to life and a British voice I recognize as my grandfather's fills the air. "Attention Vianney students and faculty. Tomorrow night there will be a public whipping in the Castle Courtyard. All are required to attend. Thank you and enjoy your day."

I stop and lean over to catch my breath. "They do whippings here?"

Corinne looks down at her black sneakers. "Sometimes. If one of our own is being punished."

I don't enjoy seeing people suffer, and I can tell Corinne feels that doubly. "Any idea who?"

Wytt shakes his head. "Haven't heard a thing about it. Weird. Usually these things are being talked about days in advance."

I start walking to my room when Corinne calls me. "Where are you going?"

I look down at my sweaty body. "To shower."

Wytt laughs and throws an arm over my shoulder. "Oh darling, you have much to learn. We have fifteen minutes to grab breakfast before our Combat class begins. Where you will just get sweaty all over again."

I slump under the weight of his arm. "Really?"

All my muscles are sore from running, pushups, sit-ups, the obstacle course and not sleeping enough. Now I have two more hours of training? At least I'm going to be in excellent physical condition by the end of the quarter. If it doesn't kill me first.

We make quick work of breakfast, with me begging off food in favor of Life Force and coffee. Turns out coffee still tastes like coffee, even with my new Nephilim taste buds.

I'm still guzzling too-hot coffee as Corinne and Wytt push me out of the dining hall.

We enter the Arena where our Combat class is taught. It looks different today, more like the empty ruins it was

95

modeled after rather than the bustling stadium it was last night. A few scraps of red cloth from discarded tokens are all that remain as a reminder of the celebrations.

There's about twenty of us waiting for class to start, and it's the first time I've seen all the Initiates in one place without the other Knights. Corinne, Wytt and I stand to the side, leaning against the Arena wall. I take the time to study the other students.

Garin and his two buddies are standing in the middle, clowning around and mock-fighting with a few of the swords that hang from a weapons' rack near them. He has a fighter's face, his bent nose looking like he might have broken it a time or two. When he sees me looking at him he sneers, but I don't turn away my gaze. I feel bad that his sister lost her spot at this school, and I hate that I'm the reason for it, but I'm not about to let my empathy excuse his bullying. So I hold his stare until he turns away and punches one of his friends in the shoulder, who yelps and punches him back.

"Do you two know everyone here?" I ask.

Wytt nods. "Mostly, yes." He points to a girl alone off to the side. She's pretty, slim, with golden brown hair in an A-line cut that shines under the sun—which finally woke up—and golden eyes. "She's a bit of a mystery. Comes from royal blood, or so I've heard. An old family, but I'm not clear on which old family." He points to the oldest member of our class. An Asian man probably in his forties, with shoulder length black hair. He's doing a graceful kata that looks meditative, like something he's done his whole life. "His name is Akio. He's been trying to get into this school for a few years and finally made it.

He's not of noble blood, but his family is well-respected in Japan and very wealthy."

I'm impressed. "How do you know all this?"

Corinne snorts. "He's a busybody."

"I resemble that remark," Wytt quips with a grin. "I just know how to ask the right questions."

I point to a guy and girl who are flirting with each other. "And them?" She's got dark hair and eyes, with a curvy body. He's tall, blond and attractive, the kind of face that could sell movie tickets.

"The girl is Lana. She's from a noble, and very rich, Spanish family. And he's Prince Jaden of Sweden. Not the Crown Prince, so he gets to have more fun."

I look around and notice someone missing. "Where's your brother?"

Corinne frowns. "He'll be here soon. Punctuality isn't his strong suit."

As if on cue, Kai comes striding in, that cocky gait to his walk, just moments before King—Master—Varian comes in with Jax by his side. The King is dressed like all the Masters, in a long black robe with the Castle crest on one side of his chest and his own Order on the other. But you can't watch him walk and not see the royal blood in him. The leader. The King. Even without the fancy outfit and crown. Even with just a leather strap holding back his hair, and his swords at his hips.

Jax looks around and stops when his gaze lands on mine. He smiles, his eyes crinkling in that way I know so well, and I smile back. For that moment, we're still just those kids who liked to build forts together in my backyard. Who played with sticks and pretended they were swords. It's all so strange, seeing him in this world. With a real sword strapped to his hip. He outranks me in every way imaginable, and yet he's still the boy I grew up with.

Everyone starts to line up as Master Varian walks to the front of the class. "You know who I am, and I'll learn about you as I see you fight. So we're going to skip formalities and get straight to it. In this class, you will learn combat. With weapons, with your hands and feet. With your mind," he says, pointing to his own head. "But first, I want to see what you're made of. So, I'm going to pair you with one of your classmates, and each team will take center stage and spar until one of you wins."

My hands start to sweat as he calls out names. Corinne is paired with Lana, Wytt with Akio…and I get stuck with a smirking Prince Kai.

Kai walks over to me and grins. "Guess my dad likes you even less than he likes me."

I cross my arms over my chest. "Really? How do you figure?"

"Because he may not like me, but he knows I can fight." He lays his hand on the sword at his hip, a sword that looks way more dangerous than any of the chipped and fading steel on that weapons rack. "If he put you with me, he wants to see you fail. I wonder what you did to anger him."

I shrug, unsure how to respond to that. We've already formed a circle around the first two students set to spar. They each pick a sword from the rack and begin on Master Varian's command. I expect to see fumbling and false starts, but they've both clearly had training. I'm getting a bit nervous. My sword fighting skills are still rudimentary at best.

I can do the Way of Nyx like a champ, but since Zorin won't teach me more until he's satisfied, I'm stuck.

And I don't know if Kai's as good as he says, but I'm not keen on losing a duel my first day.

When our names are called I walk over to the rack and look at my options. None look like they will be much of a match against the gleaming, sharpened masterpiece that Kai has. I pull one out and test the weight. Satisfied, I take my place and face Kai. He winks at me, his purple eyes offset by black hair that falls over his forehead each time he moves.

"Ready?" Master Varian asks.

We both nod.

"Begin."

We circle each other, swords held at ready. I grip the hilt, trying to keep the right amount of pressure. Not too tight, not too loose. I keep my body relaxed and focus on Kai's core. I lunge, and he parries. We're not fighting so much as testing. The clang of metal is loud.

Everything in me wants to unleash my Nephilim abilities as I fight, but I know I can't. Not here. It would be suicide.

I rein in my pulsating heart and the heat building in me as our swords continue to clash and we continue to lunge. He's playing with me, like a cat toying with a mouse before dinner. I do my best to keep a handle on my temper. Battles can only be won with cool heads.

When Kai picks up his attack, getting more aggressive with each move, I have to keep up. I twist, move, my feet kicking up dirt as I block and thrust. But he's faster, better, his skill honed since childhood.

He's getting too close. I'm losing balance, losing focus. I'm on the defensive. I can't lunge or attack, I can only keep him from cutting me. First one to draw blood wins.

I will not lose.

I use a move from the Way of Nyx, a move meant to regain the offensive when your opponent has you backed into a corner.

With it I push him forward and knock his sword from his hand. He looks surprised, shocked even, and Master Varian comes over. "Well done, Miss Night."

He looks at Kai. "I'm disappointed, Kai. I expected more from you."

When he looks back at me I can feel Kai's rage as well. "Miss Night, where did you learn that move?"

Oh, no. I think fast and decide the truth is best. "Videos of Nephilim fighting."

There's a gasp in the crowd of students and Kai raises an eyebrow.

I expect rebuke from Master Varian, but he smiles at me. "Good job. Continue."

He turns his back to us, addressing the class. "Miss Night has taught everyone here an important lesson. Learning from the enemy is the most important thing you can do if you want to defeat them."

Kai sneers at me as we begin to spar again. "Looks like being the granddaughter of the great Chancellor Forrester doesn't really translate into actual skills," he mocks, "just tricks learned from videos."

"It worked on you," I remind him. But he's right. I'm a one trick wonder, and I don't have any more up my sleeve.

He lands a hit on my sword so hard that it chips and makes my whole arm feel as if it's been ripped off. His attack is more aggressive as everyone watches to see what will happen next. I try another move from the Way of Nyx, but it's less effective and I'm back to being on the defensive, trying to keep my skin intact.

When he pushes forward again, our bodies close now, our two swords locked together between us, he clenches his teeth. "This school doesn't need any rich spoiled brats who got here on Mommy and Daddy's death card."

And all at once, it's game over. My rage, my pain, the pit of despair I keep buried deep, it all surfaces. I can't control it, not anymore, and with all of my strength, Nephilim and human, I push him forward, slashing so hard my own sword breaks on his and he flies back into the students standing many feet behind him. He knocks two of them down and they cushion his fall.

All eyes are on me now.

Because no human could have done what I just did.

Master Varian grabs the broken sword from my hand and gestures for Jax to come over. "Take her to the Council immediately, and keep her in custody until she's called in."

Jax nods and takes my arm, and I follow him without protest. I'm shaking in terror.

Once we're away from everyone, he stops and faces me. "What was that, Star? What happened?"

My eyes fill with tears. "I don't know. I just…I got so angry. He said something about my parents and something in me broke and…I don't know."

A tear falls down my cheek and he wipes it away with a finger. His face is a mix of emotion. Anger, fear, confusion.

I wish I could tell him the truth, but I can't. And it kills me.

He nods and takes me to what I can only describe as a holding cell. It's basically a tiny room with a door and two Guards placed outside of it. He squeezes my hand before leaving. "I'll do what I can to protect you."

And then he's gone, and I'm alone in the room, without Evie even, since we aren't allowed to wear eGlasses in class. I sit on the small cot, which is the only furniture aside from a sad-looking toilet and sink.

As I wait, every fear imaginable plagues me. I consider calling for Zorin using the Nephilim sign made with my blood, but what could one Nephilim do against the entire Four Orders? He'd just be caught, or worse, and I'd still be here.

So I wait, and hope I can find words to talk myself out of a death sentence.

Maybe I can control someone, if I can get close enough. Maybe Varian? He has a lot of power and influence.

It feels like hours when finally the door opens and Jax is there, a grim expression on his face. I follow him out. "What's going on? What's going to happen to me?"

He shakes his head. "I can't say anything. Just come with me. And...choose your words carefully."

He brings me back to the Council Chambers. I've been here before, but I was covered in my parents' blood and knew nothing of this world, this life. It was only a few weeks ago, but it feels much longer.

All of the Grandmasters are sitting in their marble seats above the semi-circle I stand in. This time, Master

Varian is in the seat of the Templar Order. And my grandfather is conspicuously missing.

This scares me more than anything else. I thought for sure I'd have at least one ally.

I stand before the Council and try to act braver than I feel. For all my training with my parents, I never prepared for this.

"Let's get this started," Ragathon grumbles from his seat.

"Where is my grandfather?" I ask.

Ragathon narrows his eyes at me. "We'll be doing the asking around here, Miss Night."

Varian looks sternly at his brother. "No need for hostility, brother. We'll find the truth of what happened in due time." He looks around the Council and then back at me. "Chancellor Forrester seems to be unavoidably detained, so we shall have to begin without him. As highest ranking Knight, I will direct these proceedings."

Master Varian recounts what happened in Combat Training today and I hold my head high as they all stare at me. When he's done, Ragathon leans in. "How did you keep this a secret for so long?"

Varian holds up a hand. "Let's start from the beginning. You've never been listed as a Zenith in your testing. Can you explain how you demonstrated para-powers in the Arena today? "

"I don't know. I've never had any para-powers."

Ragathon sneers. "How did you cheat the tests?"

"I have no idea what you're talking about," I say. "This is as much a shock to me as to everyone here." At least that part is true.

When the door behind me opens and everyone looks past me, I turn and sigh in relief. My grandfather has arrived.

"Excuse me for my tardiness, but I thought we might want some actual evidence before we convict my granddaughter for something she didn't do." He climbs the stairs to his seat slowly, then sits and clicks on his eGlass. "I'm synching files to each of you. These are the test results of the blood work we did when she arrived, as well as all of her tests since she was a child."

Each of the Council members click on their eGlass and look through the files.

My heart is pounding. I've been trying to find the results of my blood work for weeks, but they weren't in any of the systems. Those tests will prove I'm a Nephilim. So why does my grandfather look happy?

"As you can see," he says, "she's tested negative since she was a child. Until a few weeks ago. We just got those results back, and they show she is a latent Zenith. Rare, but not unheard of. Likely the stress and injury sustained during the attack on her family activated this latent gene."

Latent Zenith? How did the test show something like this?

My grandfather looks at me. "Scarlett, have you noticed any subtle changes in your body recently?"

I tilt my head as I consider how to answer, and I see this could be a way out of a few problems if I choose my words carefully, as Jax suggested. "As a matter of fact, I have noticed a few things," I say.

He nods. "Such as?"

"Well, I've been a bit stronger lately, though nothing like what happened in the Arena. I've been healing faster, though again, I've always been a fast healer. And...well, one other thing."

"Yes?"

"I think I'm starting to see color."

I sneak a peek at Jax, whose face can't hide his astonishment, though he recovers quickly.

"It's as I thought," Chancellor Forrester says. "She's developing her latent para-powers. The outburst in the Arena wasn't in her control. I vote we dismiss the charges against her and change her registration status to Zenith, without punishment. All in favor?"

Three voices say "Aye." Ragathon says "Nay."

"The Ayes have it," my grandfather says. "I also vote for no public identification, since she's an Initiate at our school. All in favor?"

Three Ayes. One Nay. Naturally.

My grandfather bangs his walking stick on the marble floor. "Council dismissed. Let's allow Scarlett to get back to her classes, and we can all get back to our work."

The Council room clears out quickly. I'd hoped to talk to Jax, but Varian pulls him out first thing, and I'm left alone with the Chancellor. "Walk an old man out?"

I nod and take his arm as we walk slowly through the Castle. "My test really showed I'm Zenith?"

He pauses and looks down at me, his eyes bright blue and sharp as ever. "Is that a problem?"

"No," I say as we start to walk again. "Not a problem. I'm just...surprised."

We stop again, this time in front of my room. "Good. Now, I believe you're late for class. Best get changed and hurry along. Ragathon doesn't like stragglers."

I chuckle. "Ragathon doesn't like much, it seems."

"Too true," my grandfather says. "Too true."

I place my hand against the door handle, then turn to the Chancellor. "You saved my life in there."

He reaches for my free hand and holds it. "You're my granddaughter. My kin. Yours is a life very much worth saving."

"Thank you," I say. And then I look at him and realize, I feel the same. He's kin. My kin. My last remaining family. "Thank you, Grandfather."

DAY ONE

I shower and change in record time, but I'm still painfully late to Law, and Ragathon isn't in the mood to offer any leeway given my morning.

As soon as I walk in, his eyebrow shoots up, and the corners of his lips turn down. "Thank you for joining us, Miss Night. I hope we haven't inconvenienced you in any way. Spoiled your morning?" Half the class chuckles at his sarcastic dig on me, and of course everyone knows why I'm late.

Corinne and Wytt are staring at me like I grew horns while I was gone. As I sit between them, Wytt whispers, "Are you okay?"

I nod.

"Then I'll need all the details after class."

I grin as I pull out my books. Of course he would. Wytt, our little gossip.

I sneak a glance at Kai, who's sitting across the class. He's staring at me, and doesn't break eye contact when he sees me looking, so I don't either.

I try to read his eyes, to figure out what he's thinking, but Ragathon interrupts my thoughts by standing between us. "Miss Night, are we interrupting your daydreaming, or would you care to venture an answer to the question?"

I look up. "Could you repeat it, please?"

"Repeat it? Were you not sitting right here in the class?"

Snickers drift around the room, and Corinne points down at her notebook. She wrote, *Give an example of a new law that was created after the discovery of para-powers.*

"The Standardized Registration Act was passed," I say, "requiring Zeniths to register their para-power with the appropriate agency or face fines or imprisonment."

Ragathon smirks. "I should have known you would go for the most obvious. That law is known by children learning to talk. This is not grade school, Miss Night. If you cannot manage to bring something more, I'm afraid you'll not fare well at Castle Vianney."

A voice from behind Ragathon interrupts him. "Isn't that why we're here? To learn this stuff?"

Ragathon turns in surprise to face Kai. His face softens when he looks at his nephew. "Of course, Kai. You are. But there is an expectation that you come with some semblance of knowledge before starting the classes."

"I'm sure she does," Kai says in my defense. "But everyone has their own unique skills, right? So Scarlett may not know a lot about law, but she undoubtedly knows a lot about other subjects, given her family."

Ragathon turns to face me with a look of subdued rage. "I'm sure she does…given her family." He walks to the front of the class and uses his eGlass to project a list of assignments on the board. "Write this down and complete the work before our next session. Class dismissed."

He leaves the classroom while we're all still taking notes. I wonder if this was his original homework plan, or if it was tripled on my account.

I want to thank Kai for sticking up for me, but when he passes us he doesn't look happy. "I'm surprised they let you come back," he says.

"I don't know what you mean."

"Granddaughter of the Chancellor gets special privileges it seems. Anyone else pulled that they'd be flagged for using para-powers without authorization during a training."

"Cut it out, Kai," Wytt says. "Like the son of a King doesn't get special privilege?"

He throws his backpack over a shoulder. "Being Varian's son hasn't exactly been a privilege for me."

I'm over this. I stand, books in hand and lean toward him. "At least you still have a father. Don't ever use my parents against me again, or I won't hold back next time."

I leave as Corinne and Wytt scramble to catch up. They flank me on each side. "What happened?" Wytt asks.

I explain the test results and the Council's ruling. And I tell them what Kai said to trigger me.

Corinne shakes her head, a sad look on her face. "Try not to take it personally, though I'll definitely smack him for that. Our father is a fair man, but he's also a hard man, and he's always been especially hard on Kai. It's hurt him. When we came to Castle Vianney, Kai only agreed to come for two reasons. To watch out for us, and to get away from our father."

"Looks like he failed on that count," I say, feeling a small tinge of pity for him as we head to lunch. "But he needs to grow up and stop acting like he's the only one who's been hurt by life."

...

I'm completely in my element for our Espionage class. Finally, I don't feel like the black sheep in the group. My grandfather is teaching the class, and he asks us all to pull out our laptops.

Mine looks beat up and old, but it has the processing speed of a ninja. And it's totally custom. I built it myself, so I would know.

I smile up at him as I wait for our instructions. I'm beginning to see the pattern of our first day of school. Introduce us to our subject by giving us an impossible task and seeing how we do. So far, I haven't done well. That's about to change.

My grandfather leans on his staff as he speaks to the class. "In espionage, you have to know how to access the enemy's information to use to your advantage. In today's world, that often means hacking into top secret files. This afternoon, we're going to pretend Castle Vianney is the enemy."

This gets a few chuckles, but my stomach flips a little as I remember that Castle V *is* Nightfall's enemy.

"I want you to hack into the mainframe of our library. It's got firewalls you won't even know are there, and I don't expect any of you to succeed. In fact, if you do, we may have to fire someone today."

More chuckles.

"But I want to see how creative you can be in problem solving," he continues. "So I know what we need to work on."

He uses his eGlass to set a timer. "You have until the end of class. Go!"

I boot up my computer and my fingers fly over the keyboard. I've already hacked into the Infirmary database when I was looking for my test results, so I know what kind of firewalls Castle V uses. They're good. Maybe great. But they aren't a challenge for me.

I hear Wytt curse under his breath, and I know he's not alone in his struggles. I wish I could help, but I'm hyper-focused on my task.

It doesn't take me long to locate what I need in the mainframe. I use a special program I designed last year to unravel the passcodes and sneak past the secondary firewalls that are supposed to be hidden. There's a third layer I was also expecting, and it proves more difficult, but not insurmountable.

I focus for another few minutes, brain and fingers working in sync like a machine. Nothing else exists but me and the 0s and 1s of this familiar language.

Another ten minutes, and I smile and turn my computer toward my grandfather.

He raises an eyebrow and limps over to me, his walking stick clanking against the stone floors. "Are you having some trouble, Scarlett?"

Others around me look up as he approaches. I shake my head. "No, I'm done," I say.

There's some shocked mumbling behind me that I ignore.

"That's impossible," he says. "Let me see."

He takes my laptop and looks at my work.

"It wouldn't have taken so long, but I wanted to see if I could crack the restricted file section while I was in."

He chuckles. "Don't worry, no one can get into there."

"Oh, I got in," I tell him. "And I fixed your firewalls so no one else can get in again." I also created a back door for later access. My research on Angels hasn't gone well, but maybe this section of the library will have answers.

It takes him a moment to check my work, and when he sets my laptop back down on my desk, he looks decidedly impressed. "Your mother really did teach you everything she knew."

I nod, tears stinging my eyes. "Not everything," I say, thinking of all the secrets I didn't know. "But she did teach me my way around a mainframe."

"Clearly," he says. "Well done, granddaughter. I think you just got our IT person fired."

. . .

"How did you do that?" Corinne asks as we leave Espionage and head to APD, a class I'm definitely not looking forward to.

"I've been hacking since I was four years old," I tell her. "It was part of my unusual homeschooling." I still remember my first hack. My parents set up an account that had the location of a bag of my favorite cookies. If I could hack it, I would get the cookies. It took me days. I made so many mistakes. It was embarrassing. But I was four, so there's that. I figured it out after asking a lot of questions, and

I got my bag of cookies. Best hack ever, even to this day. Chocolate mint chip with frosting. Yum.

My stomach grumbles, and I feel the heat of thirst clenching my throat. I pull out a Life Force and suck it down as we walk through the stone halls. Corinne wrinkles her nose. "You drink a lot of those things. It's not good for you. The chemical makeup alters your blood stream and can cause long term problems with your central nervous system."

I'm assuming this doesn't apply to Nephilim, so I just smile. "I'll take my chances. This keeps my brain awake."

Wytt pulls out a scrap of paper and a pen and scribbles something. "Alas, but what will keep your heart awake, fair maiden?"

I glance at his paper and grin. "Writing poetry on the go, huh?"

"He's always thinking in verse," Corinne says. "He's even been known to write on his body if no paper presents itself. One time I caught him scribbling a sonnet on his thigh in marker."

Wytt's still looking down at his paper, pen in mouth. "It was the only thing around. A poet's got to do what a poet's got to do."

"Can't you just use your eGlass?" I ask.

Wytt rolls his eyes and makes a face like I just suggested he wear tin foil as clothing. "Did the great poets create their masterpieces with an eGlass? I think not."

Corinne chuckles. "Wytt is a traditionalist with his writing. If he could find one of those ancient typewriter things that still worked, he'd use one."

When we arrive at class, Grandmaster Marian is standing with a satchel thrown over her shoulder. "Don't get comfortable. Today's lesson is going to be a field trip. We're heading to the city to introduce you to Curatio Domus, the best Hospitaller hospital and research facility in the world."

My heart is happy for just a moment. No tests!

Until...

"It's there that we will have our first test."

Great.

Corinne, however, looks like a kid at Christmas. She grabs my hand and squeezes. "This is fantastic. I can't wait for you both to meet some people there."

Wytt sticks the paper he was scribbling on back in his pocket. "She's been volunteering at the hospital since she was old enough to go into the city by herself."

"I thought you were raised in Sapientia?" I ask.

"We were," Wytt says. "But we spent our summers at Castle V for extra training."

Our entire Initiate class walks through the Castle gate and into Vianney, toward the subway.

Once in the city, Grandmaster Marian leads us at a brisk pace through the busy streets and sidewalks until we reach Curatio Domus. "Students, stay together and be respectful."

Garin and his friends are joking around, punching each other and laughing, and the Grandmaster scowls at them. "That includes you three. Unless you want to flunk this class your first day?"

They settle down enough that we are able to enter the hospital.

A beautiful young woman with chestnut brown hair and blue eyes smiles at Corinne when we walk in. "Princess, it's so nice to see you again."

"Hi, Sarah. How's our patient?"

Sarah picks up a patient chart from the front desk. "Why don't you come say hi and see for yourself?"

Corinne looks over at Grandmaster Marian, who nods. "You and your friends can say hi briefly. I'm going over hospital protocol. Make sure to explain the rules to Wytt and Scarlett."

"I will," Corinne says as we follow Sarah down a long corridor and into a private room. A young girl, no older than twelve, is lying in bed and using her eGlass to project a video onto the eScreen in front of her. She's watching a surgery of some kind, which she clicks off when she sees us.

Sarah smiles at the girl. "Hi there, Charlie. I have some friends here who wanted to come say hi, is that okay?"

Charlie grins, her dark brown eyes striking in her too-pale face. "Sure! I love having visitors."

Corinne steps forward. "Hi there. You're looking good. What were you watching?"

"Princess! I'm so glad you came by. I was just checking out videos on the surgery I'm about to have. They think they can replace my kidney with a genetically modified one from an ape that won't break down under attack from my body. I might get to finally go home soon."

Sarah looks at us. "Charlene, or Charlie, has stage 4 M. Chronic Kidney Failure, a new mutation of kidney disease where her body attacks her kidneys and destroys them. A regular transplant won't work, but through the research of the Hospitallers and genetic modifications, we might have found a cure!"

Corinne waves us forward. "Charlie, this is my twin, Wytt."

"I've heard a lot about you, Wytt. Nice to meet you. And thank you for that poem. I love it."

Wytt bows. "Anything for a lady as fair as you."

Charlie giggles.

Corinne points to me. "And this is Scarlett, a new friend of ours."

"It's nice to meet you, Charlie."

"You too," she says. "I like your eyes."

I smile. "I like yours too. They remind me of chocolate."

We chat with her for a few more minutes and then leave to catch up with our group as Corinne explains the protocol. We spend some time touring the hospital, including the labs where much of the genetic research is done. I don't know how I feel about it all, but I have to admit the facility is impressive. And it treats everyone, Zenith and human.

"The hospital is funded by the Orders," Grandmaster Marian says, "and is open to all, regardless of income. No one has to pay to be treated here. We offer cutting edge medical care and incorporate the latest in medical research into our diagnostics and treatments."

We head down a long, narrow hall and stop before a door with a restricted sign on it. "Here's where you will have your first test. Are you ready?"

No.

But we go in anyways, and in the middle of an empty, well-lit room, is a dead, naked body splayed out in all its dead, naked glory.

I pause, taking it in as the Grandmaster explains what we're to do. "You have two hours to study this body and identify all the major organs and bones, then diagnose her cause of death." She pulls out a stack of papers. "You will divide into groups of four and begin."

Corinne, Wytt and I stick together, and Kai walks over to us. "Looks like you need another member."

Corinne smiles at her brother. "Perfect."

Kai looks at me, and I hold eye contact with him. "Any objections?" he asks.

"Nope."

"Good."

Wytt chuckles. "You two will either kill each other by the end of the quarter, or fall in love. I'm not sure which yet."

I turn an evil eye on him as Grandmaster Marian hands me a piece of paper with the skeletal system drawn on it, another image with a picture of the body before us, and spaces for filling in the information.

We all move closer to the table with the body and see that it's been cut open and spread for dissection and analysis. One of the guys in our group turns away to a trash can and vomits into it while the students around him step back with cries of 'gross.'

"Begin," Marian says.

Corinne looks to all of us. "Anyone want to start?" No one speaks as we stare at the body. "Come on, guys, we all have to contribute."

I know she's right, but I'm useless here. I look down at the paper and take out a pencil. "Okay, um…Let me see." I write something on the paper, and Corinne looks at it.

"Really?" she says.

"What?"

She takes the paper from me. "Just. Stop writing. I adore you, Scarlett, and if I ever need anyone to hack into anything, you're my first call. But seriously, elbow and knee? That's the best you could do?"

"No, I wasn't done," I argue. "There's also toes, a head, legs, arms...lots of things."

Kai chuckles, and Corinne turns on him. "Care to take over, big brother?"

He waves his hands. "Nope. I'm afraid I'm as useless as Scarlett at the moment. This is your field, little sister, not mine."

"Hey!" I say, feigning offense.

He just raises an eyebrow. "Am I wrong?"

"In general, yes," I argue. "But perhaps not entirely at this moment."

He smirks as Corinne looks to Wytt. "Surely you've picked up something from me in all these years of shared DNA?" Corinne asks her twin.

Wytt studies the body. "I know there's a tibia some-where. And a fibula or something?"

Corinne sighs. "You three are hopeless." She quickly fills in the entire skeletal system and all the organs herself.

I whistle. "Impressive."

"While you were becoming the youngest criminal hacker in history," Wytt says, "my sister here was playing with bones."

Corinne puts a pen in her mouth and stares at the body. "Now's the hard part. We have to figure out how she died."

"How's that even possible?" I ask. "Don't we need to be able to run tests and stuff? Or to know something about her medical history?"

"It depends on the cause," Corinne says. "Presumably not in this case, if Grandmaster Marian believes we can actually come close to succeeding."

I'm not convinced that's true, but I keep my skepticism to myself. Kai grins at me as if he can read my thoughts, and I think we're sharing the same suspicions.

I grin back. But Corinne doesn't give up. She spends the next hour pointing out clues.

"Look here," she says, pointing to the brain. "The tissue is too soft and is atrophied. There's also some vertical enlargement. And damage of hypoxic-ischemic leuko-encephalopathy in both the bilateral globus pallidus and cerebral white matter."

I just nod, because I have no idea what she's talking about. In fact, I'm pretty sure she's just making words up at this point, but she's getting animated as our time approaches.

"I think I know what killed this poor woman," Corinne says at last.

She jots down notes on our page and draws some expertly rendered pictures of small parts of the brain in exquisite detail.

The Grandmaster comes to collect our papers, studies them, then looks up at us with a raised eyebrow. "I'm not even going to ask who came up with this." She looks at Corinne. "So your diagnosis is…"

"Acute carbon monoxide poisoning after a long-term vegetative state," Corinne says with confidence.

"That's very impressive, Princess. You do realize it's extremely difficult to make this diagnosis from an autopsy alone?"

Corinne beams. "Am I right?"

The teacher nods. "You are. You have a real future in our Order," she says.

The Grandmaster glances at me. "As for the rest of you, I really hope you have a different Order picked for your future. And you'd better hope the Princess is always around when you need her."

Wytt sighs dramatically as she walks off. "If only there were an Order devoted to the preservation of poetic imagery and language. That would surely be my calling."

I tug at Wytt's arm. "That's enough, Shakespeare. Let's get out of here. I need some fresh air that's not tainted with the aroma of formaldehyde."

...

The chemical stench still singes my nose hairs as my mind fades into the land of sleep. A voice shakes me out of the almost-dream I'm reaching for.

"Scarlett, wake up. Time to study."

I roll over, closing my eyes tighter. Nox purrs and shifts his body to lay over my neck. "Scarlett isn't here right now," I mumble. "Leave a message after the beep. BEEP."

Corinne chuckles. "So not a morning person or a night person, got it. You're one of those mid-afternoon people."

I sit up reluctantly and rub my eyes. "No, I'm just not a never-sleep-at-all person."

She grabs my hand and pulls me from the bed. "Come on, the guys are waiting for us. We're going to study in the library tonight."

"Okay, fine. Just let me get my stuff."

I stick my eGlass on my ear. Since we don't get to wear them in class, I've missed Evie. She comes to life and greets me. "Hello, Scarlett. You've been gone a long time today."

"Better get used to it," I tell her. "Classes never end here."

"You have a message from Zorin."

I sigh. "Okay, show me."

A text appears.

You coming tonight? ~Z

I reply.

Nope. Homework.

He replies immediately.

:(

I laugh out loud. I'm trying to imagine the big tough Nephilim using emoticons. It's hard to picture.

Corinne looks up from stuffing her backpack. "What's so funny?"

"Just something Evie said."

"You have an unusual relationship with your AI. You must have done a lot of customization."

I nod. "Yes, I did. I guess when you grow up a home-schooled computer geek in the middle of nowhere, you make your own friends. Literally."

She laughs, but it's a sad kind of laugh. "You had Jax though, right?"

I frown. "I suppose I did."

We grab our bags and head out to meet the guys.

"I feel sad for you," she says. "I can't imagine growing up not knowing about any of this and then finding out the way you did. I'm sorry."

I shrug. "Thanks. It's...hard, but I try not to think about it too much. I don't really have the luxury of grieving for everything I've lost."

She tugs at a stray blue hair. "Grief doesn't go away, Scarlett. Don't shut it out for too long. It'll come back and bite you when you least expect it."

She sounds like she's speaking from experience, but Wytt jogs up to us and throws an arm around me before I can respond.

"How are the two most beautiful women in all the land doing this fine evening?" he asks.

"Sleepy," I say.

"To sleep is to let in the dreams of the gods," he says.

"Then this studying is keeping me from my divine destiny," I retort.

Kai catches up with us as we head to the library. "What lessons should we work on first?"

"I don't know why we have to do this tonight," I say. "None of it's due until Wednesday."

"You don't think our classes tomorrow will have work for us too?" Corinne asks.

"Oh, right."

Kai pushes open the large, engraved doors of the library, and we step in to one of my favorite places in the Castle. Books line the three-story tower, many only reachable with tall ladders on wheels that move around the circular walls. There are wooden tables and overstuffed chairs spread throughout the library for studying and reading. We make our way to a large table in the middle and lay our books down.

The librarian smiles when she sees us, adjusting her glasses. "Scarlett, it's good to see you again. Still researching for your project?"

I smile self-consciously. "Nope, just here to study with my friends."

"How did your first day of class go?" She walks over to us, her blue dress loose around her slight frame. She has large brown eyes, fading brown hair and a small nose where her thick black glasses sit.

"They were okay. Except Law. Ragathon doesn't like me. Not sure he likes anyone."

She smiles with sympathy. "He can be a hard man to warm up to, but I'm sure it'll get easier as the year goes on. Let me know if you kids need anything."

She walks away, and all three of my friends look at me strangely.

"What?" I ask.

"You seem to come here a lot," Corinne says.

"It's been pretty quiet here the last few weeks, so I thought I'd get caught up on my politics."

Wytt gestures to the librarian. "You *do* know that's Ragathon's wife, right?"

My jaw drops. "No, I didn't. Oh man, I'm such a jerk. I can't believe I complained about her husband to her face."

Kai shrugs. "She's probably used to it. I love my uncle, but he isn't always the easiest for others to get along with."

I sink into my seat. "Let's just get this over with. I do need some sleep tonight if we're expected to do another before-dawn PT."

We all open our books and dive in, but after a few moments I look up. "Hey, is there another section to this library? Somewhere they keep books they don't want students reading?"

"You mean aside from the restricted section you hacked in class today?" Kai asks.

"Yeah, besides that."

He shakes his head. "That's it."

"Oh."

I look back down at my book disappointed. I've already perused that section. Nothing on Angels that isn't pulled from the Bible and old legends I've already heard.

An hour into our studying, as I'm writing down notes for Law, a hand lands on my shoulder, and I look up into familiar blue eyes. "Jax."

He smiles, and it still tugs at my traitorous heart. "Hi, Scarlett. I've been looking everywhere for you."

I put down my pen. "I've been here."

He chuckles. "I see that." His hand is still on my shoulder as he looks at the others. "Hi," he says to the three of them. "It's good to see you all. Mind if I borrow Scarlett for a few minutes?"

Kai frowns, but Corinne smiles. "That's up to her, obviously," Corinne says.

Jax looks down at me. "Can we talk? I want to show you something."

THE FORGE

Jax escorts me through the courtyard and down a dirt trail I've never followed. We walk for a while, and eventually the dirt is replaced with stone. Abstract metal sculptures begin to line the path through the forest. One reminds me of a woman and man embracing, another reminds me of the sea. I can't imagine sculpting such beauty. Jax leads me down three stone steps where a great forge stands before a wall of carvings. Wind howls around this monument. The heat beats against my skin.

"The carvings tell stories of great Knights, and those…" he points at a pattern of swords hanging at the top of the wall, "…those belonged to some of them."

Jax grabs an apron off a chair and puts it on. It's thick and tough and smells like leather. He picks up tongs and pulls a red-hot piece of steel from the forge. He brings it to an anvil and beings to shape it with a hammer. Sparks fly.

"I like to come here," he says over the cacophony of sounds created by metal and fire. "To think, to remember, to forget."

I never knew he was a blacksmith. "Are any of those sculptures yours?"

"Yes, a few."

"Your work is beautiful."

"Ella—Grandmaster Gabriella—taught me after..." He stops himself and slams the hammer down harder than before. "Ella taught me." The steel stretches as he works on it, turning into a blade.

"Do you like forging swords?"

He pauses. "See this steel? It's raw potential, but I give it purpose. I can change one thing to another. I can make it better." He resumes hammering.

I walk closer, but avoid the sparks. "Like the Orders?"

"Like everything." He pushes the steel into a bin of water. Steam rises. "Take you, for example. Your parents forged you into who you are. Now, you must decide who you want to be. People can change, and they can be changed. Everything can be transformed."

He lays the steel bar, now resembling a sword, down on the anvil and removes his apron. "I've thought about our talk regarding Nightfall. And though I still believe she is in the wrong, I also believe she is like this steel. She has raw potential, and if she can find the right purpose, she can do great things."

His words mean more to me than he can imagine. Or perhaps he can. Maybe that's why he said them.

I hug him, and he hugs me back. He pulls away too soon. "Scarlett, there's something I have to tell you. Tomorrow night, I will be the one whipped in the courtyard."

"What? Why?"

"The Council has determined that I must be punished for killing the Officers."

"It was Varian, wasn't it? I heard him ask if you'd ever been disciplined." I raise a fist, as if to fight Varian now.

Jax lowers my hand. "I don't know if it was Varian, but it's what the Council has decided. I will accept the necessary punishment."

He looks so calm, almost happy. I punch him in the chest. "Why'd you kill those Officers? There were other things we could have done, contact the Chancellor, or Gabriella—"

"I never told you how it happened, did I? How I killed the Nephilim girl." He sounds quiet, sad.

My anger is replaced by compassion, and I lower my fists, shaking my head, and he gestures me closer. We sit side by side on the stone steps, and Jax stares into the distant flames. "Do you know of my mother?"

"She died when you were born."

"No. My mother was a Templar, and I was born at Castle V. When my father was assigned to watch over your family, it was decided that I'd go with him, so that I could have a normal life. So I wouldn't grow up surrounded by battle and death."

I had no idea. I take his hand, my heart hurting for him. All this he kept inside. For the first time I start to see the sacrifice he's made in keeping these secrets. In living a double life.

He squeezes my hand and continues holding it as he talks. "For years, I thought, just as you, that my mother was dead. But when I discovered I was a Zenith, when I asked my father to join the Orders, he told me the truth."

It takes him a moment to speak again. "That summer, I traveled to Castle V, and I met my mother. She was beautiful, Scarlett. And kind. She was everything I'd dreamed my mother would be. She taught me how to fight, how to forge. She taught me what it meant to be a Knight. How to do the right thing, no matter the cost."

A bead of sweat runs down my forehead as flames from the forge heat up the air around us. I ignore the discomfort and focus on Jax.

"When I was fourteen, my mother and I were stationed at a Templar control center. It was a secret location, where Templars could receive and give orders. I was there to observe and learn. We were ambushed. Someone had betrayed us."

He squeezes my hand harder, his face a mask of grief and anger. "My mother killed two Nephilim while I disarmed a Zenith. We thought it was over, and then I saw her. I still remember her face. The long black hair, the cold blue eyes. She looked a year younger than me. I could have stopped her, I should have stopped her...but I didn't..."

His voice hitches and turns gravelly, almost a whisper, as he continues. "The girl charged my mother from behind, and she slit my mother's throat."

A tear trickles down his cheek. "As my mother fell to the ground, the girl turned on me, and finally my training kicked in. We fought. I kicked her, and her body fell back, impaling itself on a spear stuck in the wall behind her. It tore through her heart, killing her. I ran to my mother, to hold her, to tell her she'd be fine, but she was already gone."

He turns his face to look at me now, his eyes so full of sorrow. "I was the only one left alive. The Orders contacted my eGlass. They said someone was fleeing the area through the woods, possibly the traitor, and I was to terminate them. So I followed."

He pauses and I just hold his hand tighter, waiting for him to finish, knowing there's something more. Something even worse.

"I caught him," Jax whispers. "The traitor. It was my father."

I feel the weight of this pain, this hurt. I knew his father. Loved his father. He was family. I can't imagine being in Jax's position. Having to make that kind of choice.

"I asked him why," Jax says as he gazes back into the flames. "He tried to explain. He never believed the Nephilim were evil. The War was pointless. He'd been helping end it. I told him my mother was dead because of him. He told me he didn't know. Didn't know we were at the control center. But how could I trust a traitor?"

He looks back at me again, his eyes pleading for understanding. For absolution. For forgiveness. "I had to kill him. For the Orders. For my mother. For me." He drops his chin to his chest, his eyes closing.

"And so I did."

My heart breaks as I reach for him, wrapping my arms around his shoulders as he leans against my shoulder and cries. It only lasts a moment, and after, he stands up and faces me. His voice is hard, the tears gone. "So understand this. I don't hesitate. When those Officers threatened you, I knew I had to protect you. I knew I had to kill them. And I would do so again."

The war took everything from Jax. His mother. His father. His innocence. "I understand. And I'm sorry for what happened to you. I wish I'd known earlier, but I know now, and I'm here for you."

He sighs. "Thank you." He turns to me, his eyes watery. "Star…"

"Yes?"

"I…" He shakes his head and chuckles. "I need to get some rest. I have a big day tomorrow."

"Sure. Of course."

He escorts me back to the Initiate's Common Hall and says goodnight. I wonder what he was about to say when he called me Star. Does he care for me as I care for him?

I'm about to go inside, when someone whistles. I turn and see a familiar shadow leaning against a tree. "Zorin? What are you doing here?"

He grins. "I had to see how you're first day went."

I run up to him and quiet my voice. "And what if someone recognizes you?"

"Only a few know my face. For most, I'm just someone who lives and works on the island. So, how was it?"

I cross my arms. "Painful. I was confirmed as Zenith."

He frowns. "How is that possible?"

"They took a blood test a while ago. I thought it could detect Nephilim, but maybe it was flawed. Maybe it only picked up smaller amounts of Angel blood."

"Perhaps." He doesn't appear convinced. "Be careful of more tests."

"I will. If Varian suspects anything—"

"Varian is here?"

I sigh. "Varian teaches my combat class."

His eyes light up with concern. "Scarlett, do not train with him."

"Why not? He hasn't recognized me. This is my chance to study him. To learn his weaknesses."

"It's also your chance to eliminate him." His eyes grow dark. "Use your power to kill him."

The thought has crossed my mind. I push it away. "No. If I kill him, someone else will take his place. Then when do I stop?"

"When the Orders are destroyed."

I scowl. "I can't walk around grabbing people and ordering them to suicide. Someone will notice."

Zorin sighs. "You know, before this is over, more people will die. You can't save everyone."

He speaks a truth I've refused to face. I don't want anyone to die at my hands. "I..." I keep my resolve. "I will not kill Varian. I will learn from him. And one day, I will surpass you both." I turn and march for the door.

"And once you have," says Zorin, "what will you do?"

I glare at him. "I will advance to a Knight of the First, and I will build an army. I will turn the Orders against each other. And I will crush them."

DAY TWO

It's a grey day, full of clouds and wind with a light rain spatter. The dirt under my feet has turned to a slimy mud, and my clothes are sticking to my body as I swing my sword against an invisible enemy, practicing the attack and defense drill Jax just showed us.

"You're improving, Scarlett," Jax says as he makes his way around the arena. He puts a hand under my elbow and moves it up. "Good. Keep working on your form. You don't want to leave yourself open for attack."

"Okay," I say. I was up all night thinking about what Jax told me about his family. We need more time together, more time to talk and just be. But today we're back to our roles, and Varian has a meeting this morning so Jax is in charge of Combat.

Which makes me his student, not his best friend. So we keep it professional. But my heart is reaching out to him, to my friend, to the man I still love despite everything. How many more secrets are there for me to discover about my life and the lives of those I love?

Jax walks across the arena to help Lana on her thrust. His back is turned to me, and he's out of earshot when Garin and his friends surround me. "You may fool everyone here," Garin says, "But I know you're just a rich brat who bought her way into a spot that should've gone to someone more deserving."

They all have their swords out, and while I know they won't attack me with everyone here, my heart still beats a little faster. "I heard about your sister, and I'm sorry. I had no idea. But you need to back off and knock that chip off your shoulder."

He growls and moves closer, pushing me back against his sidekick Bartholomew, who uses his elbow to knock me forward. I rub between my shoulder blades where I'm sure a nice bruise is forming thanks to Bart.

I'm debating about whether to use my powers, call Jax, or do something else, when Kai pushes Garin away and stands in front of me. "Back off, Garin. You know as well as I do Scarlett had nothing to do with your sister's rejection. If you have a problem, take it up with the Council." He sticks a finger in Garin's chest and pokes hard. "But leave Scarlett alone."

Bart looks over at Jax, and back to Garin. "Let's go, dude. My parents will kill me if I get in trouble in the first week."

Garin glares at Kai and me. "This isn't over."

They walk away, and I turn to Kai. "Thanks for your help. Though I have to admit I'm surprised."

"Why's that?"

"You don't seem to like me much."

He presses his lips together for a moment, his hand on the pummel of his sword. "It's not that. Look, I'm sorry I was a jerk yesterday. I shouldn't have brought up your parents. Corinne reamed me hard for that one. I'm not a bad guy, honest. I just do an excellent impersonation of one from time to time."

"We'll see about that." I raise my sword. "On guard?"

He grins and raises his. "On guard."

...

We're standing, not in a classroom, but in the vast park near the arena.

"My name is Grandmaster Ella, or Gabriella, if you prefer to be more formal. I'm the head of the Teutonic Order, and I'll be teaching your Survival class this year. Today's lesson is going to test your tracking skills." The Grandmaster paces in front of us in her white Teutonic robes, her blond hair pulled back in a tight bun. She's younger than the other Grandmasters, but no less impressive.

"Since this quarter is focused on the Teutonic Order, I suggest you take this class very seriously." She points to the forest around us. "Somewhere out there, a pig has been released. Her name is Miss Piggy—"

Garin and his friends guffaw at that, and Grandmaster Ella glares at them.

"As I was saying, her name is Miss Piggy, and she's not to be hurt. Your mission is to track her, find her, and retrieve the special token inside the collar around her neck. You will be in teams of two. The first team to bring me the token will receive extra points in this class, which will increase your odds of being granted a Boon from me during your Trial. Trust me when I tell you, you'll want that Boon."

She calls out the names of the teams, pairing up everyone. When she calls my name, I step forward, and say a prayer to whatever gods may or may not exist that it's not Garin. Anyone but Garin.

"Miss Night, you and Prince Kai will work together."

Wytt looks over at us from his team with Lana and winks. I roll my eyes at him as Kai walks to me.

"Looks like fate has brought us together again," he says.

"You're starting to sound like Wytt."

"He does have a way with words. Too bad it's not appreciated more in our family," he says, the corners of his lips turning down.

Grandmaster Ella raises her hand. "Oh, and did I mention that I also released a goat and a wild boar into this forest? Just to keep things interesting. You have two hours. Good luck." She drops her hand and everyone scampers off into the forest to search for the pig. Kai and I look at each other.

"I hope you're better at tracking than you are at identifying body parts," he says.

"Likewise," I tell him.

He grins. "Fair enough. Actually, I am. We did a lot of hunting back in Sapientia."

"Good," I say. "Because I'm decent at it too, and I want that Boon. I'm sure not going to be getting one from your uncle or APD."

"True enough," he says. "Shall we get to it?"

We walk into the forest, looking for tracks against the light of the sun, which is hard given the cloud coverage and foliage. But it doesn't take long to find what we're looking for. We keep the tracks between us and the sun, so the light creates shadows in the print and makes it stand out from the surrounding soil. I point to one as we kneel in the dirt. "This isn't the pig. See how it's pointed here," I say, "That's the goat."

Kai nods. "I agree. Let's keep looking."

As we get deeper into the forest, Kai pulls out a flashlight to substitute for the missing rays of sun. We find another set of tracks, but based on the space between footprints we can tell it's the boar, not the pig.

"I'm impressed," Kai says as we keep walking. "I didn't expect this from the self-proclaimed computer geek."

"My parents did all kinds of training with me growing up." I grin. "Not anatomy and physiology, obviously."

"Obviously," he says.

"But we did this kind of thing all the time. I may know my way around a computer, but I'm still a Montana girl at heart."

He nudges me with his shoulder. "You're full of surprises."

I look up at him. "So are you, Prince Kai of the House of Ravens."

He rolls his eyes. "Please don't call me that."

"I can't imagine life as royalty," I say. "I know you think I grew up with all these connections, but I didn't know anything about my parents' involvement in this world until a few weeks ago. I grew up a normal girl with, mostly, normal parents."

His purple eyes soften as he looks at me. "I'm a real jerk, I know." He turns away as we climb over a fallen tree. "My father brings out the best in me, obviously."

"Obviously," I agree.

I look down just in time to catch the light of the sun as it lands on another track. "Kai, check it out. I think we found Miss Piggy."

He crouches next to me, our legs pressed together. "I think you're right."

We follow those tracks through the forest until we find the pig happily sunning in the one open spot in the forest. She's very pink, with coarse hair over her body that looks clean. We approach slowly, and she doesn't shy away, but instead walks toward us as if we might have a treat for her. I pull out a marshmallow I pocketed during breakfast and hold it out for her.

Kai smirks at me. "You keep marshmallows in your pocket?"

"Sometimes," I say. "What of it?"

He just shakes his head, but my marshmallow works. Miss Piggy comes over to us, her snout teasing out the air until she lands at my hand, eagerly munching up the white treat. Kai slips the collar off of her and pulls out a golden token with the Teutonic symbol on it. "Got it!"

Miss Piggy finishes her treat and trots away as we stand. "That wasn't so hard," I say.

"We make a good team," Kai acknowledges.

Something rustles in the bushes around us and Garin and Bart pop out. "That's our token, and you're going to give it to us," Garin growls.

Kai and I look at each other and smile. We both silently agree we are not giving in to this bully.

Bart puffs his chest. "What are you smiling at?"

"Just an inside joke," I say. "And I'm sorry to disappoint, boys, but we aren't giving up the token."

Kai looks at me. "Are we really sorry, though?"

I cock my head as if considering. "No, you're right. We're not really sorry. We got here first, that's the rule."

Kai turns his head to Garin. "You heard the lady. Move along. We have a token to deliver."

Garin raises his fist as if he's going to knock Kai out. Kai doesn't look worried. I prepare to use my strength on Bart, if needed, but he looks less than excited about fighting. "Dude, we shouldn't," Bart says. "You know Jax will kill you if you hurt her."

Garin throws his friend a disapproving look. "Shut up."

"It's true," Bart says. "Just let it go. There are other ways to earn a Boon."

Kai and I don't stick around to listen to them bicker, and instead cut through the forest to find Grandmaster Ella.

On the way, Kai looks over to me. "So, you and Jax?"

"What about me and Jax?"

He shrugs. "Never mind. None of my business."

...

During lunch, a group of people gathers around a circle of sand, watching as Jaden and a woman spar. I recognize the woman. She's wearing red and silver armor with an eye across her chest. She is the Seeker. Kira.

The Initiate lands a few punches.

"Drop your guard again and find yourself in the dirt," says Kira.

Jaden raises his defenses. He strikes again.

I nudge Akio with my elbow. "Why's she wearing all that armor?"

"She practice the same way she fight on battlefield," he says in his stilted accent.

Jaden strikes again, but lowers his guard. Kira grabs his arm in a hold and knocks him to the ground with her leg. "And you're dead, soldier." She addresses the crowd. "Someone care to show me something new?"

No one responds.

She snickers. "I thought not."

She acts as if Initiates are below her. It angers me. "You fought well," I say, "*if* you consider beating someone with no training fighting."

Murmurs spread through the crowd. A few Initiates sneer at me. They think I'm being arrogant. But I'm being smart. This is an opportunity to make friends.

Kira chuckles.

I study my nails, not giving her my full attention. "And..." I pause for dramatic effect. "You made three mistakes."

The Seeker raises an eyebrow and faces me. Her green eyes are piercing against her pale skin and black hair. Corinne was right, I realize. She is beautiful.

She holds out her hand. "Please, inform us, great Initiate, what were these mistakes?"

"You favored your left leg. Your kicks left you vulnerable."

Kira nods.

"Also, though you told Jaden to hold up his guard, you dropped your own twice."

Murmurs of agreement travel through the crowd. Jaden meets my eyes, nodding. Perhaps he will be an ally now.

"And finally," I say. "You turned your back to him. A soldier with his back turned to the enemy is a dead soldier."

I shrug. "Before you seek to criticize others, perhaps you should criticize yourself."

Someone in the crowd gasps.

"And do you criticize yourself, Initiate?" asks the Seeker.

"I do," I say. "Every day." The crowd grows silent.

"Then why don't you enter the ring?"

Everyone stares at me. I can't back down. I can't show weakness.

I lay my books on the ground, walk up the small hill and enter the ring. Akio wishes me good luck. Kira and I begin to circle each other. I throw a few jabs to assess her reaction. She backs away often, keeping herself out of reach, but she doesn't reposition properly. Her stance is off balance. If I could close the gap, I can hit her.

Kira strikes at my head, I block. She backs away. As expected.

Now is my chance. I dash forward.

And Kira's foot crashes into my skull.

I collapse on the sand, my head pounding, my vision fuzzy. People chuckle, others wince in mock pain. Kira grabs my head, shoving it down until I can taste sand on my tongue. She whispers in my ear. "I had five weaknesses, not three. I didn't hold my guard, so he could practice delivering a blow. I didn't reposition, so he could attempt to knock me down. I taught him a lesson. Now here's yours. You are weaker than I, Initiate. Don't act otherwise unless you're prepared."

"Leave her alone." It's Jax. He stands near the hill, though it's hard to see him through the blinding sun with my face shoved into the dirt.

Kira pushes off my head and stands up, facing him. "Her lesson is over. Would you like a turn in the ring?"

"I defeated you in the tournament two days ago. You're not ready."

"With swords. You can't match me in hand-to-hand."

"Perhaps one day we'll see. But not today."

I manage to crawl to my knees, cradling my head. It feels primed to explode.

Kira smiles at me. "You know, Jax, when you kept talking about this girl from back home, I imagined more. Shame. I don't believe she'll make it through the first Trial." She walks over to Jax and runs a finger down his shirt. My skin burns at the sight.

"Why don't you forget her now," says Kira. "Make it easier on yourself, and perhaps, give someone else a chance."

Jax grabs her finger and twists it. Kira gasps.

"Don't insult her," says Jax.

Kira escapes the hold and jumps back, face clenched in pain. "I feel sorry for you," she says. "Because one day you'll see that you and Scarlett cannot be together." She softens her voice. "I hope that day doesn't come too late."

As Kira walks away, Jax walks toward me and helps me stand. "Let me escort you to your class."

I nod, wrapping my arm around his as we shuffle down the hill. I reach for my books, but Jax picks them up first.

"Thanks," I say.

He nods and leads me through a short tunnel under a bridge that connects two buildings. I notice Kira talking with Ragathon. "What's with her?" I ask, still spitting sand out of my mouth.

"She's trained here a long time, much longer than others. She can be critical of them. But she's a great Knight, and a great teacher. She pushes people, and she does what's needed."

I'm not sure I agree, but I don't argue. Jax has known her longer. I wonder if there's something more between them. You don't touch a man like that unless you feel entitled in some way. I clench my fists, my nails digging into my skin at the thought that she might know him in a way I do not.

...

We arrive at my next class, Strategy and Tactics, and Jax says goodbye. I'm barely on time. I enter a small room with ten desks, each with an arranged chessboard on top. I find the seat opposite Corrine, who's playing with a knight piece. Varian stands at the head of the classroom, an eScreen behind him. He taps his eGlass, and an image of brackets appears on the screen.

"Are we having a tournament?" asks Wytt.

"Indeed. You will participate in a chess tournament, and I will evaluate your tactics."

Garin picks up a pawn, studying it. "What does this have to do with tactics?"

Varian glances around the room. "Anyone care to answer that question?"

I raise my hand.

He nods.

"Chess involves many aspects of tactics, including positioning, studying your opponent, and thinking ahead."

"Thank you, Miss Night." Varian waves at the screen. "As you can see, you've already been paired up. Begin."

I check my first opponent. Garin. I find him across the room and take a seat. "Let's get this over with," he says, sighing. I beat him in four turns. I don't think he understands the game.

Next is Bartholomew, one of Garin's rich lackeys. He flicks his blond hair as he makes the first move. "I apologize in advance for my victory." I beat him in seven moves. I think I traumatize him.

Corrine replaces Bart. She plays well, but her moves are too obvious. I win in fifteen turns and feel almost bad about it.

"Wow, you're amazing," she says, smiling. "Will you teach me to play better?"

"Sure," I say as she walks away.

We're left with an odd number of players. Varian pairs me with the extra. It means I need to play more games, but I don't care. I face Akio, the oldest amongst us. He's a strategic player with a calm head and a keen eye for placement. He uses his life experience to his advantage, and I admire him for that. He manages to capture my knights, but I checkmate him with my Queen. He does a slight bow as he leaves the table. "Thank you for the game, Scarlett friend," he says.

My final opponent is Lana. I'm surprised. She never struck me as the strategic type. Everyone watches the game, Wytt whispering encouragement over my shoulder and biting his nails. Lana plays well, thinking many moves ahead. But I think further. She manages to take my Queen, but it's a trap, and I checkmate her with my rook and knight. Lana grins and shakes my hand. "I haven't lost in a long time." She speaks in a cultured voice with only a trace of a Spanish accent.

"You're good," I say. "We should play again sometime."

"I'd like that." She smiles at me as she stands. "There's more to me than pretty dresses and boys."

I nod my head with new respect. "We all have layers," I say. "No one is ever really what they seem."

"I think I'm going to like you," she says, walking away.

Varian takes her place, sinking into the chair across from me. "Congratulations, champion."

It wasn't much of a challenge, but I know my fellow classmates did their best, so I just say thank you.

He picks up my Queen, turning her in his hands. "Tell me, what did you learn?"

"Nothing."

"Then you failed."

I raise an eyebrow at him. "But I won every game."

"Even your weakest opponent can teach you something."

I gesture at the board. "Maybe you can teach me."

Varian grins and puts down the Queen. I'm excited to play, to study my opponent, but instead, he stands up and walks away. "I already have," he says.

. . .

"This class is Order, and I will be your instructor," says Kira, standing at the head of the room before a giant white board. All the Initiates sit in a semi-circle or rising chairs and desks. It reminds me of a theatre.

Kira continues. "Today you will perform impromptu persuasive speeches. After I give each of you your topic, you will have two minutes to prepare." She begins to call up Initiates one by one. The topics are difficult and, to my surprise, oppose Four Order philosophies. Lana is asked to argue for the abolishment of royalty. Garin is asked to defend the terrorist group, the Red Eagles. Everyone does well. Finally, only Corrine, Wytt and I are left.

Kira calls upon Wytt first and announces his topic. "Why should Nyx have won the war?"

Wytt grins and looks a few things up on his eGlass. With a minute of prep time left, he declares he is ready.

Wytt's speech is eloquent and brilliant. He paints Nyx as a war hero, a man to be idolized and revered, and by the end, I feel as if I'd follow Nyx into any battle, no matter the cause. As Wytt performs his closing line and bows, half the class applauds. Corrine and I give a standing ovation.

Next is Corrine, who is tasked with defending the usefulness of the UFI. She does a better job than I would, citing their stellar management of transportation and construction. They are not the Four Orders. They are not powerful. But they handle the little things, and the little things can be very important. Of course, what Corrine doesn't mention is that the Four Orders could probably do better.

As Corrine wraps up, Wytt and I clap. She takes her seat, and Kira calls out, "Next."

I stand, realizing I'm the last person.

Kira smirks. "Ah, our newest Zenith. Your topic…" She rubs her chin and then smiles. "Why must Zeniths be regulated?" The first topic to coincide with Order values.

She wants to anger me, but I don't let her. I stay calm as I consider my speech. I'm outlining my conclusion when she says it's time. I walk up to the podium and address the class.

"Zeniths can be dangerous. They are born with great abilities but no training. In order to keep everyone safe, Zeniths have different rules and different laws. Unfortunately, most of these laws are focused not on safety, but on power and segregation. The government says that Zeniths are less than human. That they should be feared and need to be controlled. This is not true. And it is this mentality that breeds hate and discrimination."

I pause a moment, considering my next words. "However, if all Zeniths can be taught control over their abilities, and humans taught that Zeniths can be trusted, then the mistreatment could end. It could—"

"Scarlett." Kira raises her hand. "You're drifting off topic."

"Sorry." I focus less on Zenith mistreatment and more on how a safer world can be accomplished. "Right now, Zeniths face two choices. Live a life of limited rights, or join the Orders. For many, none of these paths are ideal. If Zeniths, at a young age, could be allowed and encouraged to master their powers, more of them could pursue a variety of careers. Some could become performers or builders. Others could manage banks. With the proper training, Zeniths would be as safe as humans. They should be treated as humans."

"Scarlett," says Kira, interrupting again. "Focus more on why Zeniths should be regulated, not how the regulations should be different."

I try to refocus. This isn't going well. "As I.... um…"
My hands are starting to sweat, and I wipe them on my
robes. "As I said, without training, Zeniths can be dangerous, but so can humans. We must all be taught what
is right and wrong. There is no reason why Zeniths and
humans must have different laws."

"Scarlett," says Kira. "What's your topic?"

"Why Zeniths must be regulated?"

"So let's get back to that. Why must Zeniths be regulated more than humans?"

I frown, facing her instead of the Initiates. "They
don't have to be. Zeniths can be regulated just as much as
humans."

She makes a clicking noise with her tongue. "Not quite
your topic."

"Why not? The topic was why Zeniths have to be regulated. I'm arguing that Zeniths and humans must both be
regulated equally—"

"Argue why they shouldn't be equal."

I shake my head. "I won't do that."

"I'm your teacher. I'm telling you to do it."

"I won't."

Kira yells, pointing at me. "How can you hope to convince someone else to see your point of view if you can't see
theirs?"

I yell back. "I do see their point of view."

"Then argue for it. Convince me."

I slam my fist on the podium. "No. I don't know if my
answer is right. But I know unequal regulation is wrong."

Whispers spread through the classroom. Garin and
Bart chuckle.

Kira snaps at them. "Do not mock her. Learn from her. Scarlett demonstrates something you have all failed to show."

I stifle a gasp, startled that Kira would defend me. Garin and Bart bow their heads and mumble apologies.

Kira turns to me and nods, and I feel like perhaps I was doing well all along. Perhaps she was challenging me to think of my topic in new ways.

The Seeker begins to pace around the classroom, studying everyone's face. "You have all spoken on behalf of an idea today. How many of you truly believed your own argument?"

I'm the only one who raises my hand. Some drop their eyes as Kira passes. After she has walked around the classroom, she stops before the board and gestures at me. "Scarlett did not compromise her ideals. She did not give voice to what she thinks is lies. If you ever become Knights, I hope you are not as easily swayed as you were today."

Jaden raises his hand, and Kira motions for him to speak. "But don't we have to listen to our superiors?" he asks.

"Why?"

"Because…. Um…because we have to…"

"Did you have to come here, Jaden?"

He grins with charm. "A Prince has responsibilities."

"And you have to fulfill them?"

"Of course."

"Why?"

"Because…Okay, okay." He nods, understandingly. "I suppose I didn't have to come here."

Kira smiles. "Do not blindly follow orders. Ask why and ponder." She glances at me. "Ask why and ponder." And she begins to pace again, but this time, there is real passion behind her voice.

"There have been many leaders who could weave words to convince others. I will not mention them all, for you know what they have done. Saved their countries. Liberated slaves. Killed thousands because they were different. They did not succeed because they were strong. They succeeded because they could inspire and because they could not be dissuaded. So learn to master language and debate, and do not fall prey to its silver tongue."

She begins to type into the keypad on her wrist, and the word *Ethics* appears on the board. She points at it. "But then, of course, who do we follow? Who is right? Who is wrong?" She pauses, letting the question sink in. Everyone is focused on her.

"And so, we arrive at our first lesson. Everyone is the hero of their own story. Everyone believes their way is right."

She writes on the board as we take notes, and I begin to understand why Kira is indeed a great teacher.

THE WHIPPING

I've been trying all day not to think of Jax or what he's about to endure tonight. He swore me to secrecy, so I can't even tell my friends. No one's supposed to know who's being whipped until it happens. I think this place likes to keep secrets just for the sake of keeping them half the time.

As we leave Order and walk to dinner, I look for something to distract my increasingly anxious thoughts. We pass the courtyard to the dining hall, and I see Kira training with her sword, doing katas I recognize from Jax.

"What do you know about her?" I ask, looking at Kira. She's an enigma to me. I thought she hated me, but then she wasn't so bad, but she clearly has a thing for Jax, and maybe he had—or has—a thing for her.

If I had an appetite, that last thought would have killed it.

"She's an orphan," Wytt says. "She was raised here and is crazy focused on her training."

"It's all she really has," Corinne says. "It's kind of sad."

That makes it harder to resent her, which is probably a good thing. I have enough enemies at the moment.

We go through the line to get our food, and I sit with them, picking at another uneaten salad as I sip my Life Force. I have to do a better job at eating human food or my friends will start to worry.

My mind is wandering when Wytt nudges me. "You look distant. What's going on in that beautiful head of yours?"

Kai is also looking at me from across the table, a small frown on his face.

"I'm...just thinking about stuff. I'm not feeling well. Tired, I think." I stand and pick up my tray. "I think I'm going to get some rest before tonight. I'll meet you all later."

"Do you want me to come with you?" Corinne asks.

"Nope, I'm good. I'll see you soon."

I head to my room as quickly as I can and collapse on my bed. Nox jumps onto my chest and curls into a warm purring ball of fur. I close my eyes, squeezing out a renegade tear. I don't want to see Jax whipped tonight. But I don't want him to go through that punishment without my support, either.

This makes me sick, that we do this to each other, that these kinds of punishments even exist.

There's a knock at my door and I groan. "Scarlett's not here right now."

The door opens and my grandfather comes in, closing it behind him. "Then she won't mind if an old man rests in her room for a moment."

I sit up and move the reluctant cat to my lap, while my grandfather sits in the chair at my desk.

"No, she won't," I say.

"Jax said he told you about tonight," he says. Nox jumps off my lap and onto my grandfather's, who pets him.

"Yeah."

"Are you alright?"

"No. It's not right, what they're doing to him."

He nods. "You're right, it's not. But it will help Jax."

"How so?"

"Right now he's the Knight who got away with murder. Tonight he will be the Knight who faced the consequences of his choices with bravery. It will help him in his career, and he will be fine. He's more worried about you than himself."

I sigh and flop back on my bed. "Sometimes I wonder if I'm meant for this world."

"I think we all feel that way from time to time." He stands. "Shall we go? I think he'd like you to be there for him."

I stand. "I suppose I should."

Nox rubs himself against my grandfather's leg. "He's a good cat, but this might not be the best place for him, cooped up in a dorm room all day."

"You're probably right," I say, leaning over to pet his head before we leave. "Perhaps he's not meant for this world either."

...

When I arrive at the courtyard, it's already teeming with excitement. It makes me sick that people take such perverse joy from seeing others hurt. My grandfather nods to me and leaves to stand at the front, where a whipping post has been erected.

Large eScreens have been placed to hover over us, broadcasting everything live as a team of Order reporters cover the story.

The council members are standing in a semi-circle behind the post as Jax is escorted out by an Inquisition Guard. He's got a robe on, which he drops to the floor. He's wearing only a pair of jeans, and his muscles flex as the guard ties his arms to the post. His eyes search the crowd, and when he finds me, I hold his gaze, willing myself not to avert my eyes no matter what happens.

He gives me a small smile, and I try to smile back. *I'm here, Jax. Whatever else is happening between us, I'm here.*

I feel a hand on my arm, and Corinne and Wytt flank me. "You knew?" Corinne asks.

I nod without breaking eye contact with Jax.

She slips a hand into mine, and Wytt takes my other hand. Their support means so much. I'm not alone in this. Jax isn't alone in this.

There's so much noise—from the people, from the televisions, from the reporters. I want to scream at everyone to shut up. Instead, I tune them out and just connect with my best friend.

Ragathon steps up with a whip in hand. I hate him. So much. He's enjoying this, and that makes my blood boil. I want to unleash my wings and fly up to him and...I squeeze Wytt and Corinne's hands and take a deep breath. I promised Jax I wouldn't do anything stupid. And I won't.

When the first lash lands on his back, splitting open skin, tearing through tissue, I sway from sudden dizziness. Jax doesn't scream. He doesn't cry. He just keeps looking at me. And so I don't cry or scream either. If he can be strong, then so can I.

Another lash of the whip. More blood. More pain.

The cameras zoom in on his back, and I feel vomit rise in my throat.

On one of the screens the image breaks into two as they continue the live coverage while showing Jax killing the Officers. I'm there, behind him. When that scene finishes, the eScreen reverts to the live feed of Jax being whipped. Next to him is an image of my face as I watch him receive his punishment. I'm huge on the screen, my blue silver eyes shining with the tears I refuse to release. My jaw locked in pain. They're saying something about me being the girl he saved. The girl he's being whipped for.

Ragathon seems to be getting angrier and angrier as he whips Jax, his punishment more cruel with each lash. I think he wants Jax to give in, to cry, to scream, to acknowledge the pain, but he doesn't.

It's becoming too much. I have to stop it. I break eye contact to look at my grandfather, but it isn't the Chancellor who steps in, it's Master Varian who rips the whip from his brother's hand. Ragathon looks ready to murder him, but Varian announces that Jax has accepted his punishment with the bravery of a true Knight.

I hear respect in his words. Admiration.

I can finally breathe again as they untie Jax. With his first step, he stumbles, his back in shreds. Grandmaster Marian offers to help him walk, but he shakes his head and takes another step, his legs shaking, then bows to the council. Varian nods his head at Jax, and Jax walks behind the Council and toward the Infirmary with Marian at his side.

Once he disappears from view, Corinne turns to me, her face streaming with tears. "Are you okay?"

I stare into the space where Jax was. "I'm not the one who was just whipped."

As we stand there, the crowd is parted by a swarm of reporters shoving microphones into my face. "Miss Night, can you tell us how it feels to watch Sir Jax whipped for standing up for you that night?" "Miss Night, what really happened that night? Can you tell us the details?"

More questions, more pushing and shoving. I'm about to lose it when Kai steps forward and grabs my hand and whispers into my ear, "I'll handle the press, get out of here."

So I do.

. . .

I walk around the Castle to avoid reporters and those morosely fascinated with the whipping. It takes me longer than it should to get to the Infirmary.

By the time I reach it, I've come to a decision. I'm going to tell Jax everything. Well, not everything. I can't tell him about Nightfall. But I'm going to tell him how I feel. He stood up there and took the worst beating of his life for me. He killed several men to defend me from an unknown fate at the hands of the Inquisition. He's the boy from my childhood I've always loved. It's time I told him the truth of my heart.

Master Varian is leaving the Infirmary as I enter. He nods his head to me. "Miss Night."

I walk past him and straight to Jax, who's already bandaged up and standing, ready to leave. He smiles when he sees me. "I'm glad you're here," he says, and my heart pounds harder.

He puts a robe over his shoulders, wincing only slightly, and Grandmaster Marian frowns. "Keep the bandages clean, and come by if it gets worse. But you should heal quickly with the medicine I gave you."

"I'm fine, Marian."

She huffs, and he chuckles as he puts an arm over my shoulder.

"Let's take a walk," he says.

"Are you sure?"

He nods. "I'm fine, honestly. It looks worse than it is."

I don't believe that, but if he's up for walking, I'll walk with him. We leave the Castle grounds and head toward the shoreline, and the sky opens up once again, showering us with rain.

"Do you want to go back in?" I ask.

"No, I like the rain. It's cleansing. Healing." He stops and pulls me to face him. "I need to tell you something."

I look up at his handsome face, a face I've had memorized since my earliest memories. "Me first," I say, before I lose my nerve. Around us, the sun sets, casting waves of rainbow light over the river as rain droplets disperse the color into fractals. It's all so beautiful, but nothing as beautiful as the man in front of me.

"Jax, I'm tired of this distance between us. I know you've had a different life than I thought, and I understand why you couldn't tell me, but I can't keep this up."

"Scarlett, I—"

"Wait, just let me finish, okay?"

He nods.

"Jax, you've been like a brother to me, but you're not my brother. You're my best friend, but you're so much more." My stomach flops around as I find the courage to say the next few words. Words that could change everything. "Jax, I'm in love with you. I have been for a very long time. I've just never been brave enough to tell you until now. But seeing you up there, whipped to protect me, it broke my heart. And I can't keep this from you anymore. I love you."

I pause, waiting, assessing his eyes, his body language, my heart hammering in my chest. My mouth goes dry, and I'm about to freak out when he lifts his hands to my face and strokes my cheek with his finger. He feels so warm, so strong.

"Oh, Scarlett," he says, and then he leans in and presses his lips against mine. They are hot, soft, then firm, familiar and new all at once. I kiss him back, moving closer so our bodies connect as his hands cup my face and mine land on his chest. His kiss deepens and unlocks more emotion than I thought I could contain.

When it ends, I feel filled and emptied all at once. I look up at him again, wondering what this means. That was not a friendly kiss. It means something, surely.

"Scarlett, I love you too. I always have—" my heart soars until his next words, "—but, things are complicated."

"Complicated? Things are always going to be complicated in our world. We can work with complicated," I assure him. Myself. Us.

"Scarlett, I'm leaving. That's what I came here to tell you. I'm leaving, and I don't know when I'll be back. I just found out tonight."

"Leaving?" I feel like something is stuck in my throat. "Where are you going?"

He looks away. "I can't tell you."

My hands drop from his chest and I step back. "Can't or won't?"

"I'm not the guy for you," he says, "even if I want to be." He steps closer and caresses my face again. "More than anything, I want to be."

RAISING A CAT

I throw a rock into the water too hard to make it skip. Right now I just want it to splash. I want to throw hard and let out all my frustration on the rock and the lake. Jax offered to walk me back to my room, but I told him I needed time alone to think.

But thinking is really not helping. Neither is being alone. But I don't want to be around anyone either. What I really need to do is beat something up. Zorin comes to mind, and I give my reflection in the water a rueful smile. That might work. Besides, I have a present for him.

I walk back to my room, still angry and sad and confused. Where is Jax going? Why more secrets? This is obviously Order business, but what? Will he be in danger? Will I ever see him again? I can't function with all these thoughts shoving paths through my mind. And that kiss. Why'd he kiss me if he was just saying goodbye? I should have hit him instead of kiss him. That would have possibly been more productive.

Corinne is sitting cross-legged on her bed sketching in a notebook when I come in. She looks up and gives me a half smile. "Hey. You okay? I saw you walking with Jax."

She sets her sketches to the side, and I see Nox is her subject. She captured his wide-eyed, bedraggled look perfectly. "I'm okay. Just. Men. You know? They are infinitely frustrating sometimes. I don't understand."

I drop onto my bed and pull Nox, who's already purring and nudging his head against my hand, onto my lap.

"They can be perplexing at times," she agrees.

"Have you ever been serious with anyone before?" I ask.

She shakes her head. "Being the crown Princess, I have to be careful with whom I get serious. It's not just my happiness on the line, but the fate of my country."

"Right. That must be hard."

She shrugs. "I guess. But I also haven't found anyone I really love, either. Let's just hope the person I end up falling in love with is also good for Sapientia."

"What will you do if they're not?"

She stares past me, her purple eyes lost in thought. "I don't know, to be honest." Then her eyes snap back to me and she leans forward. "Did something happen with Jax?"

I hesitate. I'm not used to having a friend other than Jax. It's...strange. But I kind of like it. "Um..."

She scoots forward, her eyes widening. "It *did*. What happened?"

"We sort of kissed. Kind of."

"Kind of?"

"Not kind of. We kissed. And then he told me he's leaving and not the guy for me."

She frowns. "You're right. Men are irritating."

160

"Yeah." I lift Nox up. "I need to head into the city for a few hours. We can't keep a cat here, so I'm going to give Nox to some friends."

She reaches over to rub the cat's head. "I'm going to miss him. Want some company?" she asks.

"Nah, but thank you. I need some time alone to...process."

"I understand." She picks up her sketchbook and resumes her sketching, but then looks up, a lock of now-green hair falling into her eyes. "Oh, Jax left you another note. It's on your desk."

I nudge Nox off of me and pick up the paper airplane sitting on my books. I open it and read.

No matter where I am, I'm always thinking of you.
~Friends to the end

I exhale loudly in frustration and toss the note into the trash next to my desk. I reach for my backpack, empty it and create a little bed for Nox with one of my old shirts. He doesn't make a sound as I put him in the bag and zip it half way.

I change out of my robes, throw a jacket on and grab the backpack. I'm walking out of the room when I glance down at the crumbled airplane at the bottom of the trash. I sigh, then lean down to pick it up and put it on my desk.

Men are so frustrating.

...

I love New York City at night—when no one's being executed and my hand's not being cut off, that is. Multi-colored glowing orbs dot the sidewalks casting shadows of light along the path as I walk. Genetically modified trees stretch over me with iridescent flowers that occasionally twinkle in the night as well. It's no surprise that so many couples enjoy walking hand in hand along the city streets when the sun goes down.

It's also why I decided to take the subway into the city instead of flying straight to the Cathedral from the Castle. I need this time to pause, reflect, breathe.

I pull Nox out of my backpack and hold him, stroking his soft black fur as I walk. He nuzzles into my arms, content to be treated like the royalty he surely imagines himself to be. I'll miss seeing him in my dorm room, but I know he'll have a lot more freedom at the Cathedral. And Zorin needs a pet, even if he doesn't know it yet.

My emotions are starting to settle after the whipping and kiss, and I'm wondering if things would indeed be different if Jax weren't leaving. Would we really work together? As much as my heart aches for him, my mind tells me it's a mistake. How could I be with him and still be Nightfall?

He is against Nightfall and everything I'm doing as her. What kind of life together could we really have?

I hate this. I hate that he's partly right.

It's not so much that he's not the right guy for me. It's that I'm not the right girl for him.

Or, rather, Nightfall isn't.

...

It's getting late, and I still have school, so I cut my walk shorter than I'd like. I find a private place to unleash my wings and head to the Cathedral in search of Zorin. He's sitting by the fireplace in his room, playing chess against himself. He looks up and smiles as I come in. "I thought you had homework?"

"I do. I can only stay for a few hours. But I brought you something."

I pull Nox out of my bag.

Zorin raises an eyebrow. "A cat?"

I pass him the restless feline. "His name is Nox. He needs a good home, and my dorm room is too small."

"We're raising a cat together now?"

I smile. "Yes. So don't eat him."

Zorin chuckles. "I make no promises." The cat purrs and rubs against Zorin's hand demanding to be petted. The Nephilim obliges, running long fingers over the cat's fur. I can tell they will be great friends.

Carter knocks on the door and peeks in. "May I have a moment of your time, miss?"

"Of course."

He walks in and offers me a Life Force. He also passes me a small golden box. I flick it open, revealing a key and paper. "Your apartment is set up," he says. "The address is in the box. All has been arranged."

"Is it safe to take my friends there? They want to see it."

"I think you'll find that the accommodations meet your approval."

Zorin hands Nox to Carter. "Can you get the cat set up somewhere?"

"As you wish." He walks downstairs, petting Nox as he leaves, and I sit across from Zorin and stare into the fire.

"Want to play a game?" he asks.

"No."

"Want to practice the Way of Nyx?"

"No."

He leans back in his chair, sipping from a golden goblet. "You're quieter than usual. I saw the news of the whipping. Do you want to talk about it?"

"No. Yes. I don't know." I look at him. "Why are men so complicated? Why do they have to make everything so hard?"

Zorin chuckles. "And women are so easy?"

"Jax kissed me tonight. Then told me he's leaving. Every time I think we might have a chance to make it work, something gets in the way. I don't get it."

"Some people are not meant to be together, no matter how hard they try. I once..." He stares into the fire. "I once knew a man who loved a woman. He was a Nephilim, and she was sick. She didn't look sick, but she was and, on their wedding day, she died."

"What happened?" I ask.

"Back then we had no explanation. Now, we'd call it a brain aneurysm or a stroke." He looks troubled. "The man turned his wife to save her, and they lived together for a while, but it did not last. She died too young. Even immortality couldn't save her."

"How'd she die?"

Zorin gazes at the fire, his face filling with rage. "They burned her. The Inquisition deemed her guilty of witchcraft, and there was no defense. She did not cry at the end. She did not beg. She looked happy. She told the man to live on. But how could he?" Zorin drops his head, tears welling in his eyes. "How could he?"

I touch his shoulder. "What was her name?"

He glances up, eyes red. "Who?"

"Your wife?"

"Danika," he whispers. "Her name was Danika Star."

THE FAIRY REALM

"Evie," I mumble, reaching for my eGlass. I slip it over my ear, my head still buried under the blanket, eyes closed. "Evie?"

"Good morning, Scarlett."

"Morning. What time is it?" I can hear Corinne in the bathroom humming a song. She's so chipper in the morning. It would be annoying if she wasn't so sweet.

"It's 4:30 a.m. You should get up if you don't want to be late for PT." Evie also sounds chipper.

"Evie, it's too early for you to sound so happy. Tone it down."

"As you wish, Scarlett."

Yeah, that's not much better. I groan and sit up, stretching my tired body.

Corinne comes out of the bathroom, showered and ready for class. "Morning, sleepy head," she says.

"Good morning. You have a lovely voice."

Her smile is sad. "Thanks. It's a song my mother used to sing us when we were little." Corinne sits on her bed and faces me as she puts on her sneakers. "It's one of the only memories I have of her."

"What happened?"

"She died when I was really young. From illness."

"I'm so sorry."

I wonder what's worse, having a lifetime of memories to miss, or not knowing your mother at all. I wouldn't trade the time I had with my parents for anything, but it hurts that they are gone when they were so much a part of my daily life.

Something stirs my memory, and I click through my eGlass calendar. This Friday...it's their anniversary. They always made that day special, and when I was older they included me in their celebrations. We'd get a boat and spend the day at the lake, then at night they would light a Chinese lantern and send it off into the water. They said it was to commemorate another year of spending their lives with their soul mate.

I slip on my workout gear and head to the bathroom to brush my teeth and get ready. My mouth is full of toothpaste when Evie relays messages from the Dark Templars. "Trix says another rebel group has agreed to meet with you on Saturday."

I rinse my mouth out and ask, "Which one?"

"The Gravekeepers," she says.

"Which one are they?"

"They are committed to avenging those who died during the War."

"Tell Trix I got her message and will be there."

Corinne is waiting for me when I come out of the bathroom, and we head to PT together. "How are you feeling?"

she asks. "I didn't hear you come in last night. It must have been late."

"I think I got an hour of sleep," I confess.

"You're going to be hurting today."

She's not wrong.

In fact, I spend the rest of the day hurting and falling asleep during classes. By the time Friday arrives, I'm more than ready for the weekend, and some sleep.

...

Teutonic Knights. They were formed at the end of the 12th century in Acre. They moved to Transylvania in 1211. They were expelled by.... someone. Hard to remember when I keep dosing off.

Evie is recording the whole lecture. I'll listen to it later in bed, in comfy pajamas. I nudge Corrine, yawning. "Why don't they just give us a textbook?" We've practiced nothing.

She keeps her eyes on the Grandmaster. "You can't ask a textbook questions." She raises her hand and is called on. "Grandmaster Gabriella, what's the German motto of the order?"

Gabriella smiles, looking pleased to finally receive a question. "Helfen. Wehren. Heilen. Help. Defend. Heal."

"Thank you, Grandmaster," says Corrine. As the lecture is resumed, she whispers to me. "Who are you going as for the Halloween Ball?"

It's a long time from Halloween, but this seems important to Corrine, so I try to come up with something. "Someone important. Someone who made a difference."

She raises an eyebrow. "Anything more specific?"

"Not yet, but I'm open to ideas."

She beams, clearly excited to be a part of my decisions. "I'll message you some later. If you decide soon, we can coordinate our styles."

"Sounds fun." But not as fun as sleeping for two days. Nothing sounds as fun as sleeping for two days.

"Corrine, Scarlett," says the Grandmaster, frowning. "Would you like to share your discussion with us?"

Oh no. I sit up straight, trying to look as awake as possible. All eyes turn to us, and Corrine turns red. I started this conversation, and I don't want my friend to get in trouble, so I speak up. "We were just saying how we'd like to go as famous Teutonic Knights for Halloween. We'd feel so honored."

Gabriella's frown fades. "Very well, but don't speak out of turn again."

I give her my most serious and noble of faces. "Of course, Grandmaster."

We stay focused for the rest of the class, but Corrine does spare a moment to tap something out on her eGlass. I receive the message.

Thank you, Scarlett

When history is over and Gabriella has left the room, Initiates erupt in cheers. "First week is over, ladies," says Wytt, throwing his arms around us. "We need to celebrate."

"What do you have in mind?" I ask, though this goes against my sleep plans.

"Let's head into the city."

Corrine does her 'why not' look while Wytt gives me puppy eyes.

"Let's do it," I say, feeling more energized because of my friends.

Wytt waves across the room at his brother. "Kai, why don't you join us?"

The Prince of Ravens surprises me with a grin. "I suppose someone has to keep you lot out of trouble."

. . .

The irony is not lost on me that I'm the one with mythological-inspired vampiric powers, but my friends are the ones who need no sleep and can go all night.

I would have slept from the end of History class until my meeting with the other rebel leaders tomorrow, but instead I spend the day shopping. Now I'm eating falafels at a Greek cafe in the city with Wytt, Corinne and Kai. Well, I'm mostly picking at it and pretending to eat. I miss liking food.

Wytt is telling another story, something about ancient Greece and the theatre and Dionysus, and Corinne is listening as she dips a carrot into the hummus. I eye the hummus. My brain says I should still like it, but my body disagrees vehemently.

Kai pulls a small paper bag out of his backpack and hands it to me.

"What's this?" I ask.

"Your dinner."

Curious, I open it, and find a bag of marshmallows, a chocolate bar and Life Force. I look up in surprise. "How... how did you know these things are my favorite?"

He rolls his eyes. "It's not that hard to figure out if you pay attention."

"So, you've been paying attention to my eating habits?" I ask, stuffing a marshmallow into my mouth.

"Someone has to. Should I be worried?"

I chew and swallow. "About what?"

"About you. You don't eat much, but you're training pretty hard. I know what grief can do to a person. Starving yourself isn't going to help."

I would laugh, but he's so serious and so sincere that I can't. "It's true my appetite has been…finicky, since my parents died. I think with my para-powers opening up and all the changes, it's affected me. But I assure you I'm healthier physically than I've ever been. The true threat to my health isn't lack of food, but lack of sleep. A girl needs her beauty rest." I say this last part in jest, but he cocks his head and stares at me, a serious expression on his face.

"You're beautiful enough without it."

I've just stuck a piece of chocolate in my mouth, and I almost spit it out in surprise. I'm spared from a response when Wytt stands, claps his hands and declares, "It's time to drink and be merry, since we've already done the eating part. For tomorrow we might die. And as everyone knows, it's best to die with a stomach full of ale, bread and happiness."

His words send a shiver through my spine, but I shrug it off. It's just an expression, not an omen. I hope.

Corinne stands and grabs her sketchbook. "And why are we dying tomorrow?"

Wytt shrugs. "Because it gives us an excuse to eat, drink and be merry?"

I laugh and stand, grabbing my backpack, which is now stuffed with new clothes I don't really need but Corinne insisted would look 'super fabulous' on me. In her defense, she's right. They do. Especially the silver cardigan I'm wearing now with the ultraviolet blue thread that glimmers and glows under certain light. It's made from a hybrid material that makes it soft but durable, and it conforms to my body almost like it's living. Another Eden Fashionable, a brand I've never owned until today.

Wytt seems to know where he's going so we all follow him. I'm pretty sure he has his eGlass set to find all the bars everywhere all the time. Must be a poet thing. Which I find odd, because in my limited drinking experience, drinking does not improve most people's ability to use words.

We walk a long time, passing many pubs, bars and clubs on the way. Corinne has given up on trying to draw and walk at the same time, after bumping into a few Fairy Fruit Trees and getting the sticky glowing fruit all over her sketchpad. That stuff never comes off.

Kai is quiet as we walk, and I can almost pretend he didn't just call me beautiful. I'm not sure how I feel about it. Sure, Wytt says it to me all the time, and while I'm sure he does think I'm pretty, it has a very different feel than the way Kai said it.

I'm not the kind of girl to blush and giggle and get falsely modest. I know I'm attractive. But there's a difference between someone finding me attractive and someone being attracted to me. And that's what's got me freaked out a bit. Because my heart is still reeling from Jax and the kiss and him leaving. I'm not sure what do with this.

Maybe I'm just making it all up in my head. Maybe he just meant I'm pretty and that's it. I need to stop making myself crazy over stupid things.

We finally get to where Wytt wants to go, and I'm not impressed. Neither is anyone else from the looks on their faces. We are in a sketchy neighborhood, to start. Like, abandoned buildings and cars covered in graffiti. I clutch my backpack tighter and wonder if I need to be in Nightfall mode.

The door to the club is unmarked, unless you count gang signs scrawled on it in spray paint.

"Um, Wytt..." Corinne looks around like we're about to be attacked by thugs. Which, honestly, we might.

"Fear not, fellow travelers. I know what I'm doing."

He knocks on the door, and a peephole opens. A voice on the other side of the door says, "A Knight in red must surrender—"

"To a Fairy by another name," Wytt says.

I raise a questioning eyebrow at Kai, who shrugs as the door opens and we enter another world.

Wytt raises his arms and grins. "Welcome to The Fairy Realm. The most exclusive, secret club in New York City. So exclusive, in fact, there is no VIP. The club *is* the VIP."

We all stand in stunned silence as we look around. It really is like stepping into a Fairy realm. It's dark, but everything is aglow in light. Giant mushrooms grow from the ground and glow purples, pinks and greens. Fairy Fruit Trees are also growing everywhere, the fruit and leaves brightly shining. There's dancing in the center and a long bar to the right with drinks I've never seen before. We walk over, and Wytt orders for everyone. "Give us the sampler platter," he says.

"What's the sampler platter?" I ask.

He winks at me and throws an arm over my shoulder. "You'll soon see."

We find a table that's been roped off from the rest, and Wytt pulls aside the rope and pulls a chair out for me and Corinne. "Ladies."

"Isn't this reserved for someone?" she asks.

"Yes," he says. "For us."

When our platter arrives, it's quite impressive. All of the drinks glow in different colors and have living edible fruit flowers growing out of them.

I take a purple and pink concoction and use my tongue to tease out the flavors before I commit. The flowers taste like candy, and I drink it up greedily. "This is the most amazing thing ever," I say, already feeling a small buzz.

A live band performs on a stage covered in living vines and more trees and mushrooms, their music pulsing, hypnotic.

"How did you find out about this place?" Kai asks as he sips his drink.

Wytt grins. "I have my ways, brother."

"Don't we need to show ID to prove we're at least eighteen and legal drinking age?" I ask.

Wytt waves a hand at me. "Already handled." He downs his drink in one gulp and stands, tugging on his sports coat. "And now, the ladies await."

He walks to the dance floor and has two girls dancing with him before he makes it all the way there. Incredible. "Your brother is certainly a ladies' man," I say to Kai.

Kai smiles. "He is. But some of us prefer one over many."

Corinne finishes her drink, her cheeks already pink, and she grins. "I think I'm falling in love with this place," she says.

The music stops as the band leader takes the microphone. "We've just been informed that Princess Corinne of the House of Ravens is in the house."

The crowd cheers, and Corinne looks up in surprise.

"We're also told she has a beautiful singing voice. Who wants the Princess to come sing for us?"

Again the crowd erupts in cheers, and they split down the middle to give Corinne access to the stage.

The lead singer, a tall man dressed like an elf, smiles and holds out a hand. "What do you say, Princess? Care to share your music with us?"

She shrugs and stands. "Sure."

More clapping as she walks to the stage and takes the microphone, whispering to the band.

We are served another round of drinks, and against my better judgment, I drink one more.

Kai chuckles. "I guess we found a new favorite to add to your short list?"

I nibble at the flower and smile. "Guess so." The warmth from the alcohol makes its way into my blood, and it feels good.

He leans back, his purple eyes amused. "I'm guessing you've never been drunk?"

I sit up straighter to compensate for what feels like weightlessness. "I have been! My parents actually got me drunk once and did a training exercise with me when I was sixteen. They wanted me to know what if felt like to think and work while under the influence."

"Your parents sound interesting."

"They were."

A new song starts and Corinne begins singing. She's amazing. Her shower humming has nothing on her live performance. She owns the crowd, the stage, everything, with a haunting melody in another language.

Kai grows still as he watches his sister. "I'm surprised she remembers that song."

"It's the one your mom sang?"

He looks at me in surprise. "Yes."

"Were you close to her, before she died?"

"I was, yes. Very."

I reach out on instinct and take his hand. "I'm sorry for your loss, too."

"Thanks."

"Can I ask, what happened with you and your father? Why aren't you the Crown Prince, being the oldest?"

Our hands are still touching, but I don't pull back.

"He's never liked me. I think it's because..."

His eyes look haunted as he pauses. "Because I killed my mother."

"What do you mean?"

He looks at me. "I was sick. Really sick. She nursed me back to health but she got sick, too. Only, she didn't recover like I did. It ate away at her until there was nothing left but her shell. She died in her sleep and my father has never forgiven me."

"Kai..."

He squeezes my hand. "You don't have to say anything. I know you understand."

We are silent for a few moments, listening to Corinne sing the song from his painful past. Everyone has a story, it seems. Everyone has pain.

He grabs another glass and drinks it in one gulp, then slams it on the table. "As for the crown, I don't care about that." He looks at Wytt, who's now dancing with Lana from our class. They look...close.

"Of the three of us," he says. "She's the best. Wytt and I both know it. She will make a great Queen and leader of our people. She's smart, brave, kind and honest."

"That's why you're at Castle V, isn't it? To look after them."

He glances at me. "Yes, actually. I don't care about being a Knight. But I care about them. When my mom died, she made me promise to protect them above all else. I will die before I break that vow."

Wytt interrupts as he comes over with Lana on his arm, and my hand slips back into my lap, still warm from Kai's.

"Ah, wonderful, more drinks!" Wytt says, taking one for himself and handing one to Lana.

She smiles, sips it, then looks around. "I need to use the bathroom. Be right back." She kisses Wytt on the cheek and scampers off.

Kai leans forward and frowns. "Be careful, brother. Everyone knows that girl is after a title. She's only using you for your royal blood."

Wytt's grin widens, and he holds up his drink. "Excellent, because I'm only after those lips."

. . .

177

We're all a bit tipsy as we leave the club and head to my apartment. I'd already looked up the directions so I wouldn't look like a fool when I took my friends there, but it's late, I'm tired, I've been drinking and New York is a big place.

So after turning the wrong corner and heading in the opposite direction, I stop, stumble into a Fairy Fruit Tree, and try to focus my brain.

Kai nudges my arm. "You do know where you live, right?"

I narrow my eyes at him. "Yes. But I'm still new here."

"Scarlett," Evie says into my ear. "Do you need help finding the apartment?"

"Yes!"

Kai looks at me. "Yes, what?"

"Nothing," I say, as my AI BFF rescues me from myself and talks me through the directions.

I'm getting more and more nervous as we near the building. It's an impressive-looking complex in the heart of TriBeCa, an artsy and very upscale neighborhood. Since I'm the only one here who grew up decidedly middle class, this probably impresses me a lot more than it does the royal and the rich, but even they look sufficiently pleased with the neighborhood.

"I love shopping around here," says Lana, as she hangs on Wytt's arm. "They have the best of everything."

I nod as if I know or care about 'the best of everything.'

As we approach the complex, a doorman in uniform opens the door for us. He's an older gentleman, with a tailored look and kind eyes. "Good evening, Miss Night. It's nice to see you again."

I cover the shock I feel with a smile. "Um, good evening. Thank you."

He casually taps his name badge, and I realize he must be in the employment of Zorin or Carter. "Jaspin, thank you," I say. "These are my friends."

We take the elevator to the penthouse apartment, which requires a special key, and we step directly into my apartment.

If having a doorman I've never seen recognize me was a shock, seeing my apartment is triply so. It's decorated exactly as I would have decorated if I'd had time and money to do so, with brightly colored accents and deep, overstuffed furniture. There are books on airplanes lying around and a few really beautiful framed photographs of aerial shots of Montana. There's even a portrait of me with my parents hanging on the wall. It stuns me to see them, in color, together with me. I choke back tears and stare too long.

Kai stands behind me and places a hand on my shoulder. "They look like good people. I'm sorry."

I turn to look at him, because I can't look at the picture anymore. "They are. Were. I miss them."

He nods. "I miss my mother even still. Time doesn't heal all wounds. But it does make them easier to bear."

A pillow hits the back of my head, and I turn and see Wytt grinning like a drunken fool. "Got any booze in this swanky place?"

I laugh and head to the kitchen. "I can't remember. Let me check. Thought it's not going to involve any fairy magic." I can still feel those drinks in me, and I'm convinced it's not just alcohol that's making the world so Monet-like.

Corinne tugs at my hand. "First show us around!"

"Oh, um, sure. Okay." We walk through the apartment, which doesn't take too long. The suite boats a large gourmet kitchen and spacious living room with a fireplace and a beautiful bedroom with just the right amount of lived-in mess. A few clothes in my size and style are tossed to the side of the bed, and a hairbrush with strands of what looks like my hair sits on the dresser. It's all kind of creepy and incredibly detailed. There's a spare room that's been converted into a study and two bathrooms, one in my room and one for guests.

We go back to the kitchen, and I find rum and soda and some glasses. With drinks in hand we walk onto my large balcony that overlooks the city and has comfortable lounge chairs.

I kind of love my apartment, as it turns out, and might have to find time to visit it for real.

We spend the rest of the evening talking about our lives growing up and comparing stories. I'm amazed at the differences in our childhood. They've led lives of expectation and privilege, but also with no privacy or freedom. For the first time, I'm glad my parents kept me from the Orders for as long as they did.

They gave me the one thing none of my new friends could ever have.

A normal, happy childhood.

...

It's not morning yet, but I'm pretty sure if we don't get back to our dorms soon we'll see the sun rise. And before that can happen, I have to do one more thing.

As we reach Castle V, I excuse myself. "I need to get some air before coming to bed."

Corinne nods and Wytt sings drunken songs about pirates and Princesses. Kai guides his brother back to their shared room.

I head around the castle to the water's edge. There's a full moon in the sky, full and glowing with a ring of haze around it. It's my favorite kind of moon.

I open my backpack and pull out a Chinese lantern I picked up in Chinatown today. I light the candle at its center and stare out into the water and night sky, my throat burning with emotion.

"Happy Anniversary, Mom and Dad," I say to the night. To their souls. To whoever listens to the prayers of orphaned girls. "I miss you, and I wish you were here. I've been so angry at you for not telling the truth about our life, but tonight I realized something. You protected me. You gave me a safe, normal childhood, and still found a way to prepare me in case I had to enter this world without you. I get it now. And I'm glad. I wouldn't trade the life we had for anything, not even the truth."

"Aw, how sweet, the Zenith misses her mommy."

The voice startles my foggy, alcohol addled mind, and I turn in shock just as something metal slams into my skull and sends my brain bouncing around. I crash to the ground, unable to stop gravity. The lantern's light dies as it rolls away from my outstretched hand. Pain, delayed by disbelief for just a moment, shoots through my head and reverberates down my spine.

I try to stand, to raise my head, but they are there, three giant figures looming over me, kicking my ribs, punching me, beating me with sticks.

The blows land on me like electric shocks to my nerve endings, igniting a new stream of pain with each hit. I have no moment to breathe, to move, to stand, to try to fight back. Even if I was willing to unleash my Nephilim powers, to release my wings and fly, I'm not sure I can.

As the world grows smaller and darkness takes hold of my mind, something shifts around me. They stop punching and kicking. The pain sharpens, deepens, but the beating stops. Someone else is here.

Someone who is fighting all three of my attackers. The fight doesn't last long, and they shout, curse and eventually run away. I try to pull myself up, but arms encircle me. "Move slow, I've got you."

I look up into purple eyes full of worry. Kai.

He helps me sit up, and the pain of being vertical sends waves of dizziness through me. Kai sits beside me, holding me as those waves pass and breathing becomes easier.

"We need to get you to the Infirmary," he says.

"How did you know I was here?"

"I've seen you come out here before to think. Figured this is where you'd come tonight. I had to get Wytt tucked in, but then..."

"Then?"

"Then I wanted to see you."

I lay my head on his shoulder, mostly because it feels like it's going to fall off if I don't. "I'm glad you came. Thanks for...helping."

He chuckles, and the movement of his body hurts mine, but I still like the sound. "I'm sure you had it handled. I'm just backup."

"Yeah, I had Garin and his goons in their places for sure. You just caught the let-them-think-they're-winning-by-getting-beat-up phase of my plan."

"Of course. Sorry if I stole your thunder." He holds my hand, and I let him.

"It's okay. I don't mind sharing the thunder from time to time."

I lift my head with Herculean effort and look around me. "I had a lantern. I need it back before the sun comes up."

Shades of light form in the sky, and an urgency grips me. I need to finish the ritual before tomorrow arrives.

Kai moves a bit to reach for something and then settles back next to me. He holds a slightly squished lantern and tries to fix it. "There," he says, showing me. "I think it'll still float."

Tears burn my eyes. "Thank you." I take it from him and light the candle again, then set the lantern in the water. It floats slowly away, heading toward the emerging sunrise, and I say one last prayer for my parents. "I hope you're both at peace and together."

Now the tears fall as Kai holds my hand and stands watch with me until we can no longer see the lantern in the distance.

I look at him, my heart so vulnerable, so broken, I can't keep my walls up anymore. "I feel so...alone, without them. They've always been my lighthouse, guiding me to safety, and without them I feel adrift at sea. It's scary."

He puts a hand over my cheek and wipes away a tear. "You're not alone, Scarlett. You have us now."

He pauses, looking into my eyes. "You have me now."

And then he kisses me, and I don't think about anything else but him and his lips and his arms around me. The sun gently warms the cold earth as he warms something deeper inside of me.

DIAMOND MOUNTAIN

Kai walks me to my room and we say goodbye. But I can't sleep, can't calm down. Between the kiss and getting beat up, my mind is spinning. I can't do anything about the kiss, but I can do something about learning to fight.

I message Corrine, telling her I'm going back to my apartment. Instead, I head to the Cathedral.

Zorin notices me when I enter the main hall. "What happened?" he asks, studying what remains of my bruises.

I explain.

He opens his hand, and Umbra, his sword, materializes in his grasp. "I'll kill them."

I laugh. "A bit of an overreaction. They're just some bullies at school. Teach me to fight better. Without a sword or wings."

He nods and messages TR and Trix. We meet in the training pit within the catacombs. Zorin sits on a rock as Trix and TR circle me on the sand. "You were unprepared for multiple opponents," says Zorin, popping a marshmallow into his mouth. "That can't happen again. Never allow yourself to be directly between two attackers."

I shuffle backwards, positioning myself at the edge of the circle, so Trix and TR no longer surround me. They jump to the sides, flanking me once again.

"Keep moving," says Zorin. "Position yourself so they are in a straight line and can't both attack you at once."

I do as he says, moving around Trix and TR. They try to reposition, but they can't get behind me. "Not bad, N," says Trix, smirking.

"Now," says Zorin, "let's see how you do in a fight."

Trix lunges forward, kicking at my torso. I evade backwards and counterstrike. She blocks. I'm about to strike again, when TR punches me in the back. I forgot to keep moving. I shrug off the blow and try again. I stop striking and focus on my position and defense. I keep TR and Trix in a straight line, and only one of them can attack me at once. It makes blocking much easier.

Trix tries another kick. I deflect it.

Now, I'm ready to strike. I throw a series of punches, my third managing to hit her chest. She stumbles backwards into TR. He helps her stand.

I use their delay to throw a kick at TR's chest.

Zorin lands in front of me and blocks. "Fighting three or more is harder," he says, starting to circle me along with TR and Trix. "But the same concept applies. Move in bursts, causing your opponents to change direction. If they're close, they may trip each other. When they're off balance, focus on a single target."

I dash around the arena, trying to keep them in a line. I manage to control TR and Trix, but Zorin maneuvers too quickly. When they strike, I evade, and their blows get in each other's way. TR loses his solid stance, and I kick him behind the knee, knocking him to the ground. Someone grabs my wrist from behind and pulls me to my knees. Zorin.

He smiles. "Why are you stopping? Have you won?"

I break free and kick him away.

We practice late into the night.

. . .

We end training near sunrise and depart for our bedrooms. I feel confident in facing Garin and his friends again. Still, I can't sleep. I walk to the roof, hoping to find Zorin.

I find TR instead. He sits on the edge, staring at the horizon while nursing a beer. "You fought well, Nightfall."

I sit beside him. "You too. The military trained you well."

"Trix and I learned a lot. Too much, maybe. Sometimes, the less you know, the happier you are."

I understand. I felt the same about my parents. "Trix told me she volunteered because of a boy."

He raises an eyebrow. "Did she?"

"Did she mean you?"

He shakes his. "She meant my brother. Max, Trix, and I grew up together. We were friends. When Trix tested Zenith, we looked out for her. Then we grew older, and Max and Trix became something more. When Max was conscripted, Trix joined to stay with him. They...they married the day we departed for camp."

There's sadness in his eyes.

"Max is gone, isn't he?"

TR nods. "Max, Trix and I joined near the end of the War. Except, it didn't feel like war. We were the clean-up crew, tasked with finding the remaining Nephilim and eliminating them. We did as we were told for a long time. Did a lot of things I wouldn't do now."

I imagine a life of murder. What would that do to a person? What has it done to TR?

"One day," says TR, "we located a Sunrise family. First time I saw Nephilim children. Two of them. Max refused to kill them. We agreed, but my older brother, he led the argument like he always did. And our commanding officer shot him dead."

I clutch the Token of Strife around my neck, sharing in his pain.

TR continues. "Trix killed the officer, and we deserted. Others left the army, too. They saw the slaughter for what it was. We joined up together, bit by bit, until we had an army of our own. Trix was the Zenith, so people followed her lead. We decided to attack the Vatican. I'm sure you heard how that ended."

I nod. It ended in defeat. "I'm sorry about your brother. I lost my parents recently, and I know, the pain doesn't go away."

"There's ways to numb it." He sips his beer. "And who knows, maybe one day the pain will leave forever."

Maybe when I have my revenge. But TR had his, and he doesn't look happy. Is this the path he wants? "Why do you fight for the rebels?" I ask.

He doesn't reply.

"It's for her, isn't it," I say. "You volunteered for Trix. You're still fighting for Trix."

He matches my eyes. "She can't know how I feel."

"Why not?"

"Because she loved my brother. I can't take that away from them."

I touch his hand gently. "I told someone my feelings recently. It didn't go as I wanted, but it does feel better. And besides, doesn't Trix deserve to know? Your brother is gone. Maybe both of you are looking for something. Maybe both of you can be happy."

He chuckles. "That's what I like about you, Nightfall. You're always searching for a better day. Me, I'm content with where I am."

"You shouldn't lie to yourself."

He drops his empty beer and stands. "People like us, we all lie to ourselves. It's how we can kill and still sleep at night. It's how we can save those who deserve to be saved."

. . .

It's time to meet with the other rebel leaders, and I take a deep breath to calm my nerves. We chose a neutral location—the ruins atop Diamond Mountain. It's only a few hours from the Cathedral and was once the meeting place between the Twilight Queen and the Four Orders. It's where the Nephilim War began.

Moonlight shines off stone pillars that once made a circle. Now half of them lie crushed in the dust. The center of the mountain is carved into rows of seats like an arena. Five high podiums rise above them, evenly spaced apart. I stand on one of the podiums, Zorin and Trix at my side.

Crixus of the Red Eagles takes the podium to my right, two of his black armored soldiers at his side. His armor is even bulkier, engraved with the pattern of wings, his eagle crest painted over his chest and shoulder plate.

Adam, leader of the Sons of Eden, takes the podium to my left. Green robes sway at his feet in the billowing wind. He wears no accessories. He wears no mask. His face is etched with scars and wrinkles and his gray hair is cropped short.

Trix whispers in my ear. "It's said he's never altered his appearance through unnatural means. If you want the Sons of Eden on your side, you must oppose genetic modification."

I'm not sure that I do. Corrine has shown me many cures discovered through genetic research. But, I don't have to support that research here. "Thank you, Trix. Anything you can tell me about the Red Eagles?"

"Nothing new. They attack warehouses, collect weapons. They seem to have no other goal. However, Crixus is named after—"

"After the gladiator who marched on Rome with an army of slaves. I know." I'm glad he's already contacted me to discuss an alliance, but I don't know what he wants, and that worries me.

Smaller groups occupy the remaining three podiums. The Gravekeepers, who fight for those unjustly killed in the war. The Plebs, who oppose royalty. And the Barons, who seek to hurt the Orders.

Groups with no names, or names barely known, sit amongst the audience, along with supporters of the largest five. There are hundreds of all color and age. We are ready.

I signal TR, who rings an enormous bell at the center of the mountain. It thunders through the stone and air, quieting all.

I speak, my voice amplified and disguised by my eGlass. "United we stand. Divided we fall. Since the beginning of man, this has been true. And yet, our world stands divided. Orders and Rebels. Zeniths and Humans. Kings and Servants. Knights and Citizens. All vying for power. All vying to rise when others fall." I pause, letting my words sink in. "It is time to end the divide. It is time we stand united."

"And who will lead us?" asks Adam. "You?" The crowd echoes his question, anger radiating through them.

"One does not have to be above many," I respond. "People can choose their representatives, and thus the people lead."

Adam gestures around. "They've already chosen they're representatives. We're here, and we wonder, what do you propose we do?"

"Unite under one name. One purpose," I say. "Show the Orders they face not rebels or terrorists striving for power, but people striving for unity."

"So you want us to follow this idea of yours? And what will you do for us? What will you do about the experimentation on God's children? The unnatural modification forced upon them?"

"We'll do what everyone decides is best."

"We know what's best," roars Adam. "Destroy the Hospitallers. Stop their heathen desecration of our people." The crowd cheers at his words. I'm losing control.

"If we are united," says Crixus, his modified voice calm and soft, "each of our goals will be easier to accomplish. I am interested in Nightfall's proposal."

Adam laughs. "Of course you are. All you care about is more. More guns, more money. More people to serve you." Arguments erupt between the Red Eagles and Sons of Eden. A brawl breaks out on one side of the mountain.

"This is why the Orders are winning," I yell. "This is why—"

"I'm done listening to this," says Adam. "When I saw the video of you and Varian, I thought you had some sense. But you're just another Nephilim who thinks she knows best. We're done with Nephilim. Sons of Eden, we depart. Let the girl play with the eagles. We have matters of worth to attend to."

He leaves the podium, his supporters rushing out of the arena. The smaller groups follow. The Red Eagles alone remain.

"This is not what I expected," I say.

Zorin shakes his head. "You did what you could. Most of them never came here to listen. They came to follow Adam. And Adam came to establish dominance."

I remember my first lesson with Kira. "They fall prey to a silver tongue. I ask them to think for themselves, but why would they? For most, following is easier."

"But not us," says Crixus, approaching our podium with two soldiers. "For us, to follow something we do not believe is worse than death. You ask the people to believe. You ask them to believe in themselves. But they cannot. They are not ready."

I turn to face him. "So what can I do?"

"Let us speak in private, and I shall tell you."

I nod to Trix and Zorin. "It's okay."

Crixus gestures his guards away. Trix and Zorin follow them, though I can tell by his rigid jaw Zorin is not pleased.

Crixus sighs, sitting on the short stone wall around the podium. "Here is your answer. Give them something else to believe. It is what Adam does."

"And what about you?"

"My soldiers believe in a happy life, and I compensate them very well."

I scowl. "So you fight for profit?"

"I fight for a better world, same as you. This is what you do not understand, Nightfall. Most people are not like us. They are not leaders. They do not seek a better world. But we need them. So we must use them how we can."

His words remind me of Varian. "I believe people are more than pawns in a game."

"Tell me, Nightfall, are children not pawns? Are parents not Kings? Do they not guide their children to a better life?"

"Until the children are developed enough to make their own choices."

He shrugs, his armored suit clanking. "And what is developed enough?"

I almost say when a child becomes an adult, but I've known children with more sense than adults.

Crixus continues. "Most people are like my children. I guide them to a better life. It is my responsibility. Even if they don't like me. Even if they don't listen."

I've never thought about it that way. Are some people truly meant to guide others?

"You and I, we must be parents. We must do what is needed."

I sit next to him. "And what is that?"

"Before I tell you, you must tell me something first. How did you make Ragathon stop his forces during the Shadow of Rome's escape?"

"I…I distracted him."

"Really? Did you not order him to stop with your ability?"

I flinch. My ability is my greatest weapon in this war. It is my greatest secret. How could he know? I grab his arm, willing him to forget.

I feel nothing.

"You attempted to order me now, didn't you?"

I jump back, drawing my sword.

"You have nothing to fear," he says. "I heard of this gift during the War. It will not work through such thick armor. But it is required for my plan."

I lower my sword, but only slightly. "What plan?"

He picks up a pebble. "The people have a father right now, but he is not like you and I. He is not a good influence."

"The Pope?"

Crixus nods. "We must guide him." He crushes the pebble in his fist. "We must control him."

THANE

Crixus refuses to divulge more of his plan until later, but promises to keep in touch. I arrive back at school late Sunday night, crawling into bed quietly so I don't disturb Corinne.

In my dreams I'm kissing Jax and he turns into Kai, and my heart is so very confused. And I can't afford confused right now. Not with everything else going on. But at least those are better than the dreams of all my friends being crushed into dust by a giant fist.

I know they'll want to know what happened to me this weekend. And Kai undoubtedly wants to talk, but I oversleep the next morning and am late to PT. I don't know what I feel for Kai, so I'm not ready to talk to him.

What I need is some good old-fashioned vengeance, which is what I'm going to get today in Combat class.

But when Varian shows up with his new assistant by his side, my heart sinks. I hiss in Corinne's ear, "Isn't that Thane? The jerk you grew up with who harassed us at the theatre?"

She nods, looking equally unhappy. In fact, none of my royal friends look thrilled that Thane will be a new regular in our lives.

"I trust you'll give Thane the respect he deserves while he's working with us," Varian says.

I snicker under my breath. I can give him what he deserves. No problem. We might just have different definitions of what that is.

When Varian announces he has a meeting and is leaving Thane in charge, I want to ditch class. But I can't, because once free sparring time comes, I pounce. "I'd like to do the first duel," I say.

Thane sneers at me. "Fine. Who do you challenge?"

I look around the class and spot my three assailants. "Garin, Bart and Rex."

Garin and his buddies turn to look at me, Garin with a gloating smile. "Come get it, honey. I'll take you on any day and leave you wishing you'd never come here."

Kai frowns and looks like he's about to stop me, but I shake my head slightly. I need to do this. I'm ready.

Thane allows the fight, probably because he wants to see me lose.

The three goons come to the middle with me and we begin. They try to surround me, but I use what Zorin taught me to keep them in a line. I feel my power pouring through my veins, but I don't let it out in a great show like before, I let it trickle into me, giving me an edge of speed, of strength, of faster reflexes.

When Bart and Rex run into each other, I kick them in the knees, knocking them both down. While they limp off to the side of the sparring circle, I focus my energy on Garin, who no longer wears his cocky grin.

When I finally knock him to the ground, I lean down with my hand on his throat. I lower my voice so only he can hear me. "If you ever touch me or my friends again, I will end you. Got it?"

He doesn't respond, and I press my thumb into his trachea, cutting off airflow. "Got it?"

He nods, his face a vision of hate and loathing as he struggles for breath.

I pull away and he sucks in air.

And then something hits me in the back and I fall into the dirt.

I look up to see Thane smiling at me. "And now you're dead, Night."

"Do you always have to rely on sucker punches to win? I'm not even armed." I glare at him.

He tosses me a sword from the rack, and I catch it by the hilt. "Fight me, then."

"Gladly," I say, getting into position.

It takes him under two seconds to disarm me. It's so fast I'm not even sure how it happened.

"Pick it up and try again," he says.

I let the anger fuel my strength and try again.

He disarms me even faster.

He does it again. And again. I'm nearly in tears from frustration and no small amount of humiliation. I have to beat him, but I can't. I'm not good enough, and everyone here knows it.

"Enough!" Kai steps into the sparring circle, his own sword drawn.

Thane looks over at Kai, the same disdainful expression on his face. "Well, if it isn't the Prince of Ravens coming to rescue the damsel in distress."

He looks back at me, leaning in close. As he speaks, spittle from his lips sprays over my face. "I don't need a sucker punch to win, but I will win. Make no mistake. I will always win, and I will use any means necessary to do so."

. . .

I fidget with a pen, tapping it against the desk as I think about my next step. Corinne sits beside me, dropping her books on the desk, and Wytt flanks me on the other side.

"He's a jerk," Wytt says.

Corinne scowls at him over me. "Be nice. He's just…"

Wytt raises an eyebrow and she sighs. "Okay, he's a jerk. I know it was rough for him growing up with royalty and having the stigma of his family's betrayal. He was such a sweet kid. It's sad. But he shouldn't have treated you like that."

"He was right though," I say. "I let my guard down. I can't do that again. I need more training."

Ragathon walks in, Kai following behind him.

As Kai slips into the seat behind me, he tugs at my ponytail like a kindergartener. I turn to him and he grins. "Let me cheer you up by taking you to lunch," he whispers.

"We all have to eat at the dining hall," I remind him.

He frowns. "I see you'll need more creative persuasion. I must think on this."

He leans back as Ragathon starts the class, and I can't help but smile a little, even as an idea comes to me. Kai's at the top of the class in combat. Even Thane seemed reluctant to fight him. And he *is* Varian's son. I could learn a lot from him.

As we head to lunch after class, I tug at Kai's arm. "Can we talk alone for a second?"

Wytt and Corinne smile and nudge each other. I roll my eyes at them.

Kai nods, and we walk toward the courtyard. "You were studiously avoiding me during PT and classes this morning. Has my natural charm and good looks finally persuaded you to see the light?"

I laugh. "Not exactly, but I need your help."

"So, we're not going to talk about the kiss, and about what's happening between us?"

I can't tell if he's teasing or serious, but I'm not ready to talk about it yet. "Not now. But…we will. Eventually. I just need time."

"Okay, fair enough. What can I help you with?"

"I need to learn to fight better. I don't like losing."

"That fight with Thane wasn't a fair match, and he knew it. He's been training as a Knight since birth. He was showing off and bullying you."

I stop walking and turn to face him. "But he wasn't wrong. I couldn't defeat him, even when he made it fair. Despite my extra strength and reflexes, I'm not good enough, and I need to be. And I need you to teach me. You're brilliant with a sword. Please. Train me."

"Can't I just beat Thane up for you?"

I shake my head and cross my arms over my chest. "I need to learn to fight my own fights." Another thought occurs to me. "Why aren't you in any of the tournaments? You're obviously good enough."

He shrugs. "It's not my thing. I'm a lover not a fighter." He winks, and I laugh.

"You sound like Wytt," I say, then I frown again and tug on his robe. "Seriously, though, I need your help."

He sighs. "Fine, I'll train you. But under one condition."

I narrow my eyes. "What's that?"

"You have to go to the Halloween Ball with me next month. In full costume."

I laugh. "Do you always resort to extortion to get dates?"

He leans in and places a hand over my cheek, brushing a finger against my jaw. "Only with the girls I really like."

My stomach flutters a little at his touch. "Okay, I'll go with you. But we start training right away."

He smiles even bigger. "Deal. Meet me after classes today at the Arena."

I shake my head. "No, I mean right now. We have a two-hour lunch. Teach me how to defeat someone like Thane." *Teach me how to defeat someone like your father.*

THE BLACK KNIGHT

"You know, some of us to have to subsist on more than just air, Life Force and marshmallows," Kai says, complaining once again about missing lunch.

"Grab a sandwich on your way to our next class," I say.

He rolls his eyes. "As you wish, master."

Our swords smack together as he corrects my posture, shows me new moves and tells me to keep practicing. At the end of the two hours my arm is burning, but I feel stronger and more confident. I'm not there yet, but it's a step. As I put my sword back on the rack, I ask to see his.

He hands it to me, and I admire the masterful design work on the hilt and blade.

Evie speaks in my ear. "Scarlett, I detect an AI within this blade. It's not just steel. It carries a wealth of information on combat. With more time, I may be able to link with it."

I twirl the blade in my hand. "This is no normal sword."

Kai takes it back and slashes the air. "An Angel Sword, passed down through our family."

I gasp. "It can't be…"

"It is. This was one of the pieces that inspired our current Angel Technology."

My fingers itch to hold the weapon again, but I resist.

"I need to get my own sword," I say. Even if I have one as Nightfall already.

Kai sheathes his blade, and we walk toward our next class together. "The right sword will pick you, when the time's right."

"That sounds profound," I tease.

"I'm serious. You can't just go out and buy a sword on a whim. Well, you can," he grins, "but you shouldn't. You have to bond to your sword. It's an intimate relationship and the choice must be made with care."

Once again I wish I could use my mother's sword as Scarlett.

Kai's stomach rumbles, and I reach into my bag and offer him a chocolate bar.

"Thanks," he says, stuffing half into his mouth. "So, what's up with you and Jax?" he asks once he's done chewing. "Because, I know you want to wait to talk about the kiss, so I'm not going to talk about the kiss, but I will say that this thing," he gestures between us, "it's something. It's not nothing. So I need to know, am I poaching on someone else's girl?"

"First of all, ew. Did you seriously just compare me to a piece of property?"

He shakes his head. "No, you know what I mean. Jax is clearly in love with you. Were you dating? Are you dating?"

"What does it matter?" I ask.

"I've known Jax a long time, and I respect him."

"If you're worried about his feelings, why don't you ask him yourself?"

"He's disappeared," he says. "No one knows where he is."

"Exactly."

"I see. So, then, you're a free agent?"

"Not if you keep using these lame metaphors, I'm not."

He laughs. "Scarlett, are you currently involved with anyone?"

"No," I say honestly. "Not anymore."

"Okay then."

"But I should warn you," I tell him. We stop in front of our class, my hand on the door. "I'm not really dating material right now."

He puts a hand over mine and gently squeezes. "I'm a patient guy. And you seem like the kind of girl who's worth the wait."

"What if you're wrong?" I ask, looking into his purple eyes. "What if I end up hurting you?"

He cocks his head. "Those are two different questions. I can handle pain, Scarlett. As for being worth the wait, I already know you are. I'm not wrong about that."

. . .

The last month of training and classes seems to have flown by. The deeper I get into life at the Castle, the harder it is to get out to the Cathedral as Nightfall, but I've been doing my best. There's something all those comic books and movies don't tell you about living a double life: you don't actually get double time.

I've had to feed from blood packs a few times just to keep up my strength. Between training in class, training with Kai, training with Zorin and studying, not to mention trying to coordinate with all of the rebel groups, I'm chronically exhausted.

Evie keeps me on track with a highly encrypted memory file of both my lives. I'd be lost without her.

But right now, I'm not studying or training or plotting, I'm just hanging with my friends watching the Tournament in the Initiate Hall and talking about the Halloween Ball that's a few weeks away.

I almost feel normal.

But whenever I look down at my hand and see the missing freckle, I remember I'm anything but normal. Still, I grab the happy where I can find it, and today I'm finding it in a room decked out in the best Halloween decorations I've ever seen, courtesy of Corinne, with Wytt and Kai as her 'helpers.'

I'm leaning against Kai's arm, which is wrapped around my shoulder as we lounge on the couch. We're still stuck in this in-between thing. Not quite officially dating, but not *not* dating. I don't know what it is. All I know is he makes me laugh, and I need more laughter in my life.

And I haven't heard from Jax since he left.

"You three really outdid yourselves in here," I say. Corinne used her own artwork, combined with pieces formed from Eden Fashionables, to turn our Hall into a Goth haunted manor. There are skeletons that turn their heads to follow you around the room and bats perched from the ceiling that fly at you when you least suspect it.

Nothing like waking up to screams in the middle of the night when a student ventures into the hall and is attacked by a not-quite-alive-but-far-too-real bat.

Right now Corinne is hand-painting parts of her Halloween costume while Wytt's eyes are glued to the Tournament. Two Knights are fighting each other on a life size eScreen, the sounds of their battle echoing throughout the hall. One is wearing black armor, the other blue.

"I still don't get why we can't know who's in the costumes," Lana says, leaning against Wytt's arm. They've been together non-stop since the night at Fairy Realm.

"It keeps it competitive," Wytt says. "You can't research your opponent beforehand, so you have to rely on what happens in the arena."

"I wonder who the Black Knight is. He's good," Kai says.

Corinne holds up a silk shirt she's been painting on. "What do you think? Won't Jaden look handsome in this?" She points to the blue patterns. "This is a perfect match for his eyes."

"Are you two hanging out a lot?" Kai asks, and I can hear the protective edge in his voice.

"A bit. But it's not serious," she says with a smirk. "No need to go big brother on him just yet. He's a nice guy."

When Ragathon comes into the hall, I tense. I've never seen him here, and it feels invasive. Kai squeezes my shoulder in silent support.

Corinne smiles at him though, without reservation. "Hi, Uncle."

He sits next to her at the table and hands her a small bag. "I picked these up for you while I was in the city.

You mentioned you didn't have the right beads for your costume."

She opens the bags and examines the different colored beads with a large smile. "Thank you. These are perfect." She leans over to hug him, and I'm pretty sure my jaw drops to the floor. I've never seen Ragathon be nice before. Except in that one vision.

"You're doing a great job on this," he says, gently touching the hem. "It's lovely."

She smiles and returns to her work as Ragathon looks up at the Knights fighting. "Who's your money on?" he asks Wytt.

"The Black Knight," Wytt says. "Though I think the White Knight is going to be a close contender."

"I agree," the Grandmaster says.

Kai chuckles. "Are you two actually betting?"

Wytt looks down and grins, and Ragathon raises an eyebrow. "Of course not," says Ragathon. "It's just a turn of phrase. How's your training coming Kai?"

Kai shrugs. "As good as can be expected, given Father's growing influence."

Ragathon scowls. "My brother does have a way of ticking people off."

Sure, *Varian* is the one who irritates people.

Ragathon looks at me with another scowl, as if I'm right up there with Varian on the ticking people off scale. Maybe I am. "You two have been spending a lot of time together lately," he says to me. "It seems everywhere I turn, there you are."

I'm about to tell him that Kai is training me, but Kai responds first. "We're dating," he says, pulling me closer.

He says it in a tone that allows for no argument, and Ragathon sighs and stands.

"I'll leave you kids to it then. Have fun."

After he leaves, my body relaxes. "Your uncle doesn't like me."

"He doesn't like many people," Kai says.

"He seems to like you three," I say.

"Everyone has a soft spot," Corinne says. "He's not all bad."

There's something I've been curious about though. "He looks older than Varian, why isn't he king?"

Kai looks at his brother and sister and then at me. "He and our father both fell in love with the same woman. Our mother. She loved them both in their own way, I think, but in the end she chose our father. Ragathon banished himself to North America to teach here, and did everything he could to dissociate with our family."

"He's married now, right? With a child of his own?" The librarian, the memory. Little pieces of Ragathon that don't fit the man I see every day.

Corinne nods, looking up from her painting. "I think he loves us because of our mother. He never really got over her. He sees her in us."

"Especially Corinne," Kai says. "She looks just like our mother."

I turn to Kai. "Why did you tell him we're dating?"

"I love my uncle," he says, "But I see how he treats you, and it's not okay. This was my way of telling him to back off. You're family."

Corinne grins. "I, for one, love seeing you two together. When are you going to start dating officially?"

Wytt joins in the teasing. "Then I can write epic poems about my big brother and his great love."

Kai lightly punches Wytt's shoulder. "We'll go public with our relationship as soon as Scarlett here admits she can't stand the thought of living without me."

I roll my eyes at him. "You don't have high demands of a new relationship, do you?"

"Ah, so you admit this is a relationship, then. We've made progress."

I turn to Wytt, ready to change the subject. "What are you and Lana going as? Something dripping in romantic tragedy, I'm guessing."

"How right you are," he says with a wink.

Lana smiles too, her dark eyes happy. "We're going as Lancelot and Guinevere. What about you and Kai? What are you going as?"

"We don't know yet," I admit.

Kai nudges me. "I wanted to go as Romeo and Juliet—"

"But their love story is stupid and they both die like idiots, so...no."

Wytt jumps up and shouts, and I look up to see the Black Knight winning another round. "I cannot wait for December. This is going to be the most epic Tournament Festival ever."

. . .

My mouth is full of chocolate when my day of lounging with friends is interrupted by a message from Zorin.

Need to meet in Times Square. Important.

208

I swallow too much at once and nearly gag.

I text Zorin from my wrist keyboard telling him I'm on my way.

Now for the hard part. I stand and stretch and check the time. "Hey, guys, I'm going to get going. I want to spend some time at my apartment this weekend, and it's already getting kind of late."

Corinne frowns. "You're always taking off alone. What do you do by yourself all the time?"

This is so hard. I hate lying, even though what I'm about to say isn't actually a lie. "I'm sorry. It's just...I'm still dealing with a lot from my parents' death, and sometimes it gets to be too much. I'm not used to living around so many people. Keep in mind, I grew up an only child, homeschooled in isolated Montana."

Wytt shrugs. "Fare thee well, lovely maiden. Forget not about thy loyal friends."

I smile at him. "Never. And I won't be gone all weekend. I just need a little R&R. I'm dead on my feet from all the training, and it's impossible to sleep here."

Corinne nods, her face finally relaxing. "That's true. And you do need sleep. I can hear you tossing and turning most nights, even for the few hours you're in bed."

"I've never shared a room before," I tell her, truthfully.

"Have a nice weekend," she says. "We'll miss you." She looks pointedly at Kai.

I walk out, but Kai follows me and places a hand on my arm. I think he's going to give me a hard time, but instead he smiles kindly. "I know it's easy for everyone to forget what you've gone through. You handle it so well, and life at Castle V makes the world out there seem less real at times."

He holds my hands between his, warming them. "But I get it. Just know I'm here for you if you need me."

He kisses my forehead and walks away, and I feel like the worst human being ever for lying to such good people. For lying to my friends.

. . .

I meet Zorin at Times Square, and we sit together on a bench. He wears a long black coat. We both stare at the city. I stopped two executions here, and the place looks alive as ever. Sounds of chatter and cars and music fill the air, eScreens light up the sky, and hundreds of people shuffle by, lost in their bubbles of media.

"So," I ask, "what is so urgent I had to leave my friends?"

He pulls Nox out of his coat. "Nox misses you."

What? I cross my arms, frowning. "You sure it's only Nox?"

He grins. "I didn't ask anyone else."

I groan, petting the cat. "Why do some people never admit how they feel, Nox?"

He purrs in response.

"Yeah, you have no trouble sharing how you feel, don't you, my kitty? I'm glad the big bad Nephilim didn't eat you in your sleep."

Zorin joins me in petting the cat, and our hands touch for a moment. "How was your day?" he asks.

"Great. I'm trying to pick a Halloween costume for the ball."

"You can go as Lilith, the first Nephilim to be turned."

"Right, Lilith at Castle V. I might as well dress as Nightfall." We both chuckle, though Zorin sounds half-hearted.

"Are you going with anyone?" he asks.

His tone is serious. Is he…jealous? No, he doesn't see me that way…does he? "I am," I say, deciding the direct approach is best. "With Kai."

He raises an eyebrow. "The Prince of Ravens?"

"He's a good person."

"He's the enemy."

I lower my voice, but I can't hide my frustration. "My goal is to tear down the Orders, not kill everyone affiliated with them."

"And what is Kai's goal? Corrine's? Wytt's? Will they stand by idly as you destroy the Orders?"

I shiver, trying not to imagine the future as he does. "Maybe they'll join me."

"They are Varian's children."

"But they are not him."

Zorin sighs. "Believe me when I say, it's easy to fight an enemy. It's much harder to fight a friend."

I'm tired of his opposition. "Is there anything else you need to say?"

He frowns at my response. "Yes…" He pauses. "The Nephilim."

I wonder if he asks just to irritate me. "We're not creating more."

"You will need them to win this war."

I snap at him. "Because they won the first time?"

He freezes. His eyes are sad. "You want to know how I feel, Scarlett? When Danika died, I dedicated myself to protecting those prosecuted by the Inquisition. Zeniths, Nephilim, humans who made enemies. And now, the Nephilim are nearly gone, the Zeniths are treated as less than people. I failed, Scarlett. I don't want you to fail as well." He squeezes the bench railing, bending the steel. "I can't have you fail."

CURATIO DOMUS

The night of the Halloween Ball, the Castle is abuzz with madness of the fun kind. Everyone's getting into the spirit, including the resident Knights and faculty. And our dorm room looks like an evil seamstress cursed us to be buried alive in fabric.

I sit on my bed to pull on the silver boots for my costume and feel a prick of pain on my thigh. I dig and find a stray sewing needle. Holding it up to Corinne, I raise an eyebrow.

She grins sheepishly and takes it from me. "Sorry. I know it's a bit…insane in here. I'll get it all cleaned up this weekend, I promise."

I finishing lacing my boots and stand to look at myself in the full-length mirror. "It's okay. Thanks for making my costume. You did an incredible job."

My velvet red skirt falls to the ground, and thin mesh metal armor clings to my torso. Corinne can't resist making a few last-minute adjustments as I stand there. Finally she straightens up and smiles. "Perfect. But, I still wish you and Kai could have gone as something matching."

"I know we've destroyed all your dreams," I say as I twirl to look at the back of my costume.

"You have. I'll never recover. But Joan of Arc suits you, somehow. And, well, I'm not surprised my brother chose who he did."

I admire the final look. The crimson cross hand-painted onto my thin breastplate and the fake sword hanging from my hip complete the look. The sword is impressive in its detail, and looks authentic at a glance, but it would break in a duel. I still haven't found my own sword or, as Kai would say, my sword hasn't found me. Until it does, I'm stuck using the chipped swords from Combat class.

There's a knock at the door and Corinne squeals. "They're here!"

She's splendid in blue silk she painted herself, with Eden Fashionable star flowers sewn into the fabric. They shimmer silver and blossom into star patterns that glow. She wears her hair long and white with streaks of blue, and horns stick delicately out of her forehead. Her ears are long and pointed and a beautiful crown of flowers sits on her head. She's an Elf Queen straight from fantasy books.

And as she opens the door, she greets her Elf King. Jaden looks devastatingly handsome and exotic with his pointed ears and horns and long white hair. They both shimmer with silver body paint and daring eye makeup that transforms them into something magical.

I smile at them both. "You two are definitely winning the costume contest tonight."

When Kai comes into the room I burst out laughing. "You look perfect," I tell him as he pulls me into a hug.

213

He bows, his eyes twinkling in mischief. "The dashing and dangerous pirate Blackbeard at your service."

His eye patch gives him a wicked look, and the black beard he wears transforms him into someone I almost don't recognize.

He holds out an arm and I take it. "Shall we?"

Corinne takes Jaden's arm and looks around. "Where are Wytt and Lana?"

"Meeting us at the party," Kai says.

As we walk through the halls of the Castle toward the Grand Ballroom, other groups and couples dressed in every imaginable costume press through to attend the ball.

And what a ball. Already the ballroom is filled with people dancing as fog drifts over the floor, transformed by lights into something eerie and beautiful. A live band entertains the crowd from the stage, with their own backup dancers of walking skeletons.

Round tables draped in dark purple, with black chairs padded by red velvet cushions, line the outskirts of the dance floor. At the center of each table are candelabras encased in intricate spider web designs that sparkle like diamonds. Toward the back of the ballroom is a long table piled high with food and drink, all recreated in the Halloween theme. "This is amazing," I say, as we scan the crowd for Wytt.

He raises his hand from across the room. "Over here!"

We join Wytt and Lana at the table they saved for us, sinking into the plush velvet seats.

"You two make an excellent Lancelot and Guinevere," I tell them. I turn to Corinne. "I can't believe you had time to design everyone's costumes in addition to studying."

She smiles, blushing a little under the praise. "I love doing it. It's just another kind of art: a kind women were creating for centuries without getting the kind of recognition they deserved."

"I'm surprised there's such a big ball in the middle of the quarter," I say.

Wytt smiles. "It's the last hurrah before we all buckle down and get serious about the Trials and winning a Boon from an Order."

Corinne smiles. "Especially with the death last year, everyone's extra motivated."

"The party before the war, then?" I ask.

Jaden nods. "Basically."

Kai stands and offers me a hand. "Would the lady like to dance before she leads an army to battle?"

The words are closer to the truth than he knows, but I smile and accept his hand. "Yes, please."

As we dance, his arms wrapped around me, I enjoy the feel of this, of being normal and having fun for one night. He kisses the top of my head. "You've worked really hard this quarter," he says. "You've improved so much. I don't know if you see how much stronger, faster, and more focused you are now."

I look up at him and laugh. "And here I was just thinking it was nice to have a night off work and school and training."

"Fair enough," he says. "No training talk tonight. Can I at least tell you how beautiful you are?"

A warmth spreads through me. "Thank you."

I watch others dancing around us and am surprised to see my grandfather dancing with Kira.

Lana and Wytt dance and then leave to get drinks for everyone. We join them back at our table, and I nibble on a severed finger—some kind of pastry with a strawberry filling—when my grandfather walks over and holds out his hand. "Might I have a dance with my granddaughter?"

I look to Kai who smiles, and I join the Chancellor on the dance floor.

"I regret we haven't had more time to spend together since you've been here," he says. "It's been a few weeks since you last came for tea and stories about your mother."

"I know, I'm sorry. It's a lot of work, being here and keeping up."

He nods. "I understand, dear. Just know you are always welcome. You have an ally here."

"Thank you." The Seeker and Ragathon talk near the punch bowl and I nod my head at them. "I noticed you dancing with Kira earlier. I didn't realize you two were close."

His eyes drift to her. "She's been here her whole life. We are the only family she's ever known."

I feel a twinge of sadness for her. She may have known my grandfather and my best friend in ways I didn't, but she never had parents, family.

My grandfather looks over at Kai, who's watching us. "Are you getting serious with the Prince of Ravens?"

I think about my answer. "I don't know. We are kind of stuck between friends and something more, because of me. But I might be ready for that something more now."

"He's a good man," he says. "From a good family."

As the song ends, he escorts me back to my table and kisses my hand. "Enjoy your evening."

I settle into my seat, and Kai puts an arm over the back of my chair. "We were just talking about going through the Haunted House. What do you think?"

"There's a haunted house?" I love haunted houses, and every Halloween my dad would take me on a tour of them throughout our city. My mom couldn't stand them, so it was just us. I follow my friends eagerly and wait in line until our turn arrives.

Inside everything is black, dark, crazy. The spaces are tight, and we crowd in, so many people squished into the lines. There's screaming and laughing and silly, scary shocks. I love every minute of it.

When we reach a maze of mirrors, we each take a different path to see who can get to the end first. I'm just about to find my way out when someone from the shadows grabs me. I scream, but the sound is lost in all the other noises, so I turn to fight when a familiar face smiles at me.

"Jax?"

He puts a finger to his lips and pulls me outside. "I'm not supposed to be here."

I hug him, all of my frustrations lost in the joy of seeing him again and knowing he's okay. "Where have you been?"

"I can't tell you," he says, his voice sad. "But I missed you, Star. I needed to see you."

He leans in to kiss me, and I pull away reflexively, my heart breaking just a little. I was just emotionally preparing to tell Kai I'm ready to officially date him, and Jax shows up trying to kiss me? This is ridiculous. "Things aren't that simple anymore, Jax. You left. You told me we couldn't be together. You can't just come back and pretend that we're a couple."

He clenches his jaw. "Is there someone else?"

As if on cue, Kai comes out of the maze and sees us. He walks over and puts an arm around my shoulders. "Jax, we weren't expecting you here tonight."

Jax steps back. "I'm not really here." He looks at me with sad eyes. "Take care of yourself, Star. I'm glad you found someone good for you. Someone who won't have to keep secrets."

He walks into the shadows as my eGlass buzzes and Evie speaks. "Scarlett, Zorin needs you at the Cathedral right away. The Sons of Eden are holding Curatio Domus hostage and they need Nightfall."

Kai touches my shoulder. "Are you okay?"

I shake my head. "No. I'm sorry. I have to go."

I hug him, leaning my head on his chest before I turn and walk away.

...

I join Trix, TR and Zorin at our meeting room—now deemed the War Room. We gather around a large wooden table—the War Table—and discuss the hostage situation.

"The Sons of Eden are demanding the Knights Hospitaller be dismantled," says Trix.

TR scowls. "That will never happen."

"If it doesn't, then Adam blows up the entire hospital at midnight," Trix says.

I project my eGlass feed of the event on to the table. Officers surround the building. This looks too familiar. "Are we sure it's not another trap?"

Trix shakes her head. "It's unlikely, since the Sons are involved."

I nod. "What's blocking our entry?"

"Nothing," says Trix. "But if anyone is seen leaving or entering the building, Adam will set off the explosives."

I rub my chin. "We have discreet ways of entering buildings."

Trix grins. "You thinking sewers again, N?"

I pause. Varian saw that move in advance. Will Adam?

Zorin points at the exits on my projection. "What if someone leaves the building?"

"What do you mean?" I ask.

He shrugs. "There are hundreds of people in that hospital. What if one of them breaks and runs?"

"Then they'll kill everyone," says Trix.

"Is Adam in the building?" asks Zorin.

Trix nods, pointing to the center of the hospital. "He's on the roof, preaching. He says one of the detonators is attached to his heart and will go off if he dies. He's acting invulnerable."

Pieces of a plan click together in my mind. "He thinks he'll win this. He doesn't expect to die." And so he's not concerned with his opponents. He's nothing compared to Varian.

TR raises an eyebrow. "You think he's bluffing?"

"I think he's so confident in his abilities, he can't imagine losing."

TR nods. "He did seem to have a superiority complex at the meeting."

"So what's the plan, N?" asks Trix.

"Your military training cover disabling bombs?" I ask.

"Sure did," she says.

"Good." I tap the projection. "I'll speak with Adam. While I do, you three will enter the building through the sewers, find the explosives, and diffuse them."

TR studies the image of the hospital. "I estimate three bombs, maybe four. What if they're defended?"

"I'll deal with any guards," says Zorin.

Everyone nods. We've all seen Zorin kill faster than someone can pull a trigger.

We work out the details. As we're about to leave, TR frowns. "You realize if we do this, we're publicly fighting another major rebel group. The Orders will use this to discredit us."

I clasp his shoulder, meeting his eyes. "If we do this, we're publicly saving hundreds of people. They'll remember what we've done."

"If our plan succeeds, the Sons of Eden will be captured," TR says.

"That's why I'll meet with Adam. Hopefully, I can convince him to change his methods and join the Dark Templars." I grab the hilt of my sword. "But if I can't, I rather he be executed than allowed to threaten others again."

. . .

Whatever happens tonight, I won't threaten Adam. Nightfall must be a symbol for more than just threats and violence. The people need to see that the Dark Templars can negotiate a peaceful resolution.

While the others travel ahead, I find the Night Raven in the catacombs. A black roof has been installed for the chamber since I was last here, true to Zorin's words. Evie opens it for me and sets a flight path for the hospital.

En route, I ask Evie to contact Crixus.

After a brief pause I hear his voice. "Nightfall, what a pleasant surprise."

"Crixus, I assume you've seen the news about Curatio Domus?"

"Yes."

"We could use your help," I say.

"We cannot jeopardize our plan to intervene in a dangerous, and ultimately meaningless, mission. Even if you succeed, you gain our cause nothing. If you fail, we lose too much."

I want to argue, to point out why this does help us, but I don't think it will sway him. Nor will he sway me. "So you won't help?"

"No. And I would strongly advise you to stay out of it as well. Let the Orders deal with it."

"I understand your position, but I'm still moving forward." I disconnect the call.

We are nearly at the hospital when Evie says, "Scarlett, you have an incoming communication."

"From who?"

"Varian. He must have noticed the Night Raven."

I freeze. Why does he want to speak with me? "Put him through."

"I see you emerge once again, Nightfall," says Varian.

I keep my lips from shaking. "The Sons of Eden must be stopped."

"Agreed. I will not oppose you."

I can't trust him, but he has no reason to lie. "Keep the Orders away from the building. I will diffuse the explosives."

"Very well."

"Communication over," says Evie.

"Good. Trix, how are you doing?"

She speaks through my eGlass. "We're nearly in the building."

"Keep me up to date." I examine the city below. Hundreds of people crowd around the hospital. Some to cry for relatives, others to watch the spectacle, and a few to film the whole thing. If this had been a hospital strictly for Zeniths, their concern would be replaced with cheers. It makes me sad.

"Evie, take us down to Adam."

She does. No one interferes, as Varian promised. The Night Raven hovers above the hospital's roof. The cockpit opens, and I stand face to face with Adam.

He smiles, amplifying his voice with his eGlass. "Come to join the celebration?"

I feed my speech through the city's speakers. I want everyone to know I oppose this. "There will be no celebration, Adam. You will accomplish nothing today."

He frowns, his wrinkles creasing. "You are wrong. Today I will destroy the Hospitallers."

"The Orders would demolish this hospital themselves, before they meet your demands."

"Ah," he says, raising a finger. "But if they do, then they will have proven they care nothing for their people. Riots will break out. The Orders will crumble. I will still win."

I gasp. His view of himself is higher than I even realized. He may choose to be a martyr, rather than surrender today. I ask Trix for an update. They're already in the building. I have to be careful. "One day, the Orders will fall, but not in this way. Consider what will happen if others take up your example. They'll threaten innocents, kill good people for power. What will be left in the end?"

"Innocents? Good people?" He spits off the roof. "They are sinners. They believe they know better than God. They believe mankind must be altered, when it is already perfected."

I shake my head. "Not everyone in this hospital is part of Hospitaller. There are innocent patients."

He chuckles. "I know you do not believe my arguments, but consider these patients. They have decided that humans are better than Zeniths, that Nephilim should not even be allowed existence. Yet are we not all God's children?"

I must be careful how I respond. His question is a trap, asking me to choose between humans and Zeniths. "If we are all God's children, then why do you threaten to kill hundreds of them?"

He frowns. "If they die tonight, then I have saved them from further corruption. It is my duty to protect their souls."

Evie interrupts. "Scarlett, three minutes left until midnight."

Trix updates me. "We've disabled the first explosive. Zorin knocked out the guard."

I turn my attention back to Adam. "And what of *your* soul? Is it your destiny to die tonight? Is there no more good you can do?"

He raises his hand, and I spot the detonator in his grasp. "What I accomplish today," he says softly, "will echo through the ages."

"You have three minutes left," I remind him, scared he's ready to pull the trigger.

"Two minutes now," he says. He trembles. Is he losing his courage?

"Leave now," I tell him. "Join me, and we will create such an echo, it will surpass anything you have imagined." I play to his ego, hoping the promise of victory and the fear of death sway him.

His eyes are sad. "They annihilated nearly the entirety of your race. How can you protect them? How do you not hate them?" His words feel personal. Does he remember he speaks to a crowd?

"I hate what occurred, but...a friend once told me, vengeance and justice cannot be the same. And I would rather have justice."

Another update. "Only one bomb to go, N."

"One minute left," says Evie.

I need to keep Adam talking and unaware of time. I don't think of my lessons in speech. I don't think of what I believe. I let the words take hold of me. "The people you will kill today did not destroy my race. They did not draft the laws that torture Zeniths. Are they innocent? No. None of us are. And we all are punished for it. So if you are to punish these people, be fair. Be just. Do they deserve to die?"

Adam flinches, his lip quivering. He speaks quietly, as if to himself. "It's too late, now. I have no choice. They killed my people. They..."

What does he mean?

"They turned the world against us. I did not want anyone to know, in case they hated me, in case they found me…but, now in the end…" A silver glow surrounds him.

No. He can't be.

And Adam unleashes his wings. They drift in the wind, silver, like mine. He raises the detonator. The last bomb is still active.

"Now," says Adam. "I rejoin my people." He presses the trigger.

The corner of the hospital explodes. The building shakes beneath us as metal, glass and fire rain down on the people below.

I fall to my knees, tears burning my eyes. "Trix, Zorin—"

"We're still here," says Zorin. "I'm sorry, we weren't fast enough."

Adam raises his arms, no doubt expecting the explosions to reach him. They do not.

His eyes widen in panic. He presses the trigger again. It doesn't work.

Adam drops the trigger, his eyes red. He looks to me. He looks peaceful.

And then a gun fires.

The bullet hits Adam in the head.

And he falls to the people below.

TESTED

Adam was torn apart by the mob. The Inquisition Officers did nothing to stop it. I closed my cockpit and disappeared into the sky.

Now, I'm back at the War Table with my Dark Templars. Trix is flicking a coin so that it spins upright. Zorin is reading an old black book. And TR sips on a beer, laughing at something funny on his eGlass. None of us want to face what just happened.

I consider asking about the media response, but I don't. People died in that hospital because we weren't fast enough, weren't smart enough. And they died at the hands of a Nephilim.

I've never felt great pain for the loss of Nephilim. I suppose I never truly considered them my people. But today, I saw that pain in Adam's eyes.

The world did a terrible thing when it nearly annihilated my kind.

I can't let it happen again.

But today, there is no more work.

So I allow everyone their distractions. Because we tried our best. And tomorrow we will try again.

Ours is a hard life. No reason to make it harder.

...

It's with a heavy heart that I leave the Cathedral and return to Castle V. Too many lives lost, all in the name of justice. I'm starting to wonder what I'm doing as Nightfall. Am I making a difference for the better, or am I making everything worse? I just don't know anymore. And I feel tired to my core. So tired.

When I arrive at the Castle, I find Wytt in the Common Hall alone.

He looks up when I come in. "Where have you been?" he asks. His eyes are red-rimmed and he seems angry.

"At my apartment," I say. "I needed space after everything with Kai and Jax."

"Did you hear about what happened at Curatio Domus?"

I nod. "I came back as soon as I heard. Is Corinne okay?"

Wytt shakes his head. "No, she's not. She got a call from Sarah at the hospital. Charlie—the girl you met—was killed tonight by the rebels. She'd just had her transplant, and it was working. She was getting better and was about to be discharged from the hospital for the first time in years. Now she's dead. Corinne could have really used her best friend."

I'm stunned for a moment, first at the news that the sweet girl I met on the first day of APD is dead, and then at Wytt calling me Corinne's best friend. But I guess he's right. We are best friends. All of us. I hang my head in sadness. I've failed them again. It seems no matter what choice I make, I fail someone.

"Where is she now?"

"She went back to the hospital. There's a memorial."

I turn to leave, and Wytt speaks again, stopping me. "She went by your apartment. You weren't there."

I don't know what to say to that, so I don't say anything.

To save time, I use my wings to fly into the city as discreetly as I can, and head to the hospital. I was here as Nightfall, now I'm coming back as Scarlett.

I find Corinne kneeling in front of a memorial left on the steps of Curatio Domus. Already pictures of those who lost their lives have been erected, and Eden Flowers are swaying and changing color, blooming and releasing beautiful scents into the night air. There are candles burning and crosses erected, and Corinne is crying at the picture of Charlie.

I sink to my knees beside her and put an arm around her. "I'm sorry."

She turns to me, her face red from crying. "Why did you bail again, Scarlett? Where are you always going?"

"I'm so sorry, Corinne. I should have been there. I didn't know." Tears fill my eyes, and her face softens.

She hugs me and our tears mingle. "I'm just glad you're here now. Thank you for coming."

We look back at the face of the young, beautiful girl whose life ended too soon.

"Why?" Corinne asks. "Why hurt innocent people? How is that supposed to bring peace or whatever it is they want? How does killing this girl make the world a better place for anyone?"

...

Pain has a way of testing us. It either breaks us or makes us stronger. Corinne threw herself into her studies even more after Charlie died.

We've all taken our studies more seriously since the attack on Curatio Domus. It's the second half of the quarter, and the Trial is around the corner. We all want to be ready. So, here we are, noses buried in our books.

Kai places a steaming mug of coffee in front of me, and I inhale it gratefully. "Thank you." It warms my hands as I sip on the delicious nectar. I already drank a packet of Life Force, but nothing can replace my love for coffee.

He kisses the top of my head and sits next to me, his books already spread out over the table. "You're welcome. How's it going?"

I look down at the law book laying open in front of me, full of highlighted sections and notes in the margins, all mine. "It's going...slowly."

Corinne grins over at us, and I can see her mind spinning. She loves even the smallest display of affection between us, as she believes it will lead to more soon. Maybe it will. We've been taking it slow since Halloween. This last month has been about us getting to know each other better, training, studying.

It seems that after Halloween comes the panicked cramming and studying phase of the quarter. For the last several weeks our trips to the city and nights hanging out chatting have gotten further and further apart as our workload in our classes increase. Now we only have a few more weeks until finals, and my eyeballs feel dead in their sockets from all the reading.

Wytt and Lana have become glued at the hip. Jaden and Corinne aren't dating, but he's joined our little gang of friends and brings his own charm. And even Akio is here, his wisdom adding something special to our interactions together.

"Who do you think's a shoo-in for the Boons from each Order?" Jaden asks.

Wytt looks up from his computer, where he's trying to hack into a dummy account I created for each of them to practice on. "I definitely won't be getting one from the Templars. But Scarlett, you'll get something, I'm sure."

"Maybe," I say. "It's the class I'm strongest in. But Wytt, you're awesome at Law and Order. I bet Inquisition has you tagged for something."

He rolls his eyes. "Wouldn't that make me instantly evil or something?"

Everyone laughs.

"What about you, Akio?" Corinne asks. "Have you given more thought to which Order you want?"

"I stay with Teutonic," he says. "It my only choice."

I frown, worried my new friend won't make the cut for that Order. "It's a tough one to get into if you're not a strong fighter. Have you thought about the Hospitallers? You're really good at those classes. You have the second highest score so far, next to Corinne."

He beams at the compliment but still shakes his head. "It not enough to do something you good at. Must do something that make you happy. That challenge you to be better than old self, Scarlett-friend."

"Is that why you want Teutonic?" I ask, genuinely curious. "To challenge yourself?"

"That part of it." His eyes drift as he thinks about something only he can see. "But it also for my family. My wife and children."

Corinne's eyes widen. "I didn't know you had a wife and kids. Don't they miss you?"

His eyes are sad, and my heart clenches as I sense what's coming. "I miss them. Very much," he says. "Before Nephilim War, I successful engineer and bring much honor to family. But then War happened, and town became battleground between Nephilim and Orders. Our houses were destroyed, farms burned, people died. My wife and children were in our house, trapped by fire and fighting. I come home from work but could not get to them. I found them all dead, too late to save them. I vow then to become a Knight, to fight to protect others. To bring honor to their memory."

The conversation drifts, and we go back to studying, until Wytt curses and smacks his keyboard.

"Did the computer hurt your feelings?" Kai teases.

"This coding doesn't make any sense to me," he says.

To my surprise, Lana leans over and explains the hardest bit. I raise an eyebrow and everyone else is staring, too.

Kai whistles. "Impressive. I didn't realize you two found any time to study."

Lana and Wytt look at each other, and she nods and turns to us. "There's something we want to tell you," she says.

We all put down our books and wait. I have no idea what it could be. Are they getting married? Pregnant?

"Wytt and I aren't actually dating. We never were."

Corinne frowns. "Why would you pretend to be dating for so long?"

Lana sighs. "It's my parents. They sent me here, not to become a Knight, but to marry one. Preferably one with a pedigree."

"Like a Prince," Kai says.

She nods. "Like a Prince. But Wytt and I became good friends, and he agreed to fake it to keep my parents off my back so I could focus on my studying. As long as they think I'm making progress at marrying up, they won't pull me from the program."

My jaw drops. "They would actually take you out of here if you don't date someone of royal blood?" I can't even fathom this.

"They would, and they've threatened to. Which is why I needed Wytt. You can't tell anyone," she says, a look of panic on her face. "If they found out Wytt and I were just friends with no intention of marrying, it would be over for me. And I don't want to leave. I want to be a Knight. I want to make a difference with my life, not just as someone's arm candy." She looks at me and smiles. "I want to be a Templar."

"I had no idea," I say. "But if there's anything I can do to help, just say it. You're working hard to be here, more than anyone realized. You'll make a great Knight." And I feel a twinge of shame and sadness, because they are all working so hard to build something that I'm working to destroy.

But Jaden breaks my melancholy mood by throwing an arm over Lana's shoulders and smiling. "You know, I too am a Prince. If you ever need a new guy to fake it with, I'm always free."

. . .

We are all buried in books as we spend the week taking finals. We talk in murmurs in between classes, comparing answers to the tougher questions, speculating about how we each did. At lunch, gone are witty jokes and stories by Wytt, or the sketched masterpieces of Corinne. My fiends have been replaced by zombie students, eyes glazed over from the sheer volume of words being shoved into their brains. And I'm no different.

On the plus side, they no longer give me worried glances every time I pull out a Life Force instead of real food. Instead, their eyes light up with need, and I pass out packs to each of them like the drug dealer I've become.

We are all addicts now.

The day of my APD final I'm all nerves. I know I'm not getting a Boon for this class, but still, I can't just fail. I study, I cram, I do everything I can to prepare. After, my hands are shaking, and my brain feels like a Halloween pumpkin—gutted and set on fire.

Corinne joins me in the hall. "How'd you do?"

I shrug. "I don't know. Better than the first day."

She grins. "So you didn't put 'hands' and 'feet' and 'head' on your anatomy worksheet?"

I laugh. "No. I think I did pretty well on that part, actually, thanks to your torture study sessions."

We walk, enjoying a moment of non-studying before the next test. "That's great. You just need to do well enough to stay in the program," she says. "You're obviously meant for Templar, so don't stress too much about the rest."

For three days this continues, with no sleep, a lot of Life Force, and whispered pep talks until we finally make it to the last final—History, which is tedious, but not particularly hard.

What's hard is waiting to find out how we did. And who will get the Boons.

...

This is the day. With the relief of completing our finals comes the new stress of thinking about the Trial. They say without a Boon it's ten times harder to pass a Trial.

I need a Boon.

We sit in the Great Hall in full robes waiting for the Chancellor to announce our grades.

He limps up to the podium with his staff clicking against the stone floor. He looks older, more tired, than he did last time I saw him. I should visit more, find more time to talk with him. He knows stories of my mother I don't, and I'd like to hear them. We've shared tea and cookies a few times this quarter, in quiet moments after dinner, and he told me what she was like as a child and a teen. It's like getting to know her all over again. I never realized how much alike we are.

Were.

I'm shaking, and Kai reaches for my hand, holding it. My feelings for him grow stronger every day, but I know Nightfall will always stand between me and anyone I might come to love.

"You have all worked hard this quarter in the most physically and mentally challenging program in the world," my grandfather says. "Your scores broadcasted here today are a reflection of that work. But this is only half of the puzzle. Next comes the Trial. Some of you will have help. Others won't. And still others will not make it through to next quarter."

My hand sweats against Kai's, and I pull out of his grip to rub it against my robe.

"Without further delay, here are your scores."

The eScreen behind the podium shifts from an image of the Castle V logo to an Initiate and their marks for each class. We clap politely as each student is displayed, and we wait for our names. Wytt's face appears on the screen, his impish grin larger than life. He got tens in Law, Order and History, but average to poor in his other classes. Jaden smacks him on the shoulders. "Might want to reconsider your stance on the Inquisition."

Wytt scowls at him.

Corinne's next and no one is surprised at her tens in APD and EMT. Her Combat score was the lowest, but still she's happy with her average.

Jaden gets sevens in everything. "How is that even possible?" I ask.

Jaden puffs up his chest and smiles. "I have mastered the art of being mediocre."

I chuckle. "Indeed."

Kai's scores come up next. Tens in Combat and Survival, decent scores in everything else.

I'm happy my friends have done so well.

Lana did better than I expected, getting a nine in Espionage and excellent scores across the board. Wytt hugs and congratulates her. She smiles big, and I feel a twinge of sympathy. She's working so hard and her parents don't even care.

Akio's face appears, and we all wait nervously. His combat score is a six. It's not bad, and it turns out to be his lowest grade. He receives a ten in Survival. Life experience helps a lot, it seems.

And then my face appears and I freeze, sucking in my breath. I get tens in Tactics and Espionage. Nines in Combat and Survival. My APD score is my worst. A three. I get a four in Law, a six in Order, and sevens in EMT and History. My overall score isn't great, but considering my double life, and how hard I've been training, I'm pretty happy by the results.

Once all the scores have been displayed, our quarter is basically over, other than the trial. Wytt hoorays at the top of his lungs and we all cheer as we leave the hall.

"We must celebrate!" he says. "Eat, drink and be merry—"

"For tomorrow we will surely die."

The Trial

I'm dreaming about mazes and mirrors when something lands on my face. I wake, unable to breathe, struggling against a large dark form pinning me down. There's a cloth over my mouth and nose that smells chemical, and it's clouding my mind. Something sharp pricks my arm and warmth spreads through my body. I hear murmurs of voices, someone says my name—

And darkness.

. . .

I groan, my eyes still closed against the light of early morning. The ground beneath me is hard and lumpy. My head pounds, and my body wakes slowly with pins and needles shooting through flesh.

A bird tweets in a tree nearby, and in the distance a waterfall crashes against a cliff. With reluctance, I open my eyes and lift my tired, sore body off the ground. The light blinds me for a moment, then color trickles in until I can see clearly. I'm outside, the sun is just coming up, and I'm surrounded by an expanse of tropical forest.

And I'm alone.

I look down, taking stock of myself and my supplies. I'm still in underwear and my Nox Aeterna shirt, and next to me is my backpack. I search it, finding jeans, shoes, socks, a bra and jacket. I also find a black box with a silver V on it, and a flare gun with one flare.

From everywhere and nowhere a voice fills the sky, startling me. It sounds like Grandmaster Gabriella, the leader of the Teutonic Order. "Rise and shine, Initiates," her voice says through hidden speakers. "You are officially participating in your first Trial. You have three days to find the Teutonic base on this island and enter it. Once you cross the threshold within the seventy-two hour time frame, you pass. If you give up by shooting your flare, or fail to reach the base within the allotted time, your Initiate training will come to an end. If you won a Boon from an Order, you will have it with you now."

The speaker crackles before her voice resumes.

"Good luck, Initiates, and Godspeed."

. . .

I dress quickly, then open the small black box. Inside is a note that says, *Good luck! ~Templar Order.* I pull open the tissue to find my eGlass. I slip it on.

"Hello, Scarlett."

"Evie! It's so good to hear your voice. Here's the deal. I'm at my Trial, and they've dropped me on some island. I need to know where I am. Can you get a satellite view?"

While she does her thing, I stick the box back into my backpack and sling the bag over my shoulders. First things first, I need to find a water source. My stomach growls. A marshmallow tree would also be fantastic.

I start walking toward the sound of the waterfall when Evie chimes in. "I'm sorry, Scarlett. Something is blocking the satellite feed, and I can't override it."

If only they'd also included my laptop. "Do you have any idea where we are?" I ask her.

Evie scans the area around us. "I would place you somewhere in the middle of the North Pacific Ocean," she says.

"So maybe Hawaii?" I ask. "Or somewhere near it?"

"Your vegetation suggests that is a plausible option."

The vegetation starts out normal enough. Coconut trees and banana trees and other tropical life.

But as I move deeper into the forest, things get... strange.

I pass by a row of purple bushes with green berries on them. The berries are spotted yellow and come in a variety of star shapes. I don't touch them, but I scan them and ask Evie, "Can you identify these?"

"No," she says. "These should not exist."

"And yet they do," I say, backing away from them. If anything screams poison, it's those berries. "How am I supposed to know what's safe to eat and what's not if they've filled this island with genetically modified plant life that's not identifiable?"

"Do you need to eat berries?" she asks.

"Well, no. Not specifically. But I could be out here at least three days, and I have no Life Force. I can't go that long without something."

The water finally comes into sight, and I see Amber near the water's edge filling up something. "Hey!" I wave my arms, still too far out to reach her. "Amber!"

She looks up from the water, then turns and runs off in the opposite direction.

Weird. Granted, we aren't exactly best friends, but why wouldn't she want to work together in a place like this?

I reach the water but realize I have nothing to purify or carry it with. I look around, hoping to find something useful. The bushes rustle behind me, and I turn to face Garin. He smirks. "Looks like the wannabe Princess is finally alone." He cracks his knuckles and punches a fist into his hand like we're in a bad movie.

"Do you really want to do this right now, Garin? In the middle of a Trial?" I stand and walk toward him. "I don't need a sword to defend myself," I say.

With a surge of power, I push my body forward so fast the wind rips through the air, and I stop just in front of him, my hand on his throat. "So I'll ask again, do you really want to do this right now?"

His eyes go big, and from behind us someone claps. "Well done, lovely maiden. I always enjoy seeing the bullies taste their own bitter medicine."

Wytt walks up to us with a big grin on his face, and I let Garin go.

"Hi!" I hug Wytt, and he squeezes me tight. "Have you seen Kai? Corinne, or the others?"

He shakes his head. "You?"

"I saw Amber earlier, but she ran off. Other than that, just this thug." I point at Garin, who glares at me.

"Hey you got Evie," Wytt says. "That's brilliant."

I tap at my eGlass. "Yeah, but she's not much help so far. What about you?"

He hands me a small book, and I flip through it. "Inspirational Quotes from the Pope?" I ask.

He nods and takes it back. "The Inquisition felt this little gem of wisdom would help me find my way. Allow me to share the beauty." He opens to a random page and reads, "To those who strive for greatness, I tell you, strive for goodness and greatness will follow."

I laugh. "That's...lovely."

"It's rubbish," he says. "Worst Order to get a Boon from ever."

"We should keep moving while we have daylight," I say. "Maybe we can find the others. The base would need to be near fresh water, so I suggest we follow the river and see if we can get a feel for where we are and how big the island is."

Wytt nods. "Sounds like a plan."

We both look over at Garin. I wave. "See you around."

Garin jogs over to us. "No way. I'm coming with you. Better odds."

I frown, about to argue, but Wytt shrugs. "He's a jerk, but he's right. We're safer in groups."

I sigh. I haven't forgotten about Garin beating me up, but I also want to win this Trial. "Fine. You can come. But if you so much as blink at us wrong, it's over."

He nods, and the three of us start walking. While we do, Garin picks up three sturdy sticks and uses a sharp rock to carve points into the tops of each.

"What are you doing?" I ask.

"Making spears for us," Garin says. "Have you noticed how quiet the forest has gotten?"

I hadn't, but now that I listen I realize he's right. It's spooky quiet.

"That's not normal," he says. "There's something out there. Something bad. This is the Teutonic Trial, and that means combat."

He hands me a makeshift spear, and I grip it in my hands. "Thanks. I hate to admit it, but I'm impressed."

He hands one to Wytt. "Being raised by a single mom in a bad neighborhood, you learn to be resourceful."

The walking becomes monotonous, and Wytt distracts us by reading out of his book of quotes. For hours. And hours.

"Okay!" I say, spinning on him. "That's enough from the Pope. How about a story? Or a song? Or even silence. Just please, for the love of all that's holy and just in the world, no more from the Pope."

Wytt laughs and shoves the small book into his pocket. "Not a fan, huh?"

I shrug. "There's something about him. I don't know. He rubs me the wrong way when I see him in interviews."

When we pass by a coconut tree, we agree to stop and pick some coconuts for the food and hydration. We use large rocks to knock the them off the trees, then break them open. We save several for later, and each take one to drink and then eat the meat out from inside. I can't stand the taste, but I know my body needs something, and it does help clear my head.

We hike for several more hours, mostly in silence, though Wytt and I do talk about where to go, how to find the base, and Garin chimes in from time to time with his thoughts.

When the sun begins to set, Garin looks up and frowns. "We should stop somewhere for the night. Build a camp."

"We should keep walking," I say. "We can't waste a third of our time. We don't even know where the base is yet."

He doesn't argue, but I can tell he wants to. Wytt looks back at him and leans in to whisper, "He's probably right. We don't want to be stuck out here when it's fully dark. We won't be able to see anything, and we don't know what's out here. Better to sleep a few hours and start again in the morning."

I hate stopping, hate slowing down when we haven't accomplished anything, but I sigh and agree. "Let's look for shelter."

It doesn't take us long to find a cave carved into the side of a mountain.

"Be careful," I say. "It may be occupied."

Wytt raises an eyebrow and takes a step back. "How about we just sleep under a tree or something?"

"Too exposed," Garin says. "We need something we can defend."

He steps into the cave, and I follow. Something scurries through the darkness and shadows. Garin throws his spears and an animal screeches, then silence. I shiver. We don't even know what that was, and he's already killed it without thought.

There's still enough light to see a bit in the cave, and Garin holds up his hunt. It's a small lizard with feathers. "Looks like we have dinner."

I want to argue, but then I smell the blood, and I nearly leap on it and suck it dry right then and there. "Make mine rare."

...

We stayed up far too late last night trying to warm ourselves in front of the fire as Wytt told us ghost stories. Just as I had sunk into a deep sleep, the sun comes up, and a foot nudges me in the shoulder. Garin stands above me, packed up and ready to hike. "Get up, Sleeping Beauty. We can't afford to sleep the day away."

I want to slap him. I'm the one who pushed to keep going last night. But I get up, eat, drink from a coconut, and head out with Wytt and Garin for more exciting walking.

"I'm surprised at this," I say a few hours into the day.

"At what?" Wytt asks.

"This!" I look around at more of the same. Trees, bushes, plants. "I get the survival element of it, but it seems...random. How are we supposed to figure out where the base is in three days, unless the island is small enough to completely discover all its parts in that time? There's got to be something we're missing."

Garin scoffs. "Just like the entitled to think that things should be easier because of who they are. Do you think most people get life handed to them on silver platters, Princess?"

I glare at Garin. "And just like a bully to think that his sad background gives him an excuse to be a jerk. You don't know anything about me, my life or my friends. You don't know what we've had to go through, or what pain we've endured. You complain about being from a single mom, of having to struggle? At least you still have a family. My whole family died. And I didn't grow up with silver spoons, I grew up in rural Montana. So just shove that chip you're carrying on your shoulder up your—"

Wytt grabs my arm and I stop, listening.

He covers his lips with a finger and points to the left. I turn to look, but see nothing through the dense foliage. Whatever I thought I heard, I can't hear anymore, and I let out a breath.

Wytt looks around, still too spooked to speak for a moment. "You did hear that right?"

I nod. "Yeah, it sounded big. But far away. I think we're okay for now."

Wytt nods and we start walking. It's another long series of taking one step, then another. I've lost track of how many times I've wanted to unleash my wings and fly over everything to see where we are, but I can't. Too many people would see me. So I have to keep walking. So slow. So tedious. So ineffective, because for all we know we're walking in the wrong direction.

Wytt pulls out his little book of quotes and starts reading again. Garin groans, and I laugh. "Remind me to punch Ragathon when we see him again," I say. "How could he think this would be helpful?"

Wytt shrugs, flipping through the book. "Look, it even has a dedication. 'To the nineteen nights who saved one hundred and fifty witnesses.' But it's weird, they misspelled Knights."

His words drift through my mind, as they have for the last hour, but this time they stick. I whip my head around. "Read that again."

He does, looking up at me oddly. "What?"

I stop walking and take the book from him. "This isn't a dedication. It's a map. Nineteen nights. Nights is spelled wrong because it represents North. Nineteen degrees North and one hundred and fifty witnesses is one hundred and fifty degrees West. Those coordinates are in the proximity of Hawaii, which is where Evie speculated we were. This must be where the base is!"

Wytt smiles widely. "You are truly a gorgeous genius!" He kisses my cheek.

I laugh and click my eGlass. "Evie, map these coordinates, and tell us where to go." I give her the numbers and she says the most beautiful thing I've ever heard. "Scarlett, walk north fourteen miles."

"Guys, we are officially on our way to the base."

They both cheer as we alter our direction. Wytt walks next to me, staring at the book in his hand. "I'd never have figured that out," he says. "So why did I get the book?"

I shrug. "You would have figured it out eventually."

He looks down again. "Maybe."

The walking doesn't get any more exciting, but knowing for sure we're heading in the correct direction helps a lot. We make good progress over the next few hours, despite sore feet (all of us) and a deepening thirst for blood (I'm hoping just me).

We're stopping for a quick lunch of more coconuts—yay—when we hear it again. The huge thing. This time, though, it seems a lot closer. Around us the ground shakes, the coconut milk splashing up from the shell, and then a sound sends shivers up my spine. A kind of growl that's more dinosaur than anything.

"We have to hide," Wytt says. "That thing is getting closer."

He's right. It's running now, and it's coming straight for us.

We drop our coconuts, grab our backpacks and scurry away from the beast, tripping over rocks and bushes until we find a large dead tree to crawl into and hide. Our breathing is heavy as we crouch in the darkness. Bugs scurry from their hiding places, crawling over my feet and hands in their quest to escape.

I peek through a hole in the tree bark and see bits of something giant with scales that glow green.

Wytt looks through the hole as well and pulls back, his face white. He holds up the spear Garin made. "I don't think these sticks are going to do the trick."

A tree branch snaps in the distance and through the hole in the tree I watch the beast turn, distracted, and run away from us.

"I think we're safe," I say.

"The danger's not over yet," says someone outside our hiding place.

"Kai!"

He crawls into the tree trunk with us, and I scoot over to him.

He hugs me and kisses my cheek. "I've been looking everywhere for you. Is Corinne here too?"

"No," Wytt says. "We can't find her."

He frowns and I ask, "Do you know what that thing out there is?"

He drops his hand to the hilt of his sword—his Boon was useful at least—and shakes his head. "No. But whatever it is, it's been hunting me for the last two days."

THE BEAST

"What do you mean hunting you?" I ask, gripping his arm.

"I don't know," he says. "But I haven't been able to lose its trail for long. It seems to be tracking me."

Garin glares at Kai's sword. "Of course you got a weapon. You all got Boons, naturally. Connections."

I don't even bother responding. We wait in the tree quietly for what feels like forever, just to make sure the beast is truly gone. When we think it's safe, we crawl outside, and I take a deep breath and stretch, my body cramped from crouching for so long.

Kai brushes a strand of hair off my face. "You should go on without me. If this thing is following me, I don't want you and Wytt at risk."

"I agree," says Garin. "That's an excellent plan."

"Nope," I shake my head. "We're not leaving you."

Wytt agrees. "We stick together." He looks over at Garin. "You're free to go if you're scared. But my brother stays."

Garin grunts. "Fine."

"Besides," I say with more excitement. "We have coordinates for the base camp. They were part of Wytt's Boon."

Kai raises an eyebrow. "That's excellent. Let's get going. But we need to stay where the trees are thick. And if we see the beast again, run while I distract it."

I'm about to argue but he stops me. "I have a sword. It makes the most sense."

I reluctantly agree, and I explain the route Evie has laid out for us. As we start to hike again, my head feels dizzy, and I know I need blood or Life Force soon or I'll be too weak to keep going. I might have to sneak off and eat an animal without anyone seeing, and hope there are no cameras watching me.

We're hiking up a large hill, my thighs burning the higher we go, when we hear someone scream. Kai looks west and points. "It came from a field over there."

"We should see if they need help," I say.

Garin shakes his head. "Let the loser save himself. We have enough problems."

The man screams again, and Wytt sighs. "We should go help. It's the right thing to do." He doesn't sound happy about that, but we head west and find Bartholomew fiercely battling…bunnies?

I look closer. "Are those bunnies or…"

"Hybrid bunnies with cat DNA," says Wytt. "At least that's what they look like."

It's true. They have bunny ears, but the long tail of a cat. They're adorable, and small and seem relatively harmless. Though Barty boy appears to disagree.

"Hey Bart, need some help with the kitty-bunnies?" Kai calls.

Even Garin snickers at that, despite this being one of his friends.

"These beasts are not cute, they are evil!" Bart shouts.

We walk over and the creatures run off into the bushes, more scared of us than we are of them. But Bart is still running around screaming like his pants are on fire. Kai smacks him in the face. "Shut up. We can't make noise right now."

Bart stares at Kai, shocked. "Did you just hit me?" He shoves Kai in the chest, and I step next to Kai.

"Back off, Bart," I say.

"Bartholomew. My name is Bartholomew. And when my father hears about how I've been treated here—"

"Shut up, dude," says Garin. "No one wants to hear about your father."

Bart glares at his friend. "Why are you even hanging out with these losers?"

I laugh. "You know what? You two go on. We can handle the rest of this ourselves. It's time to break up into groups."

"No way," says Garin. "You got maps and eGlasses and swords."

Bart looks at Kai's sword and sneers. "Of course they got the best Boons. Doesn't matter. With my skill and expertise, I don't need one."

"I'm over this," Kai says. "Which way next, Scarlett?"

I point north, and we start walking with Wytt by our side. The rest can figure out what they want to do.

I hear Bart arguing with Garin, but unfortunately for us, they do keep following. I wish we could mute them.

Kai reaches for my hand and I let him take it, enjoying the feel.

"I was worried about you," he says.

"I was hoping we'd find you," I admit.

We walk in silence for a while, listening for sounds in the forest.

We're getting closer to the base as the sun sets on our second day, and I feel confident we'll have no trouble reaching base by lunch tomorrow—plenty of time before deadline. We still haven't seen Corinne yet, and Kai is worried.

"She's okay," Wytt says as we search for a place to rest for the night. "She got high grades. She probably got a map and a truck or something."

I laugh. "No doubt. That'd be nice."

It's getting much darker, hard to see even a few feet in front of us, and we still haven't found a place to sleep. "We need to stop," I say. "We're going to be tripping over ourselves soon."

"Agreed," says Kai.

I let some power flow through me to increase my night vision until I see more around us. I point to our left. "There's a grove of trees over there. We can camp in the middle with some shelter at least."

Kai squints and frowns. "I can't see it."

"Trust me," I say, pulling him forward. They follow me, Garin and Bart finally quieter after hours of arguing.

We don't have much to make camp with, so we do the best we can with brush and leaves and settle in. Kai, Wytt and I sleep close to each other for warmth. Kai holds me in his arms, which isn't unpleasant, and I lean my head on his shoulder and listen to his heartbeat.

Bart starts rubbing wood together for a fire, and Kai stops him. "No fires. There's something dangerous out there and we don't want to draw its attention."

"But I'm cold," whines Bart.

"Suck it up, buttercup," says Wytt.

Garin snorts and leans back against a tree. "I'm out. Tomorrow this will be over, and we can all go back to hating each other."

"Who said we stopped?" says Bart, rolling over and facing away from us.

I doze on Kai's shoulder, falling into a half-sleep haunted by shadow dreams, when something wakes me. My eyes open, and I see Bart sitting in front of a small fire warming his hands.

He grins. "Care to join me?"

I sit up and my movement wakes Kai and Wytt. "You have to put that out, idiot."

"Forget it. You don't make the rules for me," he says stubbornly.

"Then leave. Go find another group," I tell him.

Kai puts his hand on my arm, and then I hear it. The ground rumbles. A great roar fills the night sky.

The beast has found us.

We scramble up and use whatever we can find to diffuse the flames, but it's too late. The beast is hunting us, moving closer as it smells our fire, or our fear—I don't know which.

"Should we run or stay put?" asks Wytt.

"For now, stay under the cover of the trees," I say.

We push into the spaces within the large trees and wait and listen.

Our breathing is so loud I feel like we can be heard for miles. And it's getting louder.

Bart starts to hyperventilate. He begins groaning and drops to his knees. "I can't do this," he says. "My father would never allow this if he knew."

I kneel to face him. "Bartholomew, look at me. Look at my face." He looks up, and I hold eye contact with him. "It's going to be okay, but you have to calm down. We'll get out of this. Just breathe."

I think I'm getting through to him. He takes a breath. Then another. Then the creature roars again, and Bart can't keep focus. He screams and jumps up. "No! No!" Then he runs out of the grove and into the night, screaming.

We all follow him, calling his name. Once out of the cover of trees, the full moon brightens our path, giving us just enough light to see the beast, a great shadow like a mountain, with teeth the size of my hands and sharp as swords. It's scaly with big glowing green eyes.

And as Bart runs through the brush, the beast turns his head.

I have no time to react, to run or help or stop him.

In one move, the beast opens its giant jaws and drops them onto Bart, eating him in one horrifying crunch.

...

I'm paralyzed as I stare in horror at the bloody remains of the man who stood there a second ago.

Garin's shaking from rage...or maybe fear.

Kai tenses next to me as the beast turns his focus on us again. "I'm going to distract him while you three escape," he whispers.

I grip his arm. "Not alone."

He kisses my head. "I have to. It's me he's after, and I'm the only one with a weapon." His purple eyes are filled with concern, but not for himself. "Get my brother to safety. Please."

I swallow the lump in my throat and nod. He'll be distracted if he thinks Wytt's in danger. I can protect him better by doing as he asks. For now. I nod. "I'll keep him safe. Don't die."

He grins in that cocky way I've come to love. "You can't get rid of me that easily, Night."

And then he runs out. The beast swerves its head to follow the scent of Kai, and I tell Wytt and Garin to run in the opposite direction.

Legs pumping, heart pounding, I try not to look back, not to think about what's happening with Kai as we run for a rock formation that should offer us a way out.

We arrive at the rocks, and I push Wytt to climb up first. "Go! Don't argue."

"I'm not leaving you out here alone," Wytt says.

Garin pushes past him. "Then I'll go." He climbs up the rocks and disappears through a crevice.

"Wytt, I promised your brother I'd protect you. I'm Zenith, you're not. Go!"

He obeys, reluctantly, climbing through the crevice as I stand guard with my spear.

I hear Kai yell at the beast to keep its attention. The beast charges and traps Kai between a mountain and itself.

Wytt calls for me from behind the rocks. "Scarlett, hurry up."

"Kai needs help. Go! I'll catch up."

Wytt yells for me. "No!"

But I'm already running toward Kai. I can't let him die. Can't let him get hurt. I did what he wanted. Wytt is safe. Now I must save him.

I'm running faster than I ever have, my powers surging through me. I want to unleash my wings, but if I do, it's all over. I can't take the risk. Not yet. There's still time. Kai is fighting the beast. He's not injured. I can make it without revealing who I am.

When I'm within reach, I take my spear, aim, and using extra force and power, I throw. The spear impales the beast's backside, and it cries out in pain and turns toward me. "Kai, run!"

The beast isn't slowed by a piece of wood sticking out of it. It probably feels like a splinter. I've basically just made it mad. And now it's chasing me. I run away from Kai, away from Wytt, but Kai isn't getting to safety, he's following me and the beast, and now the beast is confused. It wants to attack us both.

It changes directions, chasing Kai again, who's running fast but not as fast as needed and in the wrong direction. "Kai, the cliff!"

I try to catch up, to stop him before it happens, but I'm not fast enough. Not without my wings.

Time slows as the beast and Kai run to the edge of the cliff. Kai realizes his mistake at the last minute and turns to face the beast, sword held high to fight. But the beast is huge and doesn't have the breaks required to stop in time. It crashes into Kai, and they both disappear over the ledge.

"No!"

I have no choice. It's not even a thought, just instinct. My wings of light stretch out from my shoulders and I fly, swooping down over the cliff. I see the beast and Kai both falling. I push myself faster, passing the beast and reaching for Kai. "Grab my hand!"

He reaches for me. Our hands link. I try to hold onto him, but his hand slips away.

He's too close to the ground. I push harder, flying faster. My heart is beating so hard it hurts my chest. I reach for him again. Our hands clasp and I pull. Hard.

My arms wrap around his waist and I hold him tight against me as I slow our descent.

We crash into the ground, but without the fatal splat I feared. The beast falls next to us, shaking the earth. Instead of dying as I'd hoped, it rolls onto its legs and charges us.

It's so close I can smell its rancid breath.

I grab Kai's sword from his sheath, spread my wings and fly straight at the beast. It swipes at me, gouging my arm with its claws.

I push the sword through its eye.

It twitches, lunging once more at me, but it can't complete the move. As death steals its life, it falls to its side.

I crumble to the ground, my wings still flicking silver white light behind me. My arm burns, and I feel dizzy, sick.

The sun is just starting to glimmer in the sky, but the moon hasn't yet retired for the day. It's mostly dark as they share the sky. I look around, trying to breathe, trying to focus my thoughts. We're in some kind of grove where glow-in-the-dark mushrooms and bugs create a magical ambiance. Night flowers glow in pink and yellow and orange lights.

I pull Kai's sword out of the beast's eye and try to stand, but I stumble and fall to my knees as he walks over, a bit wobbly himself. I'm scared of what happens now. My wings are still out. He's seen everything. I wait, gripping my arm as my body works to heal it.

He kneels before me and smiles, caressing my cheek. "You look good with my sword."

I blink. I'm ready to mind control him, but I don't want to. Did he hit his head in the fall? Isn't he freaking out? I'm so confused. "Um...thanks?"

He grins. "You look good with the wings, too."

I suck in my breath. My body is shaking. "Do you understand what I am?" I cock my head, trying to read him.

"You're Nephilim," he says, as if telling me I'm blond or that I have blue eyes. "And...you're Nightfall."

My heart skips a beat. "You seem awfully...calm."

He takes his sword out of my hand, sets it to the side, and holds both of my hands in his. "It doesn't change how I feel about you, Scarlett. And I'm not going to tell anyone, don't worry about that."

"You...accept this?"

He nods. "I've actually suspected for a while, but I didn't really care either way. I still don't, though I'm glad I know for sure, and I'm glad you know I know."

"But your father, your uncle..."

He frowns. "Scarlett, I've grown up in the Orders, in politics. I know the kind of corruption that runs rampant in this world. And it shouldn't. My family shouldn't get to rule just because we're born to it. Zeniths shouldn't be mistreated just because they are born different. It's not right. My country is one of the lucky ones. My father is a just ruler, even if he and I don't see eye to eye on everything, and Corinne will be even better. She's the best of us all and will be a great Queen. But what if that hadn't been the case? My country shouldn't be stuck with someone awful just because of a bloodline. Many things need to change."

I'm still trying to absorb what he's saying because it feels impossible that this is really happening. "So you support Nightfall's cause? My cause?"

"Yes, I do. I support you as Scarlett and as Nightfall. The world needs Nightfall, and I need you." He leans in, his body so close to mine now. "Scarlett," he whispers as he runs a hand through my hair, "I love you. All of you."

When he kisses me, I melt into his arms, responding with equal passion and desire. But I can't stop the tears. To be loved like this, to be accepted for everything I am, is the greatest gift to receive and I don't know how to accept it, but I try. I try because this beautiful, frustrating, amazing man in front of me has seen all the parts of me and still loves me.

He pulls back and wipes away a tear. "Have I made you sad?"

I shake my head. "No. Happy. Very happy." I smile through the tears. "I think I'm ready to officially date you now, Prince Kai."

He laughs. "If I'd known all it would take is a near-death experience, I would have put myself in harm's way long ago."

I slap his arm. "No! No harm. Stay out of its way and we'll be fine."

He cradles me in a bear hug, and I rest my head on his chest as he strokes my hair. "Fair enough, Scarlett. I'll stay safe if you promise to do the same."

When he squeezes me harder, my arm burns and I flinch, my vision growing cloudy again. He looks down at me. "Are you okay? These cuts look bad."

"I heal fast," I tell him. "I'm just hungry."

He holds my arms. "You're shaking. I can hunt up some berries."

I look at him a moment, my wings flickering behind me, and he smacks his forehead with the palm of his hand. "Right. So, Life Force, is it—?"

"A blood substitute," I tell him.

"And marshmallows and chocolate?" He grins.

"Most human food tastes like sawdust now and makes me sick. Those are still gloriously delicious."

He nods. "I don't have any Life Force. Or marshmallows."

"I know. It's okay. I'll be fine."

He tilts his neck, exposing his pulsing vein. "Feed on me, Scarlett."

I recoil. "What? No!"

"You've done it before, yes?"

"Yes."

"Did you kill the person?"

"No." I can't possibly tell him the first person I fed on was his beloved uncle.

"Then do it. How else are you going to be my knight in shining armor and fly us out of this ravine?"

I look around and realize he's right. There's no way in or out without my wings. The Orders never expected any of us to end up down here. Which means my secret might still be safe if they didn't place surveillance in this area. But it also means I'll have to fly us out, and I'm too weak to walk, let alone fly.

He looks at me, his smile sincere. "I can take it."

I nod. "Only to get us out of here."

"Fair enough." He tilts his head again, and I lower my mouth to his neck, my teeth stretching as my appetite grows. I'm starving and need this. And I want it.

I bite into his neck, and he doesn't even flinch. I take only what I need, stopping long before I'm full. But it's enough. I pull back and lick the last traces of blood off my lips as my wounds heal themselves and my body grows stronger. I stand, my wings fully extended and powerful.

He looks at me wide-eyed. "Wow, the networks don't do you justice. Though, I thought you'd be taller."

I slap his shoulder and laugh. "The cameras add a few inches."

I hold out my hands and he embraces me.

Our faces are inches apart as I push off of the ground and into the sky. His smile broadens. "There are perks to dating you," he says as I fly us out of the valley. Just before we land, he closes the small distance between us with a kiss that leaves me lingering in the air.

When I land and retract my wings, I look at him. "You can't tell anyone about me. Ever. Not even your siblings."

He pulls me into his arms again. "Scarlett, your secret is safe with me. And so is your heart."

I laugh. "Do you tell all the girls that?"

He kisses my forehead and grins. "Only the ones who can fly."

...

We walk the rest of the way to base with light hearts, hands held and with time to spare.

It's a great feeling.

The base is a large grey building of metal that doesn't look inviting until we enter. It's set up to receive tired and hungry students with sleeping mats, a buffet table with food, and bathrooms with showers, all of which are in use.

My grandfather is there, which surprises me. He smiles when he sees me and limps over with his cane. "I had no doubt you would fare well," he says, kissing my cheek.

"It was a close one," I tell him as Kai grabs two plates and fills them with food for us.

"What happened?" he asks, concern in his blue eyes.

"There was a creature, a giant dinosaur-like beast, that hunted Kai the entire three days. We escaped and killed it, but barely." I shudder thinking about it.

"That's highly unusual," he says. "I'll look into it."

Kai brings me a plate of food—marshmallows and chocolate and three packages of Life Force. "Thank you," I say, as I down all the Life Force and stuff my face with the rest.

He laughs. "I found Corinne and Wytt."

I follow him over to a table where Corinne is eating and chatting with Wytt, Jaden and Lana. I'm happy to see all of my friends safe and back in time.

Wytt looks up at us and smiles. "Thanks a lot for leaving me alone with Garin. He's a real charmer."

Kai and I take seats, and I ask," How did everyone else do?"

"I found Jaden and Lana and we teamed up," says Corinne.

Jaden nods. "Our girl here had all the Boons. A first aid kit, a dagger and an encrypted map that Lana deciphered. We've been back since yesterday."

Lana looks over at a table where one guy I never knew well sits alone. "Not everyone did so well. He used his flare."

I frown, feeling bad for him.

"But I can't believe Bartholomew died," Lana says. "And you were there."

I nod. "It was awful."

Garin passes us with a plate of food, and Corinne calls out to him. "I'm sorry about Bartholomew. I know he was your friend."

Garin bares his teeth at her. "He wasn't my friend. And just to be clear, neither are any of you. It was only about survival."

He stomps away, and I'm not sure who I feel worse for, the guy who died, or Garin, who will spend his life forever angry and alone.

Kai puts his arm around my shoulders, and I lean into him. We share a look and communicate so much. He knows. He knows me and he loves me. All of me.

That alone is worth all of this.

THE RIVER HOUSE

Trial celebrations last the whole weekend. Even the death of one of our classmates isn't enough to stifle the cheer. Probably because he was a jerk to everyone and no one liked him. I'm not glad Bart's dead. I don't think anyone is, but it doesn't weigh on my soul.

And so we spend a few days attending parties and having fun. The only damper happens when Bart's family comes to collect his belongings. There's no body, since the beast ate it, and his father shouts at the Chancellor so loud it travels through the Castle as he demands some kind of recompense for the death of his precious son.

They leave empty handed, and life returns to normal.

We all attend a congratulatory ceremony in the Main Hall. There are now eighteen of us left from the original twenty.

"Each quarter you will lose more," my grandfather tells us, "until the end, when only the true Knights shall remain."

We leave, relieved that we have a few weeks off before this crazy starts again.

While a few of our classmates have left for their respective homes for the holidays, most have stayed in New York to attend the Tournament Festival after Christmas. The way Wytt tells it, the entire week between Christmas and New Year's is an epic celebration of chivalry, revelry and wonder not to be missed, culminating in the final Tournament battle and a New Year's Ball.

Kai and I are going together, of course, and this time we are coordinating. I'm having a dress made in his house colors, with black and gold and accents of black feathers. It's going to be stunning.

A few days before Christmas, Corinne ropes us into helping decorate the Initiate Hall.

Wytt is grumbling as he strings lights over the fireplace. "Isn't there a staff for this?"

"You're such a scrooge," she says, smiling. "This is fun."

He glares at her. "For you, maybe."

But in the end, the hall is a winter wonderland, and we all agree it was worth the work as we sit around drinking hot cocoa and talking about our plans for the holidays.

"We should do something fun," Wytt says, his arm draped over Lana's shoulders. They're still close, even if they're not dating.

"Like what?" Jaden asks.

Wytt shrugs. "How about a cabin? Just the six of us. We could bring a tree, exchange gifts, go sledding, sing carols and drink spiked eggnog. It will be epic."

Corinne grins. "That actually does sound fun. Let's do it. Kai, Scarlett, you in?"

I look to Kai, who smiles. "I'm in if Scarlett's in."

I nod. "Sounds fun. Where do we want to go?"

Wytt clicks on his eGlass and opens his laptop. "I'm on it." After a few moments of mumbling and typing he looks up. "I've booked us the perfect place." He smiles and clears his throat, to indicate he's getting his *speaking voice* on. "In the heart of the Catskill Mountain, outside the Village of Athens, through the deep old growth forest of Shakespeare on the Hudson, on the majestic Hudson River, lives the Hudson River House. An eleven-bedroom, six-bathroom mansion that will be home to our first Christmas together."

He closes his laptop, satisfied.

"When do we leave?" Jaden asks.

"Tomorrow morning," Wytt says.

We are all packed and ready the next morning. Zorin isn't happy I'm leaving for the weekend, but while I wait for more details on Crixus' plans, there's not much for Nightfall to do, and I'm only going to be gone a few days. I need a break.

Wytt has secured a limousine to drive us there. I guess being a Prince has its advantages. We climb in as the driver loads our bags into the trunk. For three hours we talk, laugh, drink and eat. Some of us also kissed. There's a lot of happy.

The mansion is everything Wytt promised and more, with a hot tub, pool, rooms enough for everyone to have two if they want, and a huge fireplace and gourmet kitchen.

"Who's cooking this weekend?" Lana asks.

Wytt rolls his eyes. "My dear Lana, do you not know me at all?"

Corinne laughs. "In her defense, she's never seen you cook."

"Fair enough," he says as he runs his hands over the marble kitchen counters. "But let me assure you, your culinary delights are handled."

Kai looks at me and winks and I blush. It's so strange, being around someone who knows the truth. Until now, Zorin was the only one who knew both sides of me, and it's different with him. I'm still mostly Nightfall with Zorin.

But with Kai, I'm Scarlett. I'm me. But I'm also her.

Since the Trial, we have grown so much closer. We've spent nearly every moment we can together. I have no secrets from him now, and he never had any from me. We talk about everything. I told him about my parents' death, about what happened after. I shared my deepest fears about being Nightfall, about the cost, the risks. I tried to warn him away from me, but he held on tight and shook his head. "You can't scare me away. I know what I'm getting into, and I accept the risks. You are worth the risks."

There's also been a fair share of kissing, I'll admit. But we will still be in our own bedrooms this weekend.

We all choose our rooms and unpack and Wytt starts whipping up something for dinner while Kai pops open a bottle of champagne. He pours a glass for each of us and we all toast. "To us," he says. "For surviving. To our friendship. To our futures." He holds my gaze as he says this and clinks glasses with me.

I smile and sip, happy to note that it tastes good. Fizzy and fun.

After dinner, which I'm sure was exquisite, but which tasted like cardboard to me, we venture out to buy a Christmas tree. "We can't do our gift exchange tomorrow without one," Corinne argues.

It's Christmas Eve, and there aren't a lot of options left, but we find the perfect one to fill our temporary living room. The guys insist on dragging it in and setting it up by themselves, and we all decorate it with baubles we bought at the store next to the Christmas lot.

When it's all set up, Kai hands me a box. I raise an eyebrow and open it. It's a silver star for the top of the tree.

He whispers in my ear. "I know that's your nickname. I wanted to get an Angel, but I figured I should be a little more subtle."

I kiss his cheek. "Thank you. It's beautiful."

He gives me a boost so I can reach the top to place the star, and then we plug in the lights. They twinkle white and gold.

Soft instrumental music plays in the background as we sip more champagne and tell stories of each of our Christmas traditions and memories. It's enlightening hearing how my friends grew up, with their different cultures, countries and traditions. But there's a spirit that binds us together, that makes all of this feel somehow familiar. Familial even. We belong together, the six of us. We fit.

It's late as Kai and I sit on the floor in front of the fireplace. Everyone else is in the game room playing pool, but we choose a few quiet moments alone instead.

I run a finger along Kai's jaw. "You seem...melancholy. You okay?"

Fire reflects in his purple eyes as he stares into the flames. "My mother died on Christmas Eve," he says. "Did I tell you that?"

My breath hitches. "No, you didn't."

He looks at me, his face a mask. "Have you ever had to kill someone? As Nightfall?"

I blink. "Not directly. But in a way."

"It does something to you," he says, looking back at the flames. "Taking a life with your own hands. It changes you."

"You've had to kill before?"

He nods. "I told you. I killed my mother."

"Oh, Kai. That wasn't your fault. She got sick. Varian never should have made you feel responsible for that."

"She didn't die from the illness," he says.

My heart skips in my chest. "What do you mean?"

"She nursed me back to health and got sick, that part is true. But she didn't die. She recovered. At least...it seemed like she did. We thought everything was back to normal. Until—"

He pauses, pain evident on his face.

"Until?" I ask, softly.

"Until she changed. She started having serious mood swings. Not just happy and sad, but violent. She'd hurt herself or the staff at the castle. My father once found one of the maids in her room, dead. My mother was crying over her body saying 'I'm sorry. I'm so sorry.' It turned out the maid hadn't changed the sheets fast enough and my sweet, kind, gentle mother beat her to death in a rage."

"That's horrible. I'm so sorry."

He nods, still staring at the flames. "My father loved her so much. Too much. He couldn't accept that her mind was lost to us. He clung to her lucid moments and assured everyone it was temporary. That she'd heal."

I can feel something momentous coming, and I hold his hand more tightly.

"She was supposed to have a nurse around the clock to keep her—and others—safe. But the nurse fell asleep on duty one night on Christmas Eve, and my mother snuck out to see us. When she came to the nursery she was normal, happy, our mother again. I ran to her and hugged her. I missed her so much. Corinne and Wytt were still babies—almost toddlers. They were in their crib, and my mother wanted to see them, too."

Kai reaches for his champagne and takes a sip. "She took them both out and held them, singing that song Corinne sang. And then, she changed. Her face disappeared, and in its place was a madwoman full of rage. She dropped both the babies to the ground. They cried, screamed, more from fear than pain. They landed on blankets and weren't badly hurt. She paced the room screaming obscenities at us all. She told the babies to stop crying, but they didn't. And she slapped them both, yelling at them to be quiet. I begged her to stop, to leave them alone. But she wouldn't."

I'm holding my breath as he talks, knowing the worst is still to come.

"When she picked up a heavy wooden toy and held it over them, I knew she would hurt them. Kill them. I couldn't let her do that. I had to protect them both. I used all the strength I had in my nine-year-old body and ran into her. She had her back to a window, and she crashed through it, falling to the ground two stories down."

A tear slides down his cheek, and he takes another drink. "I cried and ran through the castle to where she fell. Pools of blood surrounded her, but she was still alive. Barely. She grasped my hand and begged me to forgive her.

I did. Then, as she died, she made me swear to always protect Wytt and Corinne, no matter what."

We sit in silence for a long time. As the fire dies, Kai moves to add more wood. "That's why I don't fight in the tournaments."

"What?"

"You asked once why I don't fight in tournaments. This is the real answer. I don't ever want to kill again, unless I have to. I fight to protect, not for sport."

"I understand," I say.

He sits down and looks at me. "Please don't tell Corinne and Wytt. They don't know. They think she died from sickness. That's what everyone believes. It would crush them if they knew the truth."

"Your secret is safe with me."

...

The next morning we all wake excited to find Christmas presents under the tree. Jaden, who woke up first to bake, passes around a plate of ginger cookies shaped like hearts, stars and goats. The house smells like a ginger cookie factory.

"These are pepparkakor," he says, holding up a cookie. "They're a Christmas tradition in my country."

I eat one and am sad to discover this doesn't make my short list of yummy foods. Kai sneaks my other cookies from my plate to his. "I've got your back," he says with a wink.

"Such a Prince," I tease. "Making a sacrifice like that."

Corinne scoots near the tree and starts passing out everyone's gifts. We drew names for our gift exchange, a first for me.

I look at the tag on the beautifully-wrapped silver box in front of me. It's from Corinne, and I smile.

"Who goes first?" Wytt asks, holding up the gift I got him.

"You go," I say.

He rips open the package and groans. "Seriously?" He holds up a book of quotes by the Pope and everyone laughs.

I pull another package from behind the tree. "I couldn't resist," I say. "But here's your real gift."

He smiles and opens it, then gasps. "This?" He runs his hand lightly over the cover of the leather-bound book. "This is..."

Kai nudges me. "Three cheers for Scarlett. The first person in the history of mankind to render our brother speechless."

Wytt grins and holds up the book. "A limited edition book of poetry by Robert Frost. I don't even know how you found this! I've never been able to find one."

"I have my ways," I say. Actually, Carter has his ways. He helped me find the book, but of course I can't say that. I just smile, happy he likes it.

"You go next, Scarlett," Corinne says.

I nod and carefully open my present. My breath hitches as I pull a painting out of the package. It's of me and Kai together. We're sitting in the Castle Courtyard with our swords to our side, my head on his shoulder. "I remember when this happened," I say. "But...how did you see us, let alone capture all the details so perfectly."

She grins. "I have my ways, too."

I lean over to hug her. "This is amazing."

Corinne opens her gift from Lana next. It's an old record player with real records. She holds one up, staring at it wide-eyed. "These don't exist anymore."

Lana smiles. "It's been in my family for generations, but no one ever plays it. I know you love music, and I thought you'd get better use out of it than we have."

"Oh my goodness," she says. "This is incredible."

She taps her eGlass to turn off the music currently playing and plugs in the record player, choosing the first record on the pile. I've never heard anything like this. It's got a grainy quality that should sound bad, but somehow gives the music an added dimension missing from digital music.

The record plays as Lana opens her gift from Kai. I already know what it is, and I'm excited to see her expression when she figures it out.

At first glance, it's an expensive Eden Fashionable bracelet, a beautiful flower. She puts it on, admiring it. "It's lovely, Kai. Thank you."

He leans over and shows her something. "Push that, carefully."

She does, and a deadly blade releases from under her wrist. "Oh my!"

"I had it made for you," he says. "Beautiful on the outside, but deadly and never to be underestimated."

There are tears in her eyes when she looks up. "Thank you," she says.

There's so much power in being seen, in truly knowing that someone sees you and knows you. Kai didn't give her a bracelet for Christmas, he gave her something so much more. He saw her. I squeeze his hand, this man who is so amazing.

This man I am starting to fall in love with.

Kai looks at his gift from Jaden and shakes it. Jaden laughs. "Just open it," he says.

He does, revealing a raven carved from a polished black wood with something gold sparkling inside.

"That's wood from an Onyx Tree," Jaden explains. "It's a rare tree found only in my country and protected by the royal family. Very few people even know it exits. It's nearly extinct, but I had a small piece gifted to me as a child. I've been waiting for the right thing to make. The wood wanted to be carved into a raven."

Kai clutches it in his hands. "It's beautiful. Thank you."

Jaden opens his gift last and slaps his leg at what Wytt gave him.

Wytt grins. "It's a starter tree for another rare tree," Wytt says. "It grows multiple fruits year round. This hybrid isn't for sale, but I have some connections."

"I've heard of these and wanted one very much," says Jaden, caressing his pot. "Thank you."

As everyone settles in to read, talk, eat more cookies, or just relax, Kai pulls me outside. We walk around the snow-covered hills toward the Hudson River. "I had to get a gift for you," he says, pulling out a small box.

"Me first." I hand him a box, and he smiles and opens it. Inside is a knitted black scarf with a gold raven on it. "I know it's not much, but I made it myself. It's the first time I've tried to knit, and the last."

He laughs and wraps it around his throat. "I will cherish it always."

He hands me the small box. "Your turn."

I pull the red bow off and open it. Inside is a black pearl wrapped in white gold and diamond swirls, like a tiny universe. I pull it out, and Kai helps me put it on.

"This is beautiful."

"It reminded me of you," he says. "Nightfall trying to hold the world together. Nox Aeterna."

Tears sting my eyes, and I reach up to kiss him when my eGlass beeps. "Scarlett," says Evie.

"Not now." I mumble through his warm lips.

"It's urgent. Zorin needs you. The Red Eagles want to meet."

"Tell him I'm busy," I say, still trying to salvage the mood.

"You'll have to tell him yourself. He's waiting for you behind the house you're staying at."

I look up at Kai, who can only hear my side of the conversation. "Something wrong?" he asks.

"I have to go," I say sadly.

"Superhero business?" he asks.

I laugh. "Something like that. I'm sorry."

He kisses my head. "Don't be. I'm a big boy, and I know what being Nightfall means. Go. Do your superhero stuff. I'll cover for you."

I pull at his hand before he walks away, so awash in feelings I have to speak out loud. "Kai!"

He turns, our fingers intertwined. "Yes?"

"I love you."

His smile lights up his face, and he crushes me in a hug against his body. "I love you, too." He kisses me then pulls away. "Now go save the world."

. . .

I meet Crixus at the center of Diamond Mountain. There are no crowds this time. Only Zorin waits in the distance as a cold wind howls through the night.

"What do you know of the approaching Tournament Festival?" asks Crixus, looking at the moon.

His question startles me. I try to recall what I've heard from Wytt. "The Knights are anonymous. Many will attend the final match. The…" I gasp, realizing his plan. "The Pope will attend."

Crixus nods. "Have you seen the Black Knight fight?"

I smile. "He's the one I'm rooting for."

"Good. He is one of ours."

I see where this is going. I'm impressed.

Crixus continues, "When he wins, he will be granted a Boon from the Pope. He will request a personal meeting with His Holiness."

"And you want me to be at that meeting?"

He nods. "You will don the Black Knight's armor. You will get close to the Pope, and you will give him an order."

I frown, noticing a problem. "My gift doesn't last very long. He won't join our side."

"He doesn't need to. You will order His Holiness to commit suicide."

I grit my teeth. To kill someone who is not posing me danger…even if I could…"What would that accomplish? Someone else will just take his place."

"We have an agent amongst the Cardinals," says Crixus. "We will make certain he is elected as the new Pope."

"Who is it?"

"Forgive me, but I cannot say. If our plan was to fail…"

275

"Then I'd be captured."

"Yes, and I would rather have our agent's identity a secret." He holds out his hand. "So, do you agree?"

I pause. This plan can give me access to the most powerful person on earth. This plan can end this war years before I imagined. This plan can change everything. But there is something I must know. "Why do you fight against the Orders?"

Crixus drops his hand. He sits on a stone, drawing circles in the dust. "When the war began, my parents supported the Nephilim in secret. They understood there was no reason for the fighting, only a reason for a strong leader to keep the peace." His voice loses its normal calm, turning to rage. "They were discovered, and they were executed. I will not forget what they taught me. I will find the leader they spoke of. And I will bring peace."

He follows his parents, as I do. I hold out my hand. "Perhaps together we can be that leader. Perhaps together we can bring peace."

"Perhaps." He shakes my hand.

I grip his hand harder. "No one but the Pope must be harmed."

"Other than the White Knight, no one else will be." He lets go of my hand and walks away.

I join Zorin on the podium to explain our plan.

He doesn't respond for a while. When he does, he doesn't face me. "If it's between killing the Pope or staying alive, stay alive."

I touch his face with my hand, turning his head toward mine. "I will."

. . .

When I return to the cabin, I can tell the mood has shifted, and it's my fault.

I enter, kicking snow off my boots at the door, when Corinne grabs my hand and pulls me back outside.

"What's going on?" she asks.

"I just needed some time alone," I say. "I'm sorry. I didn't mean to spoil the fun."

She does this cute scrunched up thing with her face that makes her look like an angry puppy, and I resist the urge to laugh.

"Scarlett, I know there's something more." She tugs at a strand of red hair. "And I know for whatever reason you can't, or won't, tell me. But my brother is in love with you. And I don't want to see him hurt."

My heart has felt so much lighter since the Trial, since Kai found out about me and still accepted me. But I hate lying to my other friends. It hurts them, and it hurts me. I put a hand on her shoulder. "I promise I won't hurt him. I love him, too."

Her eyes light up. "You do?"

I nod. "I already told him. We are official. We were going to tell you this weekend."

She squeals and hugs me while jumping up and down. "That's the best thing I've heard in a long time." She pulls away, still smiling. "And you're happy?"

I smile big this time. "I am. Very happy."

"And he's happy?"

I laugh. "I sure hope so."

She squeals again. "We are so totally going to be sisters-in-law someday. I can feel it."

I can't help but hope she's right as we head into the den of warmth and holiday cheer and Kai hugs and kisses me. He tastes like peppermint.

For the first time since my parents died, I feel like I could be happy. Truly happy.

THE WHITE KNIGHT

When we return from the cabin, I make excuses, kiss Kai goodbye and fly to the Cathedral.

When I enter, I'm greeted by Carter, who is weaving fragrant garland and white blinking Christmas lights over the bannister. The rest of the Cathedral could pass for Santa's Workshop, with lights, a huge tree, and decorations everywhere.

"Wow, it looks amazing," I tell him.

He smiles. "Thank you, miss. Everyone's in the War Room waiting for you."

"You should join us," I say. I hold up my bag of gifts. "One of these is for you."

He tilts his head, an unreadable expression on his face. "For me?"

"Yes, of course. It's Christmas, after all."

"I don't believe anyone has ever given me a holiday gift before," he says.

"Really? That's awful." I reach for his hand. "Come, join us."

I lead him up the stairs. "By the way," I say, "I realized I never properly thanked you for my apartment."

"You thanked me when I gave you the key," he says.

"But I didn't thank you after seeing it. I don't know how you did it, but that's the apartment of my dreams."

He bows his head. "I'm glad it pleases you, miss."

We enter the War Room. There's another Christmas tree with blinking lights and a glowing angel at the top. On a table near the tree is another angel, this one spun from colored glass and surrounded by baby angels. "What's that?"

Carter walks over. "That is Lilith and her children."

"They sell these in stores?" I ask, shocked.

Carter chuckles. "No, I made it."

"Beautiful."

I walk over to the table, which is laden with cookies, drinks...and two goblets of blood. Zorin is raising one to his lips, the other is placed in front of the seat next to him.

I sit and sniff the contents. "I take it this one is for me?"

"I don't think TR or Trix would particularly enjoy it," he says.

Trix turns from the Christmas tree and smiles. "He's right about that. But you two come over here. It's time!"

TR turns on Christmas music, and we all move to sit around the fireplace as we exchange gifts. "Me first," I say, passing out boxes wrapped in reindeer paper. "You have to open them at the same time."

They all tear into their gifts, and Zorin holds his up first, a small frown on his face. "Pajamas?"

I nod, smiling. "Look at the shirt. Nox Aeterna. And the bottoms are made of silk."

He shakes his head. "I cannot wear this to bed."

"Why not?" I ask.

He looks at me, a sly grin on his face. "Because I don't sleep in pajamas."

It takes a moment to catch his meaning, and I blush. "You can wear them around the Cathedral then," I say. "For casual days."

He looks at me as if the concept of casual days is repulsive to him, and I laugh.

TR pets his pajamas and smiles. "So silky, so soft. I can't wait to put these on. Thanks, Nightfall."

Trix grins at TR and holds the shirt up to her chest. "I love it. Thank you."

Carter is still acting oddly, his face a perplexing combination of sadness and happiness. "I am speechless. I will treasure this always. Thank you."

"It's a tradition in my family," I explain. "Or was… each year my parents would buy me new pajamas for Christmas." I clear my throat. I've tried not to think about how this is my first Christmas without them. It's too hard. "You're my family now," I tell them. "So I wanted to share this tradition with you."

Zorin reaches over to put his hand on mine. "Thank you."

I nod, swiping away a tear. Zorin hands me a gift wrapped in black sparkly paper with a silver bow. "From all of us."

I open it and smile. Inside is a new cloak, black with silver hem, black leggings and a black tunic with a silver tree of life embroidered on the chest. The material is soft, light, exquisite. Eden Fashionables. "You had this made? For me?"

Zorin nods. "We did."

Trix grins. "It can't be comfortable wearing your full armor here all the time. We thought this might help."

"There's more," says TR.

I pull out a long black gown embroidered with the silver tree.

Zorin smiles. "In case you ever feel like wearing a dress."

"It's...stunning. Thank you all so much." I fold everything and put it back in the box as Zorin hands me a small black pouch.

"This is from me," he says.

I open it and find a tiny silver cylinder.

"Turn around," says Zorin.

I raise an eyebrow, but do as he says, turning away from everyone.

Zorin touches my mask and gently begins to remove it.

"What are you doing?"

"Trust me," he whispers, his breath on my neck.

I nod, and he finishes removing my mask. He installs the cylinder onto my eGlass. He clicks the top.

And a thin mask stretches over the top of my face.

I grin, turning back to my friends. "How's this possible?"

Trix relaxes in her chair. "It took some modification of the current EZ technology, but it wasn't too hard."

"Thank you all. These are amazing."

Carter excuses himself to bring us more refreshments, and Trix and TR leave to try on their pajamas. Zorin stays with me, his eyes distant.

"I don't like you going to the tournament alone," he says. "I should be there."

"You and the other Dark Templars would be recognized," I say. "It's going to be fine. I'll watch the tournament with everyone else, and when it's time to face the Pope, I'll be in full armor. I'll be okay."

He turns to me and grips my hand. "I hope you're right, Scarlett. I can't lose you."

. . .

A few days after Christmas, the festival begins. Lottery winners all over the world arrive at the island, partaking in the exclusive events. They purchase replicas of ancient swords at the market. They view exotic animals at the zoo. A mime follows unsuspecting visitors, changing into different colors. A Zenith juggles fireballs. A lady selling black market puppies engineered with wings argues with an Officer. There is no end to the entertainment.

Wytt drags me to some of the events, but mostly I avoid the commotion. Soon, the Pope will arrive, and I will have to face him. My stomach turns at the thought.

And it's what I think of most.

At the week's end, the tournament begins. Thousands of people file into the arena which, while always impressive, is now doubly so with colorful flags positioned throughout and banners draped over rock and stone. "How will the people at the top see anything?" I ask Wytt as we search for seats.

"They'll watch it on the screen."

"What screen?"

His eyes light up. "You'll see."

We pass all kinds of people. Some dressed in armor, some dressed in Eden Fashionables, and some wearing nothing but underwear, their bodies painted in white and black.

The siblings dress in elegant clothing fit for royalty. Corrine wears a stylish pink and white gown, while Kai and Wytt wear gold and black vests. Kai's sword hangs on his hip. It's for the cameras, they tell me. Since I'll likely be on those cameras as well, I'm wearing my fanciest jeans. As one who is dating the Prince of Ravens, I have responsibilities.

My friends and I find the special area reserved for royalty and guests. We're near the bottom and will see all the action up close. To our right, a part of the arena juts forward, offering the best seats of all. "Will the Pope be there?" I ask.

Wytt nods. "Along with his personal guard and guests."

My grandfather, who is in a special booth for the Grandmasters and Order leaders, waves me toward him. I excuse myself and weave through the crowds.

"Are you enjoying the festivities?" he asks.

"It's amazing," I say, my stomach full of fluttering butterflies.

"I haven't had a chance to speak with you in some time, but I wanted to let you know I looked into the situation with the creature who attacked you and your friends."

He has my full attention. "What did you find out?"

He shakes his head, his long white hair parted and wrapped in leather strips. "Not much, I'm afraid. There's a top secret government research facility on the island, and they confirmed that just before the Trial, one of their... specimens...escaped. They haven't confirmed how, but it matches what you described. It could be an unfortunate coincidence."

I narrow my eyes at him. "I don't think you believe that. And besides, you weren't there. You didn't see how laser-focused it was on Kai. It was sent to hunt him. It was no coincidence."

He nods with a small frown. "I was afraid you would say that. I will keep looking into it. Now go, enjoy the show."

"Thank you, Grandfather."

I head back to my seat as a battle begins below us. This isn't the final fight, but entertainment while people are seated. A projection appears on the other side of the arena, showing the Blue and Red Knights fighting. It's using the people and seats as its canvas. It's the largest display I've ever seen.

"Amazing, huh?" asks Wytt.

I nod.

An hour passes, and the Pope arrives, the crowd standing as he is seated. The entertainment ends.

The Black and White Knights emerge, and the people explode with cheers. These two are amongst the greatest fighters in the world and have made it to the championship. To most, they represent the pinnacle of society, the heroes children strive to be. To me, they are pawns in a much greater game.

I try not to think of their families and friends. This fight is to death or yielding, and no one has yielded in years. One of the Knights will die, and it must be the White.

The competitors march to the center of the arena. They both wear heavy plate and wield giant blades the size my body. I nudge Kai, who sits beside me. "Their swords remind me of yours."

He nods. "Their sponsors provide them with the best equipment possible, and these two have accrued many sponsors."

"Who do you think will win?" I ask, remembering that Kai is good enough to compete himself.

"The White Knight," he says.

Wytt *tsk*s beside us. "So sad that you are wrong, brother. The Black Knight exceeds in form."

"But not in discipline," says Kai. "He knows more techniques, but his foundation is weaker."

"Care to place a bet?"

Kai shakes his head.

Wytt rolls his eyes.

I sigh, hoping Kai is wrong. For if the White Knight wins, our plan fails. I message Crixus.

Remember, no one must be harmed.

He responds verbally. "Have I not earned your trust yet?"

The Pope stands, covered in a white hood and robe. He lifts his arms and addresses the crowd. "May the games begin."

A horn blares through the arena.

The Black Knight dashes at the White, striking with no pause. His assault is relentless, driving the White to the edge of the arena.

Wytt grins at Kai. "Still confident in your predictions, brother?"

Kai shrugs.

Corrine's eyes are glued to the match. "They're so fast."

I nod. If I'd never seen Varian and Zorin fight, I'd think faster was impossible.

The White Knight spins around the Black, reversing their positions. Now, he is on the offensive. His strikes are precise. His footwork impeccable.

I understand what Kai meant. The Black Knight is ferocious, but that ferocity works against him. The White Knight is calm and collected. He is like the mountain against the storm. The mountain always wins.

I message Crixus.

It's not looking good.

He doesn't respond.

The Knights lock swords and push each other away. They both take a moment to circle each other, resting. The crowd roars for more.

Crixus responds. He sounds winded. "Don't worry. The match has been adjusted in our favor."

How?

The White Knight begins to attack, but his strikes are sloppier, easily deflected.

"Looks like he's getting tired," says Wytt.

I message Crixus.

He's poisoned.

The Black Knight kicks the White back.

Crixus responds. "Like I said, don't worry. He won't last long." He sounds happy and tired. His responses have come slowly. My breath hitches as I realize what's happening.

You're the Black Knight.

He laughs in response, and the Black Knight strikes again.

Kai grips my arm. "The Black Knight…" he says, his eyes focused. "The way he fights…"

"What?" I ask.

He frowns. "I'll tell you later. When I'm sure."

I turn my attention to the fight. I hate that it isn't fair, but I'm glad our plan is secure.

The White Knight begins to stumble. He's struck in the shoulder. He falls to his knees. The poison must be taking hold.

The Black Knight, Crixus, pauses, soaking in the applause.

My friends don't smile. I wonder if they sense something is wrong.

Kai sneers. "The better man loses."

The Black Knight raises his sword for a final strike.

And the White Knight lunges forward, splitting his own blade into two. He spins, driving the Black Knight back. The arena shakes as the crowd stomps their feet and screams.

The White Knight strikes the Black twice. He is faster. Stronger. He was the mountain, but now he is the avalanche. He is unstoppable.

How could this be happening?

Who is this man who can ruin our plan?

The way he fights…

It can't be.

I whisper. "Evie, zoom in on the White Knight."

She does. And then I see it.

I gasp, shaking.

Kai grabs my shoulder. "Scarlett, what's wrong?"

"I know…I know who the White Knight is."

"Who?"

Tears build in my eyes. "He wears pilot wings on his collar. He left us to train. He left us to fight," I whisper. "Jax is the White Knight."

Corrine jumps in her chair. Wytt drops his jaw. Kai's eyes fill with sorrow. Then awe. "He's…he's incredible."

"He is," I say.

The White Knight lands a strike, knocking the Black to the ground. All he needs is a final blow. He raises his swords. He hesitates. The poison.

Crixus slashes Jax's arm, slicing through the armor. The White Knight stumbles back. He falls to his knees.

This is it.

I must choose. Jax or Crixus.

There is no choice.

"Evie, hack Crixus' eGlass. Distract him with something loud."

She does, and the Black Knight grabs his ears.

Jax can barely stand, but stand he does. He charges forward.

And rams his sword into Crixus' side.

The Black Knight collapses, bleeding onto the sand. He holds up his hand. On the projection, I see he holds up two fingers. The old symbol for surrender.

The crowd gasps. Then cheers.

Jax removes his helmet. His brown hair falls in his eyes. He smiles.

And everyone is silent. Murmurs spread. *"A Zenith?"* *"I never thought...he was incredible."* The Pope rises, quieting all.

"Kneel, Sir Jaxton Lux, Champion of Vianney. And tell me, what do you wish for your Boon?"

He kneels. "I desire to be a Knight of the Third."

"Granted. Now rise—"

"And I desire a title and lands."

The crowd gasps. A second Boon. He asks too much.

The projection shows the Pope, his face young and cold. He grins. "So be it. You shall no longer be Sir Jaxton Lux, Knight of the Fourth, but Lord Jaxton of the House of Argent, Knight of the Third, Champion of Vianney. Rise, White Knight."

He rises.

And the crowd erupts in cheers.

Jax raises his sword. "Upon my land, I shall build an Academy. And there, all Zeniths will be welcome to train and master their abilities. All Zeniths will be treated as people. Because it is what all Zeniths deserve."

As the cheers continue, I study the royalty and grandmasters around me. Most look stunned. Ragathon is seething. But Varian...Varian nods, a proud look in his eyes.

And I realize, he was Jax's first sponsor.

Few of the royalty appear to share his view. But this fight wasn't for them. This fight was for the people. Thousands of them fill the seats. And they begin to chant.

"All Zeniths. All Zeniths."

I wonder if they believe their words, or are they so easily persuaded by charisma.

And then their chant changes.

"Jax. Jax. Jax."

He's doing it. He's rising up the ranks, and he's changing the world.

I smile and meet his eyes.

For the first time, he notices me. He grins.

And then he collapses, shaking.

I jump from my seat. The poison isn't done.

Crixus begins to stand. He talks into my eGlass. "This isn't over. We can still win. Red Eagles, these people have lost their way. Destroy them."

Explosions tear apart the arena, blowing the people across from me into bits of flesh and bone. Soldiers of black and red jump from the roof, slowing down with thrusters. They land in the sand and begin to fire.

Crixus stands over Jax. He places a blade at his throat. He speaks, his voice amplified for all to hear. "Goodbye, Lord Jax of the House of Argent. The others of your kind will soon join you."

He raises his sword.

And Kai jumps into the arena. His blade extends into a whip, yanking Crixus toward him.

The Black Knight twists free and counterstrikes.

Kai blocks.

And they fight.

. . .

I am surrounded by smoke and fire and dust and death. I am surrounded by the consequences of my actions. I sided with Crixus. I encouraged him to be the leader his parents dreamed of.

And that leader does not lose.

The Pope disappears into the arena. The Red Eagles jump after him.

I jump after Kai.

The people I care for will not suffer because of me.

Kai and Crixus trade strikes. Crixus is injured, but Kai has no proper armor. They are matched.

"Evie, hack Crixus' eGlass again."

"I can't," she says. "He's disabled it."

Then I have to fight.

Dust and smoke spiral around me, clouding my vision.

I stop at Jax. He's trembling, but he's alive. I grab one of his swords, and charge at Crixus.

The Black Knight spins away, striking me with an armored fist. I fall to the sand. Kai attempts to take advantage, but Crixus blocks in time. Kai strikes again, driving him back.

I need to help, but they are far more skilled fighters, and my ability won't work through the Black Knight's thick armor. I need another weapon.

I find a fallen Red Eagle.

I grab their gun and aim at Crixus.

I fire.

The Black Knight's shoulder plate explodes, and he stumbles back. Kai charges, ready to strike.

He stops.

His eyes narrow at something through the dust.

A Red Eagle.

Holding a blade to Corrine's throat. Her dress is torn and blood-splattered, her eyes an inky mess from tears and makeup, but she doesn't look harmed. Not yet.

"Let her go," yells Kai.

"Drop your sword," says Crixus.

No. This can't be happening.

No.

Kai drops his sword.

"You were always so loved by everyone, Prince of Ravens," says Crixus. He raises his hand.

And the Red Eagle slices Corrine's throat.

A thin red line forms on her pale flesh, spreading as she crumbles to the ground, her head flopping back at an unnatural angle.

Pain claws its way out of my throat as a primal scream.

"Now," says Crixus. "It's my turn."

He lifts his sword.

And runs it through Kai's heart.

Brother and sister lay in the sand. Their hands reach for each other as blood pools around them. As the life leaves their eyes. As death claims them.

I fall to my knees, weeping. Emotions overwhelm me. Rage for Crixus. Sorrow for Kai and Corrine. Disgust at myself and what I have wrought.

Crixus gestures to his soldier, and they disappear into the smoke and dust. Nothing can be seen around us through the billows of brown clouds.

There is still something I can do.

An impossible choice stands before me. One I must make in between heartbeats. Save Kai, or save Corrine.

293

I can't save them both.

Whichever choice I make will weigh on my heart forever.

I look over to Kai, who has fallen. Is dying. And I hear his voice in my head. In my heart. *I came here to protect them. To protect Corinne, especially. She's the best of us all. I would give my life for her.*

And I know the choice I have to make. The choice that will break me.

I turn away from Kai and run to Corinne. I save the person he would want me to save. And I let Kai die.

AFTERMATH

I am not injured. My body isn't, at any rate. My heart, well, I will have to think about my heart later. I can't process what I've done. I can't hold that level of loss in my mind right now. I would break, and too many people are hurt. I can't break right now. I try to block out what just happened.

The choice.

The blood.

The taste of Corinne's life on my lips as I chose her, saved her, left Kai. I went back for him, but it was too late. Even my powers couldn't bring him to life. But at least I found Jax alive, if unconscious. He was taken away, taken to heal. I tried to help in whatever ways I could, finding those hurt or injured, getting help to those who needed it. Now that things are settling, now that the Pope is safe and the area secured, I have to find my friends. I need to know they are okay.

The Infirmary has spilled out into the courtyard as the injured take up more beds than the room can hold.

But Corinne, Wytt and Jax are inside. They are the only people I care about right now.

As I walk through the beds, stepping around busy Hospitallers trying to treat all the wounded, I click on my eGlass. "Evie, get me Zorin."

"Are you okay?" he says.

"Physically, yes. The rest will have to wait. First, you need to organize the Dark Templars to find Crixus."

"Already done," Zorin says. "But he's disappeared, gone into hiding. We can't track him."

I want to punch something. "Okay, keep trying and keep me posted. I have to go."

I click off my eGlass and walk into the Infirmary. I see Corinne sitting up on a stretcher drinking some Life Force. She's going to be drinking a lot of that now. This isn't the time to tell her. I don't know when will be the time, but not now.

I walk over and hug her. "Are you okay?" I ask.

"Miraculously, yes," she says. "I know this sounds crazy, but I thought...I just have this feeling that I was hurt a lot worse. But I seem to be okay." She places a small hand over her throat, which is covered in a gauzy white bandage.

"It looked a lot worse," I lie. "The cut didn't go deep. It should heal fast."

Her eyes fill with tears. "Scarlett, how could this happen? I don't understand. How could Kai..."

She can't finish the sentence, and I don't blame her. I'm not ready to cry. I can't. So I hug her again and sit next to her on the bed. "I know. I know."

She sniffs. "Wytt's okay. He's hurt, but not horribly. He's flirting with all the nurses of course." She kind of laughs, though I can see it hurts her heart. I kind of smile. We will all kind of be okay, and kind of not. Because how are you ever okay after something like this? "I think he can't accept what happened to Kai yet. He's not ready."

I nod. I'm not ready either. "Have you heard anything about Jax?" I ask.

She shakes her head. "They aren't telling us much. And they aren't letting me or Wytt go, even though these beds would be better used for someone truly injured." She glares at the staff bustling around. "Just because of our royal blood. We don't deserve special treatment."

I kiss her forehead. "Just rest. Everyone who needs a bed, has one." I have no idea if that's true or not, but it seems to make her feel better.

"I need to find Jax," I say, squeezing her hand. "Will you be all right?"

She shrugs. "I guess we all have to be all right now. Don't we?"

I nod. "I guess so. I'll check on you soon."

It takes me a good twenty minutes of panic-induced searching to find Jax. Corinne was right that no one's being forthcoming with any information. When I do track him down, he's in his own room and is still unconscious, from the poison or injury I can't tell.

"Evie," I say to my eGlass, "can you hack into the medical records and find me anything on Jax's condition?"

"I've tried, but they aren't using the database. It seems in the chaos, they are using paper charts."

"Great."

I lay my hand on his, my heart torn apart. "I can't lose you, too," I tell him.

Tears flow then. I can't stop them. I rest my head gently on his chest to hear his heartbeat. It does, strong and rhythmic and my tears spill onto his chest, bandaged up and covered.

"Be well, okay?" I run a finger over his forehead, pushing aside a strand of hair. "I need you."

I stand and walk toward the door when I hear his scratched voice call out my name.

"Scarlett?"

I turn, tears still falling down my cheeks. "Jax?"

I run back over to his bed and hold his hand. He pushes himself up and wipes a tear from my cheek. "I'm okay."

He pulls me into a hug, and I try not to squeeze too hard. "I missed you."

He speaks into my hair, holding my head in his hands. "I missed you too, Star."

...

I spend the next two days hovering over the people I love but also wishing I could disappear and be alone. I'm watching Corinne constantly, looking for signs of her transformation, trying to think of how to tell her what I did. And what it cost us all.

We're sitting in the dining hall. I'm sipping a Life Force and watching Corinne, who pushes food around on her plate. Wytt leans in. "You sick?"

She shrugs. "Just not hungry."

"You have to try," he says. "We all have to try."

He's not just talking about eating. A piece of us is missing. We all feel it. Jaden and Lana bring their trays over and join us, but don't say much. The mood everywhere at Castle V is somber.

My eGlass buzzes in my ear, and Evie's voice alerts me to a new message. I click to play. It's Trix asking what they should do next. I type a message on my eBand.

Can't talk now. Don't know next step. Need more time alone.

They won't like that answer, but I'm not sure what else to say. I don't know where we go from here. Crixus has disappeared. No one knows where to find him. And I...

I just need time.

Halfway through lunch, Corinne excuses herself to go back to our room. Wytt catches my eye with a worried frown. He stands and holds out his arm. "Walk with me, fair maiden?"

I give a small smile at his attempt at normalcy. "Sure."

I take his arm and we walk through the courtyard. It's still cold, and our feet leave prints in the new snow.

"I'm worried about Corinne," he says. "She's not herself."

"None of us are," I remind him.

He sighs. "That's true."

We walk in silence for a few moments.

"Kai always underestimated his role in our lives," Wytt says. "He was my hero. I wanted to be just like him. I don't think he—"

Wytt's voice catches on his grief, and I squeeze his arm. "He knew," I say. "He knew you loved him. He loved you two more than anything. He would have done anything for you." *He did do anything for you.*

Wytt looks at me with a small smile. "He felt the same about you."

I promise Wytt I'll keep an eye on Corinne, and I head to our shared room.

She's lying in bed staring at the ceiling, a blank sketchbook in her hand, when I arrive.

"Corinne?"

She sits up. "Hey."

I pick up her sketchbook, draw a line with an X through it and hand it to her. "Do you know what this is?"

Her eyes widen. "The Nephilim symbol."

I nod. "There's something I have to tell you."

PRINCESS OF RAVENS

After I finish explaining, Corinne is silent, but a war rages on her face. How could it not?

Her best friend is Nephilim.

And now, she is as well.

I don't know what the future holds for us, but I hope for the best. I hold out my hand. "Let me show you something."

She turns away. "Does anyone else know?"

"Only the one who turned me."

A moment passes.

I remember Zorin's words. It's much harder to fight a friend. I pray I don't have to fight Corrine.

Another moment.

I consider what to do if she decides to turn me in. Do I make her forget this conversation? Do I expose her as Nephilim first?

I tremble, unable to think any further.

Another moment.

Corrine turns back, fire in her purple eyes.

She takes my hand. "Show me. Show me everything."

...

We drive to the Cathedral, and she watches me change into Nightfall before we approach the gates. I hand her my old black mask and an EZ-Dye pack. "You can't go in looking like the Princess of Ravens."

She nods, dons the mask and dyes her hair black like mine. Then she pulls a cloak over her head. "Good enough?"

"Your eyes," I say. "They give you away." I hand her an EZ-Eye.

When she looks up, her eyes are golden. I nod in approval and begin the tour.

First, I show her the houses and where the recruits train on a field with Zorin. I show her where the ground opens up and the Night Raven emerges. The whole time, she doesn't speak.

As we walk down the path, Allen bows at my side and holds out his hand. "A blessing, Darkness."

I touch his palm, and he returns to practicing swordsmanship.

Corrine frowns.

"It's to inspire them," I say.

She doesn't respond.

When we arrive at the Cathedral, she enters first. I start to follow, when Zorin grabs my shoulder. He whispers in my ear, "If she is not with us, she will not leave this place."

"I know."

I follow Corrine inside. She stands before the golden cross. Her hands are clasped in prayer.

"You have heard my story," I say. And I ask her the question Wytt asked me so long ago. The question I have never stopped pondering. "Am I the hero, chosen to save my people, or the monster, destined to destroy them?"

I don't look at her.

For if I look at her, and she rejects me, I will collapse. A part of me will break. Tears build in my eyes.

I do not look.

Corrine touches my hand. "You're my friend, Scarlett. You're my friend." And she holds me.

And we both let the tears flow.

...

"Are you ready to meet the other Dark Templar leaders?" I ask, after our tears have dried and we have sat in silence for some time, lost in our own thoughts. Our own sorrows.

She nods. "I am."

I lead her to our War Room where Trix, TR and Zorin sit around the War Table while Carter serves snacks and Life Force to everyone. "I want you all to meet someone." I gesture for Corrine to come in, and I introduce everyone at the table. "And this is...a friend," I tell everyone. "A new Nephilim."

TR looks up from his powdered donut, and a bit of cherry filling drops from his lips. "New Nephilim? As in just recently found, or made?"

"Made," I say. "To save her life."

"So this is a thing we're doing now?" he asks. "Making Nephilim?" TR looks over at Zorin. "Did you put her up to this?"

I bring my palm down on the table and the sound shuts everyone up. "He didn't put me up to anything, and this does not mean we have a new policy of making

Nephilim. It was an isolated situation that required an immediate action. I made the choice alone, and I alone take full responsibility for her."

"Does she have a name?" Trix asks.

I look over at Corinne. We haven't discussed code names yet.

"Raven," she says, surprising me. "You can call me Raven."

"Nice to meet you, Raven," Trix says, smiling.

TR isn't smiling though. "So another person with a secret identity you can't even share with the group?"

Zorin stands and stares down TR. "Nightfall has to keep her identity a secret from everyone, if she is to accomplish the mission we all share. She is not a known rebel like you and Trix. She is not someone who has long since been forgotten by history like me and Carter. She and Raven have identities outside these walls that help us all with our mission, and thus need to be protected from everyone. Even you."

TR sneers at Zorin. "But you know, don't you? What makes you so special?"

"He saved my life," I say. "He turned me. That is what makes him so special. And I'm done arguing about this, TR. You can stay and accept that some of us have to maintain a secret identity from even our most trusted allies, or you can leave. It's your choice."

I want him to stay. I hope he hears it in my voice. But I will not continue to defend my need to wear a mask.

He sinks back into his chair, exhaling all his rage. "You know I'm in, Nightfall. I don't like the masks, but I'll shut up about it if I have to."

"Thank you, TR." I sit at the table, Zorin to my right, Corinne to my left.

"Do we have any news on Crixus since the Tournament?" I ask, getting down to business.

Corinne flinches next to me. Her throat has healed with only the faintest scar, but the other wounds inflicted that day by the Red Eagles, those won't heal so fast, if they ever do at all.

"Still no word," Trix says. "He's like smoke, vanishing without a trace."

"Have you tracked his money?" Corinne asks. "Rumor has it he's funded by a few underground criminal groups. Dig enough you might find something that could help flush him out."

TR nods, a growing look of respect on his face. "That's not a bad idea. I'll get my people on it."

Corinne nods. "He has to be held accountable for his crimes. And the Dark Templars should publicly disavow any knowledge of what the Red Eagles did that day. You have to set yourself up as something more than just a rebel group."

I smile at her. I've seen Corinne the Healer, Corinne the Friend/Sister/Daughter/Niece. I've seen her as the Student. But I've never seen her as the Heir to the Throne. As the Queen I'm seeing now.

Trix looks at Corinne more closely. "So are you in now? Part of the Dark Templars?"

Corinne looks at everyone in the room, then looks at me. "I'm here for Nightfall. And I'm here to help catch Crixus. What my role is after that will be determined later."

We discuss a few more options for tracking down Crixus, then Carter offers to give Corrine a longer tour and introduce her to others. She looks to me, and I nod. "I'll catch up with you later," I say.

"Okay." She hugs me, then whispers in my ear. "I meant what I said. I'm here for you. Whatever happens, I'm on your side. No matter what."

. . .

Zorin and I walk alone through the long halls to his room. We don't talk, but there is much to be said. I settle into a comfortable chair in front of his fire and Nox meows and leaps onto my lap. I smile and pet him, enjoying the purring warmth under my hand. "Corinne's going to want to see you," I tell the cat. "She's missed you."

Zorin sits next to me and runs his hand over the cat. Our fingers touch, our eyes lock. "Nox missed you," he says softly.

"Just Nox?" Our parallel conversation lacks the light teasing it had once upon a time in New York.

"Not just Nox," he says.

We both continue petting the cat and staring into the fire.

"You created a new Nephilim," he says.

"Yes."

"Does that mean you agree with me?" He looks at me again, his blue eyes so full of...something.

"I don't know. But I agree there are times it is the right and just thing," I say.

"Scarlett, what happened at the arena?"

He's not asking about the politics. Or Crixus. He knows all that. He's asking a far more personal question. One I find hard to answer.

"She would have died. They killed her and Kai. I had to choose." It hurts to speak the words. To acknowledge out loud to another person what I did.

"Why her?" he asks, his voice so quiet I can barely hear him. "Why not Kai? You loved him, did you not?"

Is there pain in his voice? "Yes, I did. I love her, too. He would have wanted her to live. If I'd saved him, he would never have forgiven me, or himself. He once said she was the best of them. She will make a great Queen someday."

Zorin nods. "She will. She has what every truly great ruler should have. Compassion. Empathy. Intelligence. And courage."

"I thought you didn't like the Ravens? I thought you'd be glad Kai is dead."

He grabs my hand and looks into my eyes. "I never wanted this, Scarlett. I never wanted you hurt. I know the pain of losing someone you love. Of feeling responsible for their death. I would never want that for you."

"Your wife, Danika?"

He nods. "What do you want now?" he asks.

"I want to find Crixus. And kill him."

...

I pick up Nox, holding him against my chest, as I go in search of Trix. I find her in the North wing, in her bedroom reading. Her door is open and I knock, then step in. "Am I interrupting you?"

She sits up on her bed and puts her book on the bedside table. "Not at all. Come on in." She pats the end of her bed, and I sit down next to her. Nox squirms out of my hands in order to walk back and forth between the two of us, head nudging us for body rubs.

Trix laughs. "He loves attention, this one. Everyone here dotes on him. I think half the Nephilytes worship him."

I roll my eyes. "Like he needs to be worshipped. He already has a god complex just by being a cat."

"No kidding. They haven't forgotten their former Egyptian glory."

I look around her room. It's the first time I've really been in here. It's spacious, with bookshelves, a bed, a dresser, a desk, a reading chair and a fireplace. There are a few personal touches to brighten up the dark wood furniture: a painting of an Italian landscape, some stacks of books, her laptop. But it's the picture on the dresser that catches my attention. Three happy people with arms around each other lean against a tractor. Trix is in the middle, and TR is to her right. The other man is looking at Trix with a smile. "Is that him?" I ask, pointing to the picture.

She picks up the framed photograph. "That's my Max." She runs her fingers over the image. "Before everything."

Before the war. Before he died. Before life changed for everyone. "He looks a lot like TR," I say.

She nods, still staring at the picture.

"Do you love TR?" I ask.

She looks up, holding the picture to her chest. "Of course. I always have."

"Are you *in love* with him?"

Her breath hitches. "I…It's complicated."

"Because of Max?"

She nods.

"I understand. I just...I recently lost someone I loved. And I didn't let myself love him for a long time, because of someone else. Someone I could never be with, but who still ruled my heart. I wish...I guess I just wish that I'd lived more in the present, with the person who loved me and was there, instead of living in the past with the ghost of someone I once loved but could never have."

A tear falls down her cheek and she looks back at the picture. I put a hand on her knee. "Word of advice from someone who probably shouldn't give advice on love?" I ask.

Trix chuckles, nodding.

"Don't let memories from the past destroy what you have right in front of you."

PRINCE OF RAVENS

It's raining the day of Kai's funeral, and I send up a prayer of thanks. Had the sun shone on a day so void of happiness, I would have cursed the sky for its cruelty. But even Mother Nature knows today is a day for grief.

I was initially surprised his funeral pyre wasn't set in his own country, with his people, but it makes sense. All his family is here, as are the most powerful Order leaders in the world. There will be a public memorial for him in Sapientia. Today is more private. Or as private as something for the Prince of Ravens can be.

I still can't believe he's gone. I dreamed about him last night. His smile, his kiss, the way he always held my hand just to show me he cared, that he was close. For that brilliant moment between breaths, when I was awake but not, I could forget he was dead. But then reality crashed down on me the moment consciousness firmly took hold, and it broke me all over again.

It's hard to let go of the man who knew me inside and out, knew all my secrets, and still loved me. It's impossible to say goodbye.

Everyone is dressed in black and gold, the Raven house colors, as we walk in solemn silence to the arena. His pyre will burn all night until his mortal shell has been reduced to ash.

I walk behind the royal family, alone in my grief. Jax is there, but he is with the Knights. Corinne and Wytt with their father and uncle. We are in the center of the arena, close to the pyre that's already set up with his body.

Others fill the stadium seating, like this is a show.

But those of us here, on the ground level, we know. We feel the grief. The loss. The world is poorer without Kai's soul in it. I am poorer without him in my life.

Rain pelts down in its rage as musicians play a mournful dirge.

Varian speaks about his son in tones of monotone sadness. I don't hear his words. I'm just staring at Kai. At his body. His profile, hard to see through the wood and cloth. But there. His strong jaw, the lock of hair that always falls into his eyes, even in death. He could be sleeping. I want to reach for him, to beg him to come back.

I've gone over that night in my mind countless times. Could I have saved them both? Could I have done something different? But I never see another way out.

Except one.

I realized it after.

The horrible truth that will forever haunt me.

I killed Kai when I saved Jax.

If I had let Crixus win, his rebel group wouldn't have needed to revolt, and Kai and Corinne wouldn't have been caught in the crossfires.

A life for lives.

Choices that bleed crimson consequences.

It's silent now as Varian sets fire to the pyre. The heat whooshes around me like a living thing, burning not my skin, but my soul. The smell is spicy and smoky, incense covering the smell of burnt flesh.

The rain beats down harder, but the fire is fueled with a fast burning chemical. No matter how hard the rain—or my heart—rails against this, Kai's body will be dust by morning.

And I will not leave until the flames have died out.

I will hold vigil through it all.

The crowd in the stadium leaves after the initial ceremony, once the fire has burned its first blast.

But others stay longer. Kai's family. Jax. Kira. Thane. My grandfather and the Order Council Members.

Me.

I don't know how long I've been standing here, my legs cramping and body shivering with cold, when Ragathon walks over, his face a mask of grief and pain. The moment he steps close enough I hold up my hand, palm facing him as water streams down my face. "Please, not today. I know you hate me. I get it. But not today. Not right now. Not here." I'm pleading, begging, my voice cracked with pain and tears. I have no fight in me right now, only sadness. Only loss.

He shakes his head. "I didn't come here to fight you, Miss Night. For this night, let us call a truce. We both lost someone we loved deeply. I came here to offer my condolences, such as they are. He loved you. And I could see you loved him. You brought him more joy in these last few months than I think he's ever had in his life. I wanted to thank you for that."

Before I can say a word in reply, he walks away, his back straight, spine stiff. Something in me cracks and tears pour of out my eyes. I thought I'd used them all up. How many tears can one person produce in such a short time?

His momentary kindness has stung me more than his hatred ever could.

The long night of standing vigil feels timeless. Once night cloaks us in its blanket, the flames seem to burn brighter, stronger, filling the sky and all around me with its fierce hot light.

But as the first rays of morning sun casts its fingers over the arena, the fire dies down to almost nothing.

Only Varian, Ragathon, Corinne, Wytt, Jax and myself remain.

My eyes blur with yet more tears as the final embers fade in the pile of ash.

And then a sob escapes, clenching my chest and gripping my body with the finality of this moment.

He's gone and he's never coming back.

My Prince is gone forever.

Small crowds return to the pyre, hoping to catch a last glimpse before his remains are packaged and returned to his country. Thane and the Council Members also join the royal family. Even Ragathon's wife returns, daughter tugging at her hand, to stand by her husband.

I still stand alone in my grief, in my bitter goodbye to a great man.

I wipe my tears away when Corinne walks over to me holding Kai's sword, her own face red with evidence of her pain.

She hands me the sword, and I take it, confused.

"He left it for you, in his will. He wanted you to have it."

"But...why did he have a will?" He couldn't have known.

She gives a small, sad smile. "We are royalty. We always have instructions for the eventuality of our deaths. We updated them before the Trial, and I believe he amended his even after, to add this."

She hands me a thick cream envelope with the Ravens seal on it and my name scrawled on the front in Kai's script.

"Thank you," I say, through tears.

She nods. "He loved you. He said you're family."

It's too much. This is just too much. "I loved him, too."

Then she hugs me and walks back to her brother and father, leaving me alone with these last words from Kai.

I open the letter, letting the rain fall on the paper, smearing the ink with the tears of heaven as I read.

Dear Scarlett,

If you're reading this, I died a lot sooner than I imagined. That's unfortunate, because I had plans. Plans that involved convincing you to run off into the great world with me. I know you wouldn't have agreed. Not with your other responsibilities. But I would have tried.

Failing that, I would have stayed in this messed up political quagmire. I would have stayed, and done my best to protect you—all the parts of you. I would have tried to help you in your cause.

I would also have tried to convince you to marry me, eventually. We could have been happy, you know. I loved you enough. We could have made it work—despite everything.

But alas, like Romeo and Juliet (I told you we should have gone as them), we were never meant to be. But Scarlett, what we had, it was real. And I regret nothing.

I don't know what happened to me, but if there's any chance it involved your other life, then don't do what I know you'll do. Don't blame yourself. Don't take on my death with everything else, regardless of what happened.

I knew the risks in loving you, and I took them. I'd do it again in a heartbeat, if I still had a heart that beat.

So, now what's left? Take my sword and kick some butt with it. Make the world a better place. And know that wherever my soul is now, I'm rooting for you.

Yours forever,
The Prince of Ravens

When I look up from the letter, I can barely see through the tears. I tuck it into my cloak and hold the sword close to my chest. "I *will* make the world better, Kai," I say to his spirit, wherever it is. "I swear it."

I stand there longer, my legs already cramped, my body tired, but I can't leave just yet, so I walk over to Corinne and Wytt, who are talking softly as Varian talks to Thane. The Cardinal hadn't stayed for everything, but he'd come back this morning, apparently.

I'm about to say something to Corinne when Thane's movement catches my eye.

I turn to look at him.

He's limping, a hand on his right side.

The same spot where Jax wounded Crixus during the fight.

I freeze as the pieces fall together. Kai was going to tell me something during the tournament. He recognized the Black Knight.

Thane was the Black Night.

Thane is Crixus.

And he murdered Kai.

THE CARDINAL

The realization burns through my grief, my sorrow, my pain and fills me with rage. With the need for vengeance. For justice.

Because it all makes sense.

Thane had been a ward of Varian's, because his family had been traitors.

Crixus admitted his family had helped Nephilim and had died for it.

Crixus used illegal means to accrue wealth.

Thane possessed wealth most speculated he did not come by honorably or legally.

Thane has always been ambitious and is a Cardinal in the Catholic Church. He would be in the running for Pope should the current one die.

And Crixus wanted me to kill the Pope.

Thane hated Kai. He wanted him dead.

Anger replaces my grief, fueling a new fire in its place.

I storm over to Thane, who is standing with Varian and Jax. Corinne and Wytt watch me.

Other members of the Order are present, mingling. My grandfather is here.

I unsheathe Kai's sword. It hums in my hand as I hold it up. "Cardinal Thane, Knight of the Fifth in the Order of Inquisition, I hereby publicly and with those present as witness, accuse you of murder."

There's a gasp as everyone stops talking to stare at me, disbelief etched in every face.

"You were the Black Night who killed Prince Kai. You are Crixus, the rebel leader of the Red Eagles who caused the slaughter of so many at the Tournament Festival, and you will pay for your crimes."

Thane laughs. "I think your grief is getting the best of you, girl. You don't know what you're talking about. Maybe you should go back to your room and cry over your boyfriend alone."

I take a deep breath to stop myself from thrusting this sword through his heart right here and now. "I saw you stab Kai in the heart."

Varian walks over to us. "What is your evidence?" he asks.

"He fights like the Black Night. Kai saw it. And I have videos to prove it. He's also injured in the same place Jax injured the Black Knight during the tournament."

Varian looks at Thane. "Lift your shirt."

Thane smirks. "Surely you aren't taking her seriously?"

Varian places a hand on the hilt of one of his swords. "Lift your shirt, Thane."

Thane sighs and lifts his shirt, revealing a bandage seeping blood on his side.

"How did you come by this injury?" Varian asks.

318

Thane drops his shirt and shrugs. "During training. Accidents happen."

Varian turns back to me. "We already had the Pope confirm the identity of the Black Night. It wasn't Thane."

"That would be easy enough to lie about," I say. "Thane wore the armor after another person officially registered."

Varian is silent a long moment. My palms sweat, and I rub them against my cloak and try to slow my hammering heart.

"Take him into custody," Varian says.

Two Teutonic Knights come over and hand-cuff him. Thane is still grinning. "This is all just a big misunderstanding."

Varian faces Thane, a hard look in his eyes. "My family protected you, raised you, gave you every advantage we could. If Scarlett is right about this, you will pay for what you've done to my son."

Corinne runs up to me as they take Thane away. She pulls me to the side of the arena, her eyes huge. "What the—" She stands, mouth agape. "I can't even believe this."

"I figured it out when I saw Thane limping just now. Kai knew. He was about to tell me when everything happened."

"Are you sure?" Corinne asks. "Really sure?"

"Yes." I say.

Corinne nods. "Then the Orders will find him guilty. He will be sentenced to death. We will testify to what we know."

"What if they don't?" I ask.

"They will," she says, her face determined. "The system isn't perfect, but it does work. Trust them to do the right

319

thing. My father will never let Thane free for killing Kai. You can trust that if nothing else."

. . .

The trial is set for later today, and we all attend.

The Council Members are seated in their respective places, and though my grandfather is technically in charge, Varian has clearly been given a lot of authority in this, for obvious reasons.

Since I'm the primary witness, I testify first. With Evie's help, I show videos side by side of Thane and the Black Knight fighting, noting similar techniques and mannerisms used by each. I go through a list of all the reasons Crixus and Thane are the same person and conclude by calling on Corinne to testify about his injury. She confirms that his injury is consistent with the exact injury the Black Knight received from Jax. Grandmaster Marian speaks up. "The Princess is correct. I would have a hard time believing Thane received this wound in regular training. It's entirely too coincidental."

There seems to be no dissent in the Order about Thane's guilt and yet through it all, Thane has maintained his arrogant gloat as if nothing can touch him.

Ragathon slams his fist into his podium. "I hereby vote to convict Cardinal Thane to death for crimes against the Orders and against the people."

Varian matches eyes with his brother and nods slowly. "I've studied the videos myself," Varian says, "and I agree with Miss Night. That is Thane fighting as the Black Knight. I second my brother's vote."

Marian nods. "I agree."

Both my grandfather and Grandmaster Ella vote for his death.

Corinne looks over to me, a sad smile on her face. She was right, her system worked for us, and convicted the correct person with the correct and just punishment.

Varian stands. "I hereby declare that by the ruling of the Order Council, Cardinal Thane is deemed—"

The door to the private council chambers opens and a Teutonic Knight walks in holding a note he hands to Varian.

As Varian reads the note, revealing nothing on his stoic face, my heart sinks. Something bad has happened, I can feel it.

Varian is silent for a long time. So long it feels repressive.

Finally, he clears his throat. "By order of the Pope, our ruling is overturned and Cardinal Thane is to be released without further prosecution or penalty."

"What?" Ragathon rages at his brother. "You can't let him go. He killed your son."

Varian glares at his brother. "I don't have a choice. This goes far beyond any of our stations. He's a Cardinal and under the authority of the Pope."

Thane smiles and stands, adjusting his coat. "I wish I could say it's been a pleasure, but that would be disingenuous. I will instead wish you all a miserable day and take my leave."

We all sit in stunned silence as Thane walks out of the room. I click on Evie and tell her to alert Zorin. I'm going to need his help. Corinne was wrong after all. This justice system is too corrupt to be effective. Sometimes justice has to come from the shadows.

. . .

I leave quickly, ignoring a call from my grandfather, Corinne and Wytt.

I have to catch up to Thane before he gets away. Before I lose him forever.

The rain is once again pouring down when I step outside the castle walls. It's a dark day, with heavy clouds obscuring the sun. I pull my cloak around my head and run into it, searching for Thane.

I see him turn a corner and I follow, catching up to him several minutes later as he walks into the forest outside the castle.

He turns when I get closer, his lips pulled up in a derisive sneer. "What are you doing out here, girl?"

"How did you get away with this?" I ask, stepping closer to him.

"Get away with what?" he says with a laugh. "Didn't you hear? I'm innocent."

"You're not innocent, and we both know it." I put a hand on his arm and enter his mind. Memories flood me. I have to be sure. Before I do what I'm about to do, I have to be sure.

Flashes of his life pass before me. I see him as a boy, playing with blocks in a mansion. Varian enters and informs him that his parents were traitors, and they were executed. Thane will live amongst the House of Ravens.

He finds friends there. Two brothers and a sister.

But they grow older.

Thane tests Zenith. His abilities are pathetic. He can summon a centimeter of flame above his fingers. Nothing more.

Thane is told he is nothing compared to those he has grown to love. They are royalty, and he a son to traitors.

Thane works harder. He achieves nothing.

He begins to manipulate those around him for advantage. He creates the persona of Crixus and the Red Eagles. He accrues wealth and eliminates his competition under the guise of a rebel. As Thane, he becomes a Knight of the Fifth and a Cardinal. As Crixus, he inspires people to follow him.

He is no longer that weak boy. He knows better than everyone. They are children, and he must guide them. He will eliminate the Pope and secure his election.

He enters the tournament as the Black Knight. He defeats all opponents. His plans go well, but he is still full of hate.

Kai was once like a brother, but now he cares nothing for Thane. So Thane arranges for a vial of Kai's blood to be transported to an island and given to a dangerous creature. During the trial, Kai will die, and finally he will have revenge.

Kai lives.

But not for long.

The memories fade, and I look into Thane's eyes who doesn't know I've just seen into his soul.

He shrugs my hand off of him. He wipes the rain from his face. "Those in power need Crixus. He can do what they can't. I was never going to be prosecuted. I'm safe. Untouchable."

"You're not safe from me," I say.

And I spread my wings as my eyes glow silver.

"You?"

I nod. "Me."

"You can't take me alone, even with your wings." He holds up his hands as fire forms around them.

"Who said I'm alone?"

Zorin drops down behind Thane and strikes him in the head.

The Cardinal drops to the ground, and I stare down at him. "You will be prosecuted for your crimes," I tell him. "And you will be found guilty."

JUSTICE

"Is everything set?" I ask Evie.

"It is," she says in my ear. "Your feed will stream live across the world, interrupting all major broadcasts. I have made sure it is auto-translated into local languages."

"Good." I check myself in the mirror to make sure I haven't missed any pieces of Scarlett, but I'm all Nightfall. My silver wings glow around me and my eyes glow in the same silver hue. Beneath my chest armor I wear the necklace Kai gave me for Christmas and my father's Token of Strife. I can't avenge my parents yet, but at least I can bring justice to Kai's killer.

Corinne—Raven—walks up to me in her mask and golden eyes. "Are you ready?" she asks.

I nod. "How do you feel about all of this?"

She looks over to the room where Thane is being held. "You were right. The system failed. We need a new system, and I think Nightfall is the way to get it." She looks at me, her golden eyes unyielding. "You have to be strong. Unwavering. You have to show the people you are the leader they need."

I hug her. "Thank you."

...

I step up to the podium on Diamond Mountain. The rebel groups have gathered below. A camera faces me. It represents the face of every man, woman and child who is watching this live feed. I have to speak in such a way as to touch the hearts and minds of everyone listening to me tonight. If I don't, I will have failed all those whose lives were lost this year.

Thane is brought out gagged and handcuffed and placed on his knees next to me.

"Earlier today, the Council of Four Orders sentenced Cardinal Thane to death for the murder of Prince Kai of the House of Ravens and for inciting rebellion and terrorist acts at the arena and against the people of this nation as leader of the Red Eagles. But that judgment was overruled by the Pope." I let my words sink in a moment.

"We live in a corrupt society and it is my mission, and the mission of those who work with me, to fight that corruption. To bring peace and equality to everyone. To create an egalitarian society where everyone's voice is heard and everyone's needs are met and everyone's rights are respected. The Pope and the current world government would crumble under this system. They would lose their power, and so they fight it. It is in their best interest to keep us divided. To keep us afraid. To keep us as enemies. But I am not your enemy."

I point to Thane. "He is your enemy. The Pope is your enemy. I am one woman trying to fight for the justice I know you all deserve. I am not a terrorist. I am not a tyrant. And I will not allow terrorists to kill innocents in the name of my cause or any cause."

I hold up Crixus' helmet. "This man tried to use me and my people toward his own end, for his own political and financial gain, and he killed many in that pursuit. I commit to you now, today, that anyone who puts at risk the innocent, whether Zenith, human or Nephilim, will answer to me. Terrorism is not the way to peace. Tyranny is not the way to peace. We must find a new way. Together."

I pull the gag out of Thane's mouth, but he doesn't have a microphone on him, so no one hears as he hisses at me. "What are you going to do? Keep me locked away forever? Keep me prisoner?"

I don't answer as I draw my mother's dagger.

"You won't kill me, Nightfall. You don't have the guts."

I ignore his words. "You will never be loved."

"And you—"

I pull the sharp blade across his throat.

And he slumps over, the life bleeding out of him.

I take a deep breath and address the audience. "You can join me, or you can continue on your own. But if you do it at the cost of innocent lives, this will be your fate."

I toss Crixus' helmet to the floor and turn away. As I do, a chant rises through the mountain. "Nox Aeterna. Nox Aeterna."

It gets louder as I leave the podium.

I smile sadly. They can't believe in themselves. But they can believe in me.

They can believe in Nightfall.

...

I walk up the center of the mountain as TR catches up to me. I clasp his hand in mine. "You did good today," I say. "I was worried the chanting wouldn't work, even with you starting it up."

He squeezes my hand. "That's just it, I never had a chance to start it. They did it on their own."

Evie beeps on. "Scarlett, the chanting has spread worldwide."

TR and I walk to the edge of the mountain, where Trix, Zorin and Raven wait for us. "Show us now," I tell Evie.

She projects multiple videos from all over the globe, each one displaying hundreds, thousands of people chanting Nox Aeterna and making the sign for the Nephilim in sand, on windows, anywhere they can.

Zorin puts his hand on my shoulder. "You've done what only the most successful leaders in world history have accomplished."

"What's that?" I ask.

"United the masses to your vision. You've become their god," he says.

I shudder. "I don't want to be anyone's god."

"You shouldn't," he agrees. "Humanity has a history of killing their gods."

Tyranny and Terror

It doesn't take long for my words to inspire action. We're in the War Room talking about our next step when Evie interrupts us.

"Scarlett, I have messages coming in from many different rebel group leaders, all wanting to talk with Nightfall and join your cause."

I look over at Zorin. "It's working. They're making contact. Trix, can you start messaging the various leaders?"

"Sure can," she says, smiling.

"How will we organize them?" Zorin asks. "Are you planning on folding them into the Dark Templars, or will you allow them to keep their own groups?"

I think about it for a moment. "I think…a little of both. We make it clear that if they want in, they have to commit to being part of the Dark Templars. But they can keep their names and missions—as long as those missions are in no way in conflict with ours—and they can act as branches of the Dark Templars. Tell them each group will need to send a leader here as a representative. They will be given a room and office and will be required to work with our team on any and all missions. No more vigilantes working alone. It all has to go through us now."

"I'm on it," Trix says. She and TR leave, and I notice them hold hands as they exit. It makes me smile.

Zorin follows my eyes. "Is that your doing?" he asks when they are gone.

I shrug. "I just reminded them of what we're fighting for."

"And what is that?" he asks.

"Happiness."

"Happiness? I thought we were fighting for justice. For equality."

I nod. "But why? In the end, isn't it all so we can be happy?"

His hand falls on mine. "Scarlett..."

His eyes are intense. He stares into me.

And then he removes his hand from mine and stands. "I'll see about quarters for the rebel leaders. Like we need more people here."

I laugh at him, the spell between us broken. "You are such a hermit."

He smiles at me. "No, I just prefer more intimate gatherings."

I smile back at him. "You'll get used to it."

Corinne had to get back to her family after the execution, so she's not here. I'm left alone with Carter, who hands me a Life Force and joins me at the table. I thank him and sip on it as I think about what to do next.

"How do you feel, having killed a person for the first time?" he asks.

"This isn't the first time someone has died because of me."

"Perhaps not, but it's the first time you've killed someone by your own hand, is it not?"

I look down at my hands, one old and familiar, one new and still strange. It's the new one that held the knife and sliced Thane's throat. "It's true."

"Do you have regrets?"

I shake my head. "He was sentenced to death. He deserved his judgment. He would have kept hurting others."

"So it wasn't just revenge?" he asks.

"No. It was justice. It was to punish and protect."

"I once had to kill someone to protect another," he says, his eyes lost and far away. "Someone dangerous, who sought a path that could have hurt many. It is not an easy thing to live with, even now."

"I suppose it should never be an easy thing to live with, taking the life of another. No matter how much they deserve it."

He sighs and stands, picking up his silver serving tray. "I suppose it shouldn't."

. . .

It seems like entering another world when I return to Castle V and pretend to be just another Initiate, after everything that's happened. After everything I've done.

But I put on my Scarlett mask, as I wonder more and more often who the real me is now. Is it Scarlett Night?

The girl who lost her parents so many months ago? Or is it Nightfall? The Nephilim with a cause?

How can I be both?

How can I be either?

I'm losing myself to my roles, and it scares me. But as I sit with Corinne, Wytt, Jaden and Lana in our Common Hall, I feel for a moment like this could be real. Like whoever I am, whatever I'm doing, if I can just stay present long enough, it will be real.

Or real enough for now.

And maybe that's all we get in this life. The moment to moment sense of real. The now.

So I enjoy the now with my closest friends, even if the Scarlett mask isn't all of me, it's still me, and I can still be her.

"Are we still going to the party?" Lana asks. The mood in our little group has definitely changed since Kai died.

Corinne nods. "We should. He wouldn't want us to mope around depressed forever. He'd want us to live our lives. To enjoy our lives." She looks at me. "What do you think, Scarlett?"

"You're right. I don't like to think about it, to imagine being there without him, but you're right. We should go."

Jaden scoots closer to me and throws an arm over my shoulder. "If you need a dance partner, I'll keep my card free for you."

I smile. "Thanks. I'll take you up on that if I end up dancing."

"Have you seen much of Jax since everything?" Lana asks.

"No. He's been busy with Order business."

"What's everyone's thoughts on Nightfall's execution of Thane?" Wytt asks. "I have to admit, I'm shocked, but not displeased."

"He killed Kai," Lana says. "Right?"

Corinne and I nod. No doubts.

"Then he deserved it," she says fiercely as she strokes the bracelet Kai gave her. "And I know this is a controversial thing to say, but I don't think Nightfall's the enemy. She's doing what we can't."

Wytt, Lana and Jaden start debating the pros and cons of Nightfall, and Corinne moves to sit next to me. She leans in and whispers. "You okay?"

I shrug. "Mostly."

She holds my hand. "There's a cost to being a great leader."

I nod. "I just hope it isn't more than I can pay."

CHECKMATE

I don the gold and black dress I had made to wear with Kai, accented with black feathers he acquired for me, and I attend the New Year's Ball.

"He would have loved you in that," Corinne says as I walk over to her and Wytt sitting at our table.

"Thank you."

This ball is more subdued than the Halloween Ball. Many here are still nursing injuries, and Kai wasn't the only casualty that day. We are all still in mourning, still pulling ourselves out of that fog of grief that makes the rest of the world disappear.

I see Jax enter the ballroom and our eyes lock. He's dashing in his Teutonic Knight suit. We haven't talked much since the night of the tournament. But my heart misses him.

I stand and walk over to him as others come and go, shaking his hand and congratulating him on his promotion.

"So, a Knight of the Third," I say as I approach.

His eyes are sad. "I'm sorry. About everything."

I shrug. "We are who we are, Jax. I still—"

"Love you," he finishes. "I love you, Star. Always will."

My eyes burn, and I blink away the feelings. "Me too."

"I haven't known what to say to you. How to console you. I was jealous of you and Kai, but now—"

There's nothing left to be jealous of. But neither of us can say that.

"I never stopped loving you," I tell him. "What I feel, felt, for Kai, it didn't change what you mean to me."

He reaches for my hand and pulls me closer to him. "Will you dance with me?"

I nod and let him lead me to the dance floor.

His arm slips around my waist and our bodies press together. I can feel his breath on my neck and smell the faint mint of his shampoo. Whoever we are, whoever we become, he's still my Jax. I hold him tighter, and we don't talk, just move and feel and let the music sink into our bruised and broken hearts.

He's still my Jax.

He leaves me with a small smile and a bow. "I can't stay, but I'll see you soon, Star."

"See you soon."

I rejoin Corinne and she and I walk toward the balcony door. It's a crisp winter night, the sky full of bright stars. A fresh coat of snow blankets the world around us. Nature's way of covering the blood, hiding the flaws of humanity until the seasons change and we are stronger.

"You still love Jax," Corinne says, as a statement not a question.

I nod.

"And Kai?"

I turn to her. "I will always love him. The night of the Halloween Ball, I chose Kai."

Corinne nods, satisfied with that answer. Satisfied, I suspect, that while Kai was here, I chose him. I loved him. I didn't break his heart.

I just killed him.

"I don't know how to live this life," Corinne says. She's staring out into the night, and I follow her gaze. "Nightfall and my father are enemies. Nightfall and my uncle are enemies. One of them will die, won't they? Nightfall or them?"

"I don't know," I say honestly. "I don't want anyone else to die."

She turns to look at me. "But someone always dies in war. And this is a war, isn't it? It's a war that no one knows is happening, but it's real."

"Yes," I say. "It's real."

"And you turned me into an enemy of my own family."

"Yes," I admit. "I did."

She reaches for my hands and holds them. "But you did it to save me. To save my life?"

I nod, a tear running down my cheek. "Yes. And—"

I hesitate at this part, but I think she needs to know. I think Kai would want her to know. "Kai knew. He knew who I was, and he still loved me."

Her eyes widen. "When?"

"The Trial. I had to reveal myself to save him."

Now she's fighting tears. "He still loved you?"

"Yes. Which means—"

"He would still love me."

I nod. "Always."

She nods. "Okay then. We'll figure it out. Together, we'll figure it out. We really are family now. Kai was right."

The door behind us slides open and Varian steps out. "Ladies. It's a cold night to be standing out here so long."

Corinne turns to her father. "We were just getting some air."

"Of course," he says. "I was just wondering, Scarlett, would you care to join me for a game of chess? I believe I owe you one."

I sense something bigger is happening but I don't know what, so I nod. "Of course."

And I follow him in.

. . .

We sit in Varian's office. Black curtains with golden ravens drape the stone walls, and a fireplace burns near the ornately carved desk. The chessboard is glass and the pieces are variations of dragons. Varian plays white and makes the first move. "Thank you," he says, "for revealing my son's killer."

We play quickly, our moves almost instant. After the first few turns, its clear Varian is the greatest player I've ever faced. "I did what was right," I say.

"And you did it with honor." Varian positions his rook. "One day, you shall be a great Knight, Scarlett. What Order do you desire?"

"Templar."

He smiles. "Like your parents. Have you considered who to study under?"

I take one of his pawns. "What do you mean?"

He takes my bishop. "You shall need a Templar Knight to accept you as his Page."

"And you seek an apprentice?"

He chuckles. "Finish your Trials, and we will talk more."

"Not necessary. I will decline."

He doesn't seem surprised. "Do you fear me, Scarlett?"

I hesitate for the first time in the game. "There is nothing to fear but fear itself."

He laughs. "You've been spending too much time with Wytt."

"Your children have all had an effect on me." They showed me not all those with privilege are my enemy.

"And you changed them as well." For a moment, his purple eyes are not cold, but sad. "You made my son happy, before the end. Thank you for that."

"He was an amazing person."

He nods. "And so are you. He saw that in you. Now, I do as well."

My eyes are tearing. I don't want to talk about Kai anymore. "How are things going with Nightfall? Any suspects? The Castle is abuzz with speculation." He's more open today than I've ever seen him. I hope he lets some information slip.

"I have a few. Actually, I'm narrowing down the list."

I chuckle. "Anyone I know?"

Varian moves his Queen. "Tell me, what happens next."

That sounds familiar. I study the board. It takes me a moment to see it, but..."I lose."

He nods. Three turns pass. "Checkmate," he says, his eyes meeting mine. "Once again, you disappoint me... Nightfall."

My breath hitches in my throat. I freeze, but I need to move. I need to make him forget.

No.

I need to eliminate him.

Zorin was right. Varian is too dangerous.

I raise my hand.

Why isn't he attacking me?

"Before you do anything," says Varian, "you should know I have taken precautions. If I die, or behave in a way I would not, you, and those at your Cathedral, will be taken into custody. And you will be executed."

I drop my hand, my heart pounding in my chest. "How...how did you know?"

"I suspected for a while. You and Nightfall shared the same skills, the same ideology. Of course, that was not enough proof. But then you accused Thane, and Nightfall executed him. But I needed one more thing. I needed this game."

I stare at the chessboard, trembling.

"You and Nightfall both calculate your actions based off what is most effective. You will take the path with least casualties, but also the path that is swiftest. These paths are not obvious for most, but they are always there. And so, they can be manipulated. Every turn, I led you down the path you deemed most effective. And when you reached your destination, I was prepared."

I don't know why he's talking to me, or why this matters, but I can't resist asking. "Then how do I win?"

He leans closer. "You must be deceptive at every turn. When you are able to attack, you must seem unable. When you are close to victory, you must appear close to defeat."

I nod, finally understanding. When I went into the sewers with Trix, I did so because it was the safest path, but it was also the most obvious. When I first met Varian,

I thought I was meeting a rebel leader. I thought I was so close to taking control and winning. But instead, I'd lead myself to a superior opponent.

I bow my head, defeated. "So, what happens after you take me into custody?"

"I'm not taking you into custody."

"What? But what about your orders?"

He grins, a spark in his eyes. "I want Nightfall," he says. "But there is something I want more."

EPILOGUE

Only the dead and those mourning them are present at St. Gabriel's Cemetery the night the Princess of Ravens stands before a tombstone. She brushes off the dirt and cut grass that cover Charlie's name, and lays a bouquet of rainbow roses down. They were the girl's favorite.

Corinne doesn't have a grave to bring flowers to for her brother, Kai. She regrets that the most. There will be no quiet place to mourn him and connect to his spirit.

There has been too much loss, too much death, too much that cannot be undone. But who is to blame? Nightfall upsets the status quo, but creates choices where none exist. The Orders discriminate and abuse, but keep order and peace.

We all have different sides, she thinks. *Is one more real than the other?*

Scarlett becomes the persona of Nightfall, just as she becomes the persona of royalty when she has to. Like her, Scarlett has different speech patterns and language, a different bearing when she turns into Nightfall.

Lately, they've spent a lot of time together so Corinne can train and learn about her new skills. No matter her methods, Scarlett's heart is in the right place.

Queens, rebel leaders, we're all the same at the core, she thinks.

She hears footsteps behind her.

He's here.

She turns to the man in long robes.

"Who is that?" the man asks as he twirls his white beard, pointing at the grave.

"A friend," the Princess says, running a finger over the tombstone one last time before she stands to face him, a single rose still in her hand.

"You've lost much in the last few days," he says. "Are you still prepared?"

Corinne raises an eyebrow. "Is this why you wanted to meet? To see if I'm committed?"

He clutches his walking stick as it sinks into the moist soil. "Grief changes people. Has it changed you?"

A wind blows through the cemetery, and the Princess shivers and twirls the rose in her hand, letting the breeze catch its scent. "No. We go ahead with the plan."

The old man cocks his head, his pale blue eyes prying into her soul. "Are you sure you will be able to—"

"I'm sure." The Princess looks down at the rose she holds. And crushes it in her fist. "I will eliminate my father. I will become Queen." She matches the old man's eyes. "And I will help Scarlett destroy the Orders."

The old man smiles. "My granddaughter chose right, when she saved you."

Corrine looks away.

"Do you think me a monster, for thinking so?" he asks.

The Princess pauses. She shakes her head. "We are all monsters," she says softly.

And she unleashes her cobalt blue wings and flies.

. . .

It's not the scene he would have chosen. His wife deserves better than what he's been able to give. He knows that, and he's grateful for her patience, for her love, for her commitment to their small family. He kisses her goodbye as their daughter runs up to him, her blond pigtails slapping against her small, perfect face.

If his feelings for his wife are clouded by the pain of the woman he loved and lost, at least his love for his daughter is untainted, pure. She's the best part of him, and he knows it. He leans down to hug her.

"Daddy, look," she says, "I found a Fairy Flower. Look how the colors change."

She twirls the flower in her small fingers, and the colors shift from blue to purple to pink to yellow.

"It's beautiful," he says. "Just like you."

She giggles and runs off, and he turns to leave. His eGlass blinks, reminding him of his appointment, as if he'd forget. He clicks it off and drives to the cafe where his brother agreed to talk.

Varian is sitting at a table sipping a coffee when he arrives. There should evidence of grief on the face of a man who just lost his son. Varian shows none.

Ragathon sits across from him, and Varian smiles. "It's good to see you, Ragathon. What did you wish to discuss?"

"You know what I came here to talk about. How can you act like Kai's death means nothing? You treated him like garbage his whole life, making him feel worthless, and now that he's dead you act like he never existed. What kind of heartless monster are you?"

The false pleasantry drops from Varian's face, replaced by sorrow. "You're right. I should have treated him better. I tried. I gave him my name, my status, every privilege of a Prince, but…"

"He was your son, of course you did. That didn't make you a good father," Ragathon says, his heart still torn apart by Kai's death.

"You are so blinded by your own hate, you never even saw it, did you?"

Ragathon's heart runs cold at the sneer on Varian's face.

"What didn't I see?" he asks, his hands shaking.

"He was never my son," Varian says. "He was yours. Kai was your son, and you left him and her before she could even tell you. You stormed away like a petulant child who had lost a toy when she chose me, and I was left to take care of the messes you made. I did the best I could with the bastard son of my coward brother."

Varian slams his coffee down and stands, adjusting his suit. "She loved you once," he says. "But when you left without a word, that love died long before she did."

Varian leaves Ragathon sitting stunned at the table. Memories of Kai flash through his mind, and piece by piece it breaks him down.

He had a son.

His son is dead.

344

A sob racks his chest, and he leans his head down and grieves for all that was lost and is now forever gone.

. . .

The Cathedral is dark and silent. Zorin sits in his room, re-watching a memory. He sees the crystal coffin shatter, and a frail version of himself falls out. He notices a pale, blond-haired girl, bleeding out on the ground. She looks familiar.

There are soldiers there, dressed in gold. They do not move.

Zorin, ravaged with hunger, crawls to the girl and bites her neck. He drains her of blood, and when someone enters, he pulls away, face covered in red.

It is the Angel. His wings shimmer gold and purple. "Hello, old friend," he says.

Zorin's eyes are hazy. "Where am I?"

"You had been imprisoned. The Nephilim have been destroyed. You are the last."

Zorin shakes his head. There is silence. And then he weeps.

"I'm sorry."

"What of Marcus and Violet?" asks Zorin.

"They are dead."

"No—"

"They had to be killed. They were the ones who kept you prisoner."

Zorin turns to the bleeding body. "And the girl?"

"Their daughter."

Zorin nods. He tears open his wrist and pours blood down the girl's throat.

The Angel steps forward. "No. You cannot save her. She is too dangerous."

"She is innocent."

The Angel raises his golden sword. "I cannot allow her to live."

"You will not touch her," roars Zorin.

The Angel walks forward. His soldiers target Zorin with their guns. "I'm sorry, old friend, but the seals can never be unlocked."

Zorin stands, stepping in front of the girl. He is weak from many years of slumber, but he is strong enough for this. "You challenge the Lord of Night?" The sky darkens, and black tendrils spread from Zorin. An unnatural wind rushes around him. A sword, black as night, materializes in his hand. "You challenge death."

He charges.

The Angel attempts to defend. He is not fast enough. Each of his soldiers collapses, their necks sliced opened. When the Angel lunges to strike, Zorin slams into him, pushing them both out of the truck and into the sky.

They struggle as they fly further and further, a spiral of gold and black. The Angel pushes Zorin away and turns back for the girl. Zorin dives after him. He catches him.

And stabs the Angel through the shoulder.

They fall.

The memory fades.

"Why do you watch this?" asks Carter, standing in Zorin's doorway.

Zorin turns to him. "They should not have died."

"The girl has far too much sway over you. She leads when it should be you."

"I cannot," says Zorin.

Carter sighs. "You will tell her of the seals."

He nods.

"We agreed they must never be opened," says Carter.

"And we lost. I will not lose again." Wind rushes through the bedroom.

"Zorin, I beg you—"

"You continue to challenge me," Zorin roars and stands to face Carter. "I ordered you to stay away from her, and yet you returned here. Do not make me choose between you and the girl."

"My old friend—"

Zorin charges Carter, slamming him into the wall.

And Carter unleashes his wings.

They shimmer gold and purple.

He pushes Zorin back. "I have searched a millennium for one to lead us," he says. "You are that leader, Zorin. You know what must be done."

Zorin steps back, anger leaving his face.

And Carter smiles kindly. "You love her, don't you?"

Zorin says nothing.

"This has happened before, with another. Do not make the same mistake twice."

"I will not," says Zorin, his eyes dark. "Scarlett shall become one of the Four. And the one who betrayed us will die."

THE END

A NOTE
FROM THE AUTHORS

Call us Karpov Kinrade. We're the husband and wife team behind *The Nightfall Chronicles*. And we want to say... Thank you for reading it. It's our baby, and we hope you enjoyed it. We spent years crafting the world and characters in *The Nightfall Chronicles*, and we're thrilled to see so many readers find and enjoy this book.

Ever since our first novel, we've benefited tremendously from the feedback readers have given us, and we encourage you to write us directly with your thoughts at contact@karpovkinrade.com. The inspiration and kindness we've received from so many of you has changed our entire career.

If you have time to write a review, please know that we will read it, and that we take feedback very seriously. Each and every review is important. Each and every review makes a difference. They increase the chances of people finding this novel, and they influence how we write.

Thanks again for reading.

Want more urban fantasy? Check out *Forbidden Mind*.

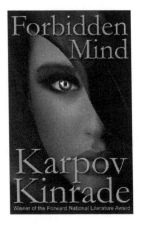

She reads minds.

He controls minds.

Together, they might get out alive.

ABOUT THE AUTHOR

Karpov Kinrade is the pen name for the husband and wife writing duo of bestselling, award-winning authors Kimberly Kinrade and Dmytry Karpov.

Together, they write fantasy, paranormal, mystery, contemporary and romance novels and hook readers into new and exciting worlds with writing that blends side-splitting humor, heart-wrenching drama, spine-tingling twists and sigh-inducing happily ever afters.

Look for more from Karpov Kinrade in The Nightfall Chronicles, the Hitched series, the Call Me Cat Trilogy, the Seduced Saga, the Forbidden Trilogy and more coming soon.

They live with three little girls who think they're ninja princesses with super powers and who are also showing a propensity for telling tall tales and using the written word to weave stories of wonder and magic.

Find them at www.KarpovKinrade.com

On Twitter @KarpovKinrade

On Facebook /KarpovKinrade

And subscribe to their newsletter for special deals and up-to-date notice of new launches. www.ReadKK.com

. . .

If you enjoyed this book, consider supporting the author by leaving a review wherever you purchased this book. Thank you.

If you enjoyed this book, consider supporting the author by leaving a review wherever you purchased this book. Thank you.